AF846520

BLACK DESERT
THE SUNDERING OF SERENDIA

BLACK DESERT
THE SUNDERING OF SERENDIA

ROBBIE MACNIVEN

TITAN BOOKS

Black Desert: The Sundering of Serendia
Print edition ISBN: 9781835414859
E-book edition ISBN: 9781835414866

Published by Titan Books
A division of Titan Publishing Group Ltd
144 Southwark Street, London SE1 0UP
www.titanbooks.com

First edition: October 2026
10 9 8 7 6 5 4 3 2 1

This is a work of fiction. All of the characters, organizations, and events portrayed in this novel are either products of the author's imagination or are used fictitiously. Any resemblance to actual persons, living or dead (except for satirical purposes), is entirely coincidental.

© Pearl Abyss 2026. All rights reserved.

Robbie MacNiven asserts the moral right to be identified as the author of this work.

No part of this publication may be reproduced, stored in a retrieval system, or transmitted, in any form or by any means without the prior written permission of the publisher, nor be otherwise circulated in any form of binding or cover other than that in which it is published and without a similar condition being imposed on the subsequent purchaser.

A CIP catalogue record for this title is available from the British Library.

EU RP (for authorities only)
eucomply OÜ, Pärnu mnt. 139b-14, 11317 Tallinn, Estonia
hello@eucompliancepartner.com, +3375690241

Without limiting the exclusive rights of any author, contributor or the publisher of this publication, any unauthorised use of this publication to train generative artificial intelligence (AI) technologies is expressly prohibited. Titan Books also exercise their rights under Article 4(3) of the Digital Single Market Directive 2019/790 and expressly reserve this publication from the text and data mining exception.

Printed and bound by CPI Group (UK) Ltd, Croydon CR0 4YY.

This book is dedicated to the fans of *Black Desert*,
veterans and new players alike.

CHARACTER LIST

THE SERENDIAN ROYAL FAMILY

Crucio Domongatt: King of Serendia

Antonio Domongatt: Prince of Serendia, Crucio's eldest son

Sergio Domongatt: Prince of Serendia, Crucio's middle son

Vittorio Domongatt: Prince of Serendia, Crucio's youngest son

Jarette Domongatt: Princess of Serendia, Crucio's daughter and youngest child

Roxanne Domongatt: Formerly Roxanne Fiazza. Adopted while still a child by Crucio, now married to Antonio Domongatt

Noble House Ducas of Serendia

Frederick Ducas: Head of the House and High Constable of Serendia

Martha Ducas: Frederick's wife

Jordine Ducas: Frederick's son and only child

NOBLE HOUSE RHUNDI OF SERENDIA

Edward Rhundi: Head of the House, known as the 'Pauper Knight'

Alfonso Rhundi: Edward's son and only child

OTHER NOTABLE FIGURES

Johann Cliff: Marshal of Serendia and Commander of the Western Marches

Guy Seric: King of Calpheon

Elysia Seric: Guy Seric's younger sister, married to Prince Sergio Domongatt

PART ONE

ONE

It was high summer in the year 275 when the court of Serendia came together to hear the last proclamation of King Crucio Domongatt.

Jordine Ducas was late for it. He and Afonso Rhundi had been drinking in the Golden Frog inn, and Jordine had lost track of time after a particularly enthralling encounter with the wife of a Xian merchant whose husband was currently selling his wares in Heidel's marketplace. Thanks to that dalliance, Jordine reached the great hall of Heidel castle just as King Crucio was completing his opening address.

'The march of ages waits for no man, be he pauper or king. I have ruled for many years now, in times both fair and ill, and always my foremost priority has been the wellbeing of the kingdom. It would be wrong of me, therefore, to continue to reign as my ever-increasing years begin to wear me down.'

A wave of muttering ran through the hall. The court of

Serendia was packed in beneath the high timber rafters, the great and the good of the land drawn by their monarch's command. Neither Jordine nor Alfonso would ordinarily have been allowed to attend, both being too young and not yet knighted, but special dispensation had been granted for firstborn sons and daughters to accompany their households and hear the king's will.

Jordine used the opportunity provided by the sudden hubbub to work his way through the gathering towards the front of the hall, to the place afforded to his mother and father, Martha and Frederick Ducas. They stood just back from where the heirs of the blood were arrayed beneath the throne and its dais, Crucio's three sons – Antonio, Sergio and Vittorio – alongside Roxanne, Antonio's wife; Elysia, Sergio's wife; and the king's only daughter, Jarette.

Frederick shot Jordine a cold glance as he reached his side.

'You stink of ale,' he muttered.

'You can't expect me to endure a full gathering of the court without a few libations to strengthen my resolve,' Jordine replied, not looking at his father.

'Because of this, and following a period of careful consideration, I have decided to take matters into my own hands,' Crucio continued, stilling the whispers of the nobility and cutting off Frederick's retort to his son. 'I do not intend to wither away on this throne, and drag the kingdom of Serendia down with me. It is therefore my intention to abdicate in favor of one of my sons. It only remains to be seen which of the three will receive my crown.'

This time the sound of the court's dismay was unrestrained, but Crucio carried on over it, the expression on his lined face one of steely determination, picked out by the afternoon sunlight streaming in through the hall's high windows.

'My sons and their qualities are known to all of you. I will not be so base as to simply surrender the throne on primogeniture. I expect whoever succeeds me to earn the right to rule!'

Jordine watched as the three princes in front of him exchanged glances. The eldest, Antonio, was the first to step forward, mounting the dais before kneeling in front of his father's throne and speaking in a tone loud enough to carry to those crammed into the very back of the hall.

'I, Prince Antonio Domongatt, pledge my life to protect Serendia. I will ensure the prosperity of our lands by conquering the insolent lords of Mediah. They still reel from past barbarian invasions and war between their merchant guilds and the Sausans. Their new capital of Altinova is ripe and ready to be plucked. With your blessings, my liege, I will lead the Serendian host there, and return to Heidel bearing all the treasures of the east.'

Those nobles aligned or allied with Antonio applauded. King Crucio, reclining now in his throne, nodded his silent approval and dismissed his eldest with a wave. Sergio took his place, kneeling and speaking with the same brash confidence.

'I, Prince Sergio Domongatt, swear to prove myself worthy of this greatest of inheritances. I will journey north, and bring the region of Balenos fully under the stewardship of the ruler of Serendia. The Bartali family have been masters of those lands in name only for more than a century, and their resistance to our overtures – even as they consort with Calpheon – is an insult. With your permission, Father, I will lead the Serendian host to subjugate Olvia and Velia, rebuild Cron Castle as our seat of power, and expand both the borders and the glory of Serendia. Furthermore, once Balenos has been added to our territories, I will cede its stewardship to our beloved younger sister, Princess Jarette, securing our lineage in the north in perpetuity.'

He gestured down at Jarette, the sunlight making her red hair blaze like fire. The court made noises of approval, and Sergio stepped down.

Jordine glanced up at his father, trying to gauge his reaction to the bidding of the first two princes. Frederick was attempting to maintain a neutral expression, but Jordine knew him well enough to sense the anger kindling beneath the surface.

The court waited, and it seemed as though the youngest of Serendia's princes, Vittorio, would not take Sergio's place before his father. Eventually he stepped up, but unlike the other two, he did not kneel.

'Father, you know the love I have for you, and for our family,' he began to say, his tone altogether less bold and confident than that of his siblings. 'Yet I confess I feel nothing right now other than dismay. Your rule has not been without its trials, as you yourself have admitted, yet we live in a time of peace and stability. We need only look around us to see the turmoil. To the east, Mediah is still struggling to emerge from internal strife and natural disasters. To the west, Calpheon is still locked in its interminable war with Valencia. Balenos to the north is barren and destitute. Yet when Antonio and Sergio spoke of their ambitions, they did so using the language of conflict. Their only suggestions were to make war on our neighbors. What can such plans bring other than bloodshed, and the specters of famine and disease that always follow? Will any loot brought back to Heidel make up for the many widows Antonio and Sergio plan on making? My brothers are blinded by their greed for the throne and seek to win your favor with lies and deceit. Hastily relinquish your throne, and the day shall come when you see your sons shed blood and tear themselves apart in jealousy.'

Stunned silence followed young Vittorio's words. All eyes turned to Crucio. The king's expression had grown dark and thunderous.

Slowly, he rose from his throne, glaring at Vittorio.

'How dare you cast such aspersions on my judgment, or speak of your older brothers in such a manner,' he said. 'I have long doubted your fitness to rule, Vittorio, but today you have proven it not only to me, but to the whole of Serendia.'

Vittorio made no effort to reply, his head bowed as the storm of his father's wrath crashed over him.

'You have at least made the matter of succession easier

for me! You will go henceforth from Heidel, this very day. I banish you from this city, and from my court. You are not fit to lay claim to the line of Domongatt. Guards, remove this impudent pup from my sight!'

Uproar gripped the court as Captain Malchevo of the royal guards mounted the dais and snatched hold of Vittorio, dragging him down towards the doors while Crucio was still delivering his final pronouncement.

'You are no longer my son! If you ever show your face in Heidel again, I will have your insolent head cut from your shoulders!'

Jordine took in the chaos, feeling a thrill of excitement twinned with amusement – he had no love for the pomposity and theatrics of the court, so something as unexpected and shocking as the scenes now playing out around him was a welcome change. That was until he felt his father's hand on his shoulder, beginning to steer him through the arguing, jostling nobles towards the doors.

'We're leaving,' Frederick told him firmly.

'Just when it was getting interesting,' Jordine replied but made no effort to resist.

Several members of the court tried to draw Frederick into their arguments as he passed by, but he was too wise to allow himself to be accosted. As the high constable and commander of the Serendian military host, he was one of the most powerful nobles in the land. As much as Jordine disliked the politicking of the aristocracy, even he understood that his father could not allow himself to become entrapped on one side or the other of a debate, not until the fallout had become clear. House Ducas would remove itself from the fray and take stock of the king's pronouncements before making its next move.

As he was led from the hall, he looked around for Alfonso, catching sight of him alongside his father, Edward Rhundi, who appeared to be locked in an increasingly heated discussion with Sir Monvald of North Bank. Jordine waved cheerily to his best friend, but Alfonso's expression didn't lighten. Whatever his father was saying, it wasn't good.

Feeling suddenly deflated, Jordine lost sight of him amidst the press, before passing through the great hall's doors.

'This is madness,' Frederick snarled as soon as he, Jordine and Martha were alone, out in the antechamber beyond the hall. 'It's one thing to declare his abdication without any recourse to the council, but to banish Vittorio while condoning the other princes' hunger for war...'

'Crucio gave no indication this was his intention before the speech?' Martha asked, looking as concerned as her husband. Frederick shook his head.

'None at all. I must find out what has caused this sudden determination to surrender the throne. No good will come of it, mark my words.'

'Jarette will know.' Jordine spoke up, causing his parents to look at him with surprise.

'Nothing happens within the royal citadel without her

noticing,' he went on. 'I can ask her as soon as the court disperses.'

'That would only add to our troubles,' Frederick said, unimpressed by Jordine's abrupt suggestion. 'The king is already displeased that you spend so much time with his only daughter, Jordine. I have told you already, you must cease meeting with her.'

'Why, because you all think I'm a bad influence?' Jordine demanded, feeling stung. 'I'm the only genuine friend she has. Crucio acts as though I am some lowly castle servant or field-peasant from Glish trying to seduce the royal princess, not the heir to one of the most prestigious noble families in the kingdom. I have every right to keep his daughter company.'

'Having the right to do something does not mean you *should* do it,' Frederick said. 'You speak of House Ducas's prestige, but that is the very same prestige you are undermining every time you anger the king. Today should serve as a clear example of how dangerous that can be.'

'I'm only offering to help,' Jordine said, but Frederick cut him off with a placatory gesture.

'I understand that, but right now you can help by returning to Shield Street with your mother. I am going to remain here and seek a private audience with the king as soon as possible. With Elion's blessings I can at least convince him to pause his abdication and not to banish Vittorio. The last thing any of us want is a succession crisis.'

TWO

As soon as Jordine returned to the family's townhouse on Shield Street, he sent a servant back to the citadel with a message. He had no doubt Frederick would have demanded he stayed in for the rest of the day, but his mother had always been far easier to convince, and she eventually permitted him to leave with assurances that he was only heading to one of his regular haunts, the Lilly Valley inn.

Instead, he went in the opposite direction, taking the eastern bridge road and then turning off it before reaching the crossing over the Demi River, which flowed to the immediate south of Heidel. He found the spot he had specified in the message he had given to the servant, beneath an old, dead elm just above the river's embankment, its branches withered and bent with age.

The young lion of Serendia stood for a while, leaning against the dry timber, trying to let the sound of the rushing waters wash away his frustrations. How often had his father demanded that he leave behind the misadventures of youth and begin to show sensibilities worthy of the heir of House Ducas? Yet now, when he offered to help his father, he was commanded instead to return home like an errant child?

As the sun sank towards the horizon and the darkness in the streets behind him deepened, Jordine looked across the river, taking in the expansive Moretti estate that began on the Demi's southern bank. Its slopes of ripening corn and vineyards were serene and peaceful in the golden light, a contrast to the chaos that had followed on from Crucio's announcement – chaos Jordine was sure had continued to spread as the dismissed court and princes broke off into their various factions, to hold secret meetings and councils of war. He could understand why his father wished to quell the king's temper and rein in the compulsive proposals of Antonio and Sergio. But Jordine could help him and was determined to do so. First, he just needed some assistance of his own.

'This is unwise,' said a voice, breaking apart his thoughts and making him turn.

A figure had approached without him noticing, cloaked, cowl raised to hide her fierce red hair from the setting sun. Jarette Domongatt, the princess royal, come alone and in secret to meet with the heir of House Ducas. Her appearance brought a smile to Jordine's face, but it was fleeting. He knew she was right.

'I used one of the serving hatches to slip out again, but my chaperone will already have noticed I'm missing from my chambers,' Jarette said, joining Jordine beneath the dead boughs, keeping her hood raised. 'And I'm fairly certain I was recognized in the streets. Father will have those ogre-brained brutes he calls his royal guards out for me already.'

'We won't be long,' Jordine reassured her, trying to mask his own anxiety with his usual confidence. 'I wouldn't have called you from the citadel if it wasn't urgent.'

She gave a short laugh. 'Now, we both know that isn't true—'

'Regardless, the kingdom is on the brink of turmoil, and you might be able to help me avert it. Did you know your father was going to announce his abdication today?'

'Not exactly,' Jarette said, glancing past the elm's trunk, watching the road back into town. 'But he's been acting especially morose these past few days.'

'Have you any idea what could have triggered this? My father says he and the rest of the king's council had no forewarning.'

'Is that why you're here?' Jarette asked with unexpected sharpness. 'On behalf of Frederick Ducas? Not to check how I'm faring amidst all this? My older brother just proposed installing me as the puppet ruler of Balenos!'

'All the more reason to stop this madness before it goes any further,' Jordine said. 'Someone or something has influenced Crucio to pursue this path, and if we know what, we might be able to stay his hand.'

Jarette was silent for a while, gazing towards the river and the vineyards beyond. Eventually, she looked back at Jordine.

'Roxanne has had several private audiences with the king lately. I began to notice his change in mood around the same time. What they discussed, I don't know, but it isn't the first time she has exerted influence over him. There was the marriage to Antonio, and he dotes on her more than he does me, his own flesh-and-blood daughter!'

Jordine considered her claim. Roxanne was now wife to Prince Antonio, but before that had been Crucio's adopted daughter. The story went that she had been taken by the king on one of the joint Serendian-Calpheonian campaigns through Valencia, when Serendia had still been a part of the Western Alliance. Roxanne's family had been killed and her home burned by the invading forces, but in a moment of remorse Crucio had rescued the little girl and brought her back to Heidel. She had been adopted into the royal family, and had taken her place in court, further securing her standing within the family through her marriage to its eldest prince.

It was no secret that Jarette disliked her adopted older sister, but Jordine doubted her accusations were wholly unfounded. There were frequent rumors about Roxanne's influence over the king, especially since the death of the queen. Jordine had heard his father speak of similar concerns. It wasn't hard to imagine Roxanne's hand at work, but if so, what was her intention behind convincing Crucio to abdicate? Was she working with Antonio to secure him the throne, and in doing so make herself queen? Certainly, there was a known rivalry between her and the wife of Prince Sergio, Elysia Seric, who was herself a princess of Calpheon, wedded into the royal line of Serendia when the two neighboring kingdoms had still been militarily aligned. Antonio had been first to respond to his father's proclamation, and had shown no hesitation in offering to strike at Mediah to the east. Were he and Roxanne colluding to pressure the king into relinquishing his crown?

Jordine did not know, but at least he had a name to take back to his father. It would surely help him in his own meeting with the king, if Jordine could get the information to him in time.

'This could be useful,' he told Jarette, but his thanks were cut off by a shout and the clatter of armor.

They both looked up to find the bullish captain of the royal guard, Malchevo, approaching from the nearest street, a troop of men-at-arms hurrying to keep up. He gestured at them both and shouted again at them to stay still.

'The Golden Frog, at sixth bell the day after tomorrow,' Jordine suggested, throwing up the hood of his own cloak. Jarette shrugged.

'We'll see what fate brings our way, Joe,' she said.

Jordine nodded, and ran.

It was dark by the time Jordine made it back to Shield Street. He had lost the guards with little difficulty, taking the back alleys behind the forges and smithies of Soot Row before circling back round to cut across the North Road, close to the central market – it wasn't the first time he had given

Crucio's soldiery the slip under similar circumstances, but his haste wasn't born solely from a desire to escape.

He reached the Ducas townhouse and burst inside, startling his mother, who was just stepping into the entrance hall to investigate the sound of running feet.

'Jordine,' she exclaimed, shock turning swiftly to anger. 'What's the meaning of all this?'

'Where is father?' Jordine panted, snatching back his hood. 'I have information he needs.'

'You weren't at the Lilly Valley, were you?' Martha snapped. 'What've you done now, you foolish boy?'

'I met with Jarette,' Jordine admitted, knowing there was no time to get bogged down in accusation and denial. 'She believes Roxanne is behind the king's announcement. I must tell father, so he can—'

'Your father left for the citadel half an hour ago,' Martha said stonily. 'He is meeting with the king as we speak.'

THREE

'What is this about, Ducas?' Crucio demanded.

'I would have thought it were obvious, sire,' Frederick said, standing deferentially back from the hearth and the chair Crucio was reclined in beside it. As was customary with a senior member of the royal council, the king had agreed to meet Frederick in his bedchamber. Darkness had fallen outside, and the only light came from the low fire burning fitfully in the grate, casting flickering illumination across the heavy silken drapes of the four-poster bed and the tapestries that hung upon the wood-paneled walls, while leaving the king's face in shadow as he looked towards Frederick.

'I was not informed of Your Majesty's intentions prior to the announcement today,' Frederick went on. 'As your high constable, that is irregular.'

'You are not the first member of the council to bring their worries to me today,' Crucio said. 'Roig Mills has only just left after complaining for the past two hours about what this announcement will do to our trade deals. I am weary, and finished with explaining myself.'

'I merely wish to understand your thinking,' Frederick said, careful to keep his tone respectful. He could tell Crucio had been drinking, both from his demeanor and the empty goblets beside his chair.

'You think me unwise, foolish,' Crucio declared, his tone accusatory. 'You come here to demand that I renege on today's proclamation.'

'I would never presume to make demands of the crown,' Frederick said.

'Yet what I say is true. You would have me undermine myself and my sons by recanting. How would the court take it? And the common people, for that matter. Should I claim I was overcome by a bout of madness? Or that I had been led astray by sinister influences?'

'Have you been?' Frederick asked, unable to keep the edge from his tone. Crucio scoffed.

'You may be one of my most senior advisors, Frederick Ducas, but I am the king. I can seek counsel wherever I please.'

'But why would you not discuss these matters first?' Frederick said. 'You speak of authority being undermined, but it damages the standing of the royal council if it seems that none of us have your confidence.'

'Please,' Crucio said, shifting in his chair and waving a hand, the firelight glinting from the golden circlet he wore upon his brow. 'You would not have sought an audience with me so desperately if you merely wished to complain about a lack of propriety in dealing with the council. It is the meat of my choices that you wish to sink your teeth into.'

'I simply do not understand what Your Majesty thinks to gain by permitting your eldest sons to make war upon our neighbors,' Frederick said, unable to deny Crucio's incisiveness. 'Relations with Calpheon have been fraught since we left the alliance, yes, but there are no signs of imminent conflict. Their host is battle-hardened and larger than ours, and the Western Marches are in a state of disrepair. We are in no position to antagonize them by laying claim to Balenos, and thereby reducing their own influence over the region. As for Mediah, it is true they have been weakened by recent conflicts and disasters, but nothing will unify the adherents of Aalism like a foreign invasion. Prince Sergio has never led a campaign before, and I fear one waged in Mediah would be his last.'

'You insult the princes of the blood,' Crucio snapped. 'Both are more than capable, and it is time they showed that, to the nobility and the wider kingdom. I had thought the proposal of fresh campaigns would be welcome news to my high constable.'

'The host of Serendia stands ready to obey your commands, and those of your heirs, always,' Frederick said, struggling to hold his rising frustrations in check. 'But are you really so eager to risk the lives of your sons in foreign campaigns, especially now that you have disinherited and banished your youngest?'

Silence followed his words. While Frederick could

not make out Crucio's face in the long shadows of the bedchamber, he knew immediately that he had pushed the old king too far.

'Did Vittorio seek you out?' Crucio demanded, voice barely audible at first over the crackle and snap of the hearth, but rising relentlessly as he went on. 'Did he plead for you, as my most trusted advisor, my old comrade- in-arms, to intercede on his behalf? What favors did he promise you, if you could convince me to change my mind?'

'I have not seen Prince Vittorio since you banished him from the great hall,' Frederick said firmly, knowing he needed to tread carefully, but also unwilling to bend wholly beneath the king's misplaced ire. 'I can only assume he is already on the road from the capital, given you did not even permit him one last night in his home before sending him away.'

'And what business is it of yours that I did just this?' Crucio said. 'Am I not master of my own household, let alone the whole kingdom? Perhaps you should show such firmness with your own boy, and he might amount to something, rather than being a wastrel who staggers from one tavern and brothel to the next, dragging all those who consort with him down into the gutter.'

'This is not some errant son we are speaking of, sire,' Frederick said, his own voice now rising to match his monarch's. 'You have sent one of your heirs into exile for no greater crime than public impertinence. With a single pronouncement you have pushed your house to the brink of war. All my life I have served Serendia, and I will not stand idly by and say nothing as the kingdom is thrown into turmoil!'

Crucio rose from his chair with a snarl of rage and effort. He stood before Frederick, a dark, dire shape framed by the guttering flames behind him.

For a moment, Frederick thought his king was about to strike him. Instead, he stood still as a knocking sound came from the door.

'Enter,' Crucio rasped, and the heavy, iron-studded timber swung open to reveal Captain Malchevo of the royal guard. The big brute stepped inside and bowed with a scrape of plate armor, glancing from Frederick to his ruler.

'Speak,' Crucio snapped.

'Your Highness, Princess Jarette has been returned to her chambers. We found her near the East Bridge.'

'What foolishness was she engaged in this time?'

'She refused to say, but my men and I caught sight of someone accompanying her. He fled on our approach, but I believe it was the young Ducas, Jordine.'

He glanced again at Frederick as he spoke, and the head of House Ducas felt a chill creep over him. Had the boy really been fool enough to meet with Jarette Domongatt now, when things were so fraught, and after he had specifically instructed him to remain at Shield Street? Was he so arrogant, so foolish, that he had failed to anticipate what would happen if he was caught?

Crucio did not even dismiss Malchevo before turning his wrath on Frederick.

'Once again, your embarrassment of a son has been

caught ensnaring a royal princess! Is he really this insolent, or is he merely following orders from his father? Perhaps you seek to corrupt my only daughter, to gain influence not just within the court, but within my own household?'

The accusations stung too badly for Frederick to restrain himself anymore. He met his king's anger with fury of his own.

'I have never condoned Jordine's actions, but he is my son and heir, and I will not have him besmirched, not even by my king. He has never treated your daughter dishonorably, and while I have only ever urged him to break off his companionship with her, it is clear to see he is her only true friend, the only one who does not treat her like a prize mare to be coddled before market day! He treats her properly, not as an afterthought forever caught in the shade of your two eldest sons!'

As the words left Frederick, he expected to feel apprehension, terror even, of the retribution he knew must follow. But he felt only relief and the sense of determined pride that came with speaking truth to great power.

At no point did Frederick Ducas regret those words, even as Crucio raged and delivered the dreadful ultimatum he had known must follow, before commanding Malchevo to haul the former high constable from his sight.

FOUR

Jordine had never known his mother so angry. He endured her fury for as long as he could, before breaking off and storming upstairs to his chamber. There he slept fitfully, until the sound of hooves on the cobbled streets outside and voices in the dining hall below drew him back downstairs.

He hovered for a while outside the hall doors, catching snatches of the conversation between his mother and father. Eventually, unable to stomach cowering on the fringes or slinking back upstairs to wait on being summoned, he entered the room and announced himself.

He was ready to face his father's rage – Elion knew, he had withstood such storms enough in recent years. A part of him still hoped that Frederick had been able to convince Crucio to see sense, as he had done in the past. All would be well once more, and everything could continue as it had done before the king's proclamation.

Jordine knew as soon as he laid eyes upon his parents' faces that such hopes were nothing more than wishful thinking. Frederick was leaning against the mantelpiece, the flames in the hearth making him look wearier than Jordine had ever seen him before, like an exhausted traveler just come in from the road. Martha stood at his elbow, poised as though to catch him if he fell, her own face riven with concern. They became silent as Jordine walked in, and said nothing for long, painful moments after he first spoke.

Eventually, his father acknowledged him.

'You were seen,' he said, his voice low and hoarse. 'By the king's guards. Seen with Jarette.'

'I only went to try and find out who had convinced the king to abdicate,' Jordine said, stepping closer, desperate to explain himself. 'It's Roxanne! She's behind it all, or much of it! Maybe Antonio too, I haven't been able to work it out yet, but—'

Frederick stilled him with a gesture.

'It doesn't matter,' he said. 'It's all too late. Too late for us, for House Ducas. Maybe too late for the whole kingdom.'

'What do you mean?' Jordine asked. Frederick looked down into the hearth, unable to speak.

'King Domongatt has banished us.' Martha spoke up, her voice hollow. 'He has stripped your father of all property, land and titles, and has disavowed you from his inheritance. We are no longer counted among the nobility of Serendia.'

Jordine felt a plunging feeling, as though he was

in freefall, the sensation so potent he had to put a hand against the wall to steady himself.

'That's not possible,' he breathed. 'He… he cannot do that.'

'He already has,' Frederick said quietly. 'He has offered us only a single means of retaining any kind of standing at all. I am to enlist as a common man-at-arms in the host I once commanded, in one of the detachments going west to reinforce the Marches and the Watchtower. Then I will at least be afforded payment, and a profession I can still take some pride in.'

'You are too old for common soldiering,' Jordine exclaimed. 'And what of Mother and I?'

'I will provide for you both. And soon you will be old enough to join me in the ranks.'

Jordine's thoughts reeled. The idea that they were no longer to be counted amongst the nobility, that he was no longer set to inherit his family's wealth and titles, that they must leave Heidel – it all seemed impossible, like a nightmare from which he wished desperately to awake.

'But what about my friends?' he found himself asking, hearing the words coming out as though someone else was speaking them. 'What about Alfonso, and Jarette, and life here in Heidel?'

'Your indiscretions with your so-called friends are half the reason we find ourselves here,' Frederick snapped, anger momentarily flaring up again. 'You are the reason it has come to this, boy. Don't you understand? You have no choice. We are banished. The line of House Ducas is at an end.'

'It is not only his fault,' Martha said, coming to Jordine's defense. 'The king has taken leave of his senses.'

'The king is no longer a man worthy of our aid,' Frederick said. 'Trust me when I say, leaving Heidel for the far-off borders may well prove to be a blessing in disguise. Dark times lie ahead for Serendia, and for the lineage of Domongatt.'

Shield Street was a scene of frenetic activity in the days that followed. The servants had to be laid off, and what items were privately owned by the Ducas family were hastily sold. Jordine participated in none of it. He was sick with anger and remorse, and after another clash with his father, decided to remove himself entirely, seeking solace in the only places that brought him joy – the taverns of Heidel.

He drank alone, until Alfonso eventually sought him out.

'So it's true then,' he said as he sat across from Jordine in the Golden Frog, nursing a flagon of ale. 'The king has truly lost his mind.'

'Careful, or he'll banish you next,' Jordine said bitterly, not looking up from his drink.

Alfonso sat in silence for a while, and Jordine assumed he was simply struggling to find the words necessary to ease his best friend's suffering. When he did speak, however, it was not the condolences Jordine had anticipated.

'There might be a way for you to stay,' he said. Jordine looked at him over the rim of his flagon, scowling.

'This is no time for your jests, Al—' he began to say, but Alfonso shook his head.

'No jest. I've already brought it up with Father, and he is open to further conversations on the matter. He agrees that the complete loss of House Ducas from the court and from Heidel would be a great blow to the kingdom.'

Jordine set his drink down and did his best to focus. His head was aching and his thoughts were far from sharp.

'What're you proposing?' he demanded.

'Adoption,' Alfonso said. Jordine began to laugh, but he carried on, seemingly finding nothing funny in the proposal.

'The Ducases might have been banished, Joe, but what if you were to break ties with your family? You know as well as I that adoption between the noble houses is far from uncommon. It normally only happens after tragic deaths, but there have been many who have avoided the disgrace and dishonor of their wider family by accepting the embrace of nobles not tainted with…'

He trailed off, realizing what he was saying could be construed as an insult, but Jordine offered no reprimand.

Alfonso was right. Adoption was a common tactic employed by houses that sought to bolster their numbers or improve the prospects of their lineage, often combining with young, up-and-coming nobles from lesser houses who sought advancement. There were a score of senior members of the court who did not hail directly from the high families they now represented. Roxanne was only the most famous example, albeit her case – a foreigner adopted by the king – was exceptional.

Yet what Alfonso was proposing would be more of an adoption in reverse. House Rhundi and its head, Edward Rhundi, were one of the poorest and least prestigious in the court – Edward's enemies scathingly called him the 'pauper knight.' By contrast, until a few days ago Jordine had been one of the most eligible young nobles in Serendia. Rather than a powerful family adopting a less prestigious youth in the hopes of reaping future rewards, the Rhundis would be enhancing their prestige by offering shelter to a well-connected young noble. House Ducas had many allies, and Jordine suspected Edward Rhundi hoped to harness those allies by bringing Jordine under his wing.

'My father would not approve,' he said.

'That is nothing new,' Alfonso pointed out. 'And with all due respect, Frederick Ducas's approval no longer holds any weight. Is it true he is set to become a common man-at-arms with the border guard?'

'It is,' Jordine said, still thinking. 'But even if it was agreed between our two houses, what of the king? If what my father says is true, I am half the reason my family are being banished.'

'There are rumors he regrets his actions,' Alfonso said. 'But you know how stubborn and prideful old Crucio is. He cannot possibly pardon your family as a whole, just as he will not go back on his abdication. But by allowing the sole heir of Frederick's line to stay, he shows magnanimity, and takes the edge off what looks like royal impulsiveness.'

'Has your father already spoken with Crucio?' Jordine said, sensing there was more at work than idle speculation by the Rhundis. 'Did he send you to try and convince me?'

'The groundwork has been laid, yes, but I come here as your best friend, not an emissary of my house,' Alfonso said. 'In fact, Edward has forbidden me from speaking with you about it until he has reached out to your father. But when have we ever obeyed our primogenitors?'

That brought a smile to Jordine's lips, and he raised his drink in salute.

'To confounding our fathers,' he said. 'May we never make life easy for them.'

Edward Rhundi visited Shield Street the next day.

Jordine had risen late, still recovering from his hangover. The townhouse was bustling with servants and laborers carrying furniture, tapestries and paintings outside, stripping the wealthy residence like carrion. It sickened Jordine, and the fact he was helpless to stop it only made it worse.

His father called him down to the dining hall. The chamber had been fully emptied, the familiar furnishings gone, the artworks and family portraits that had gazed down upon him all his life now replaced by bare walls. The space felt like the corpse of the life he had once known, at once recognizable and yet not, a dead shell that carried the weight of memories in its cold and unmoving flesh.

Frederick was standing at his place beside the barren hearth, his expression grave. Edward was opposite, face unreadable.

'I suspect you already have some inkling of what we've been discussing,' Frederick said.

'House Rhundi seeks to offer us a lifeline,' Jordine replied.

'House Rhundi seeks to offer *you* a lifeline,' Frederick corrected. 'I'll confess, it is not something I had anticipated, nor have I yet found it in myself to approve of what is being proposed.'

'I am to be adopted,' Jordine surmised, looking from Frederick to Edward. The head of House Rhundi nodded.

'If you are willing, yes,' he said. 'I have made no secret of how I disapprove of both the king's abdication and his treatment of your noble family. House Rhundi has long stood aligned with House Ducas, and I am always mindful of favors granted by your father in the past. I pray to the gods you will both see this as a favor in kind.'

'One that will surely benefit House Rhundi in both the short and long term,' Frederick pointed out, his tone factual rather than accusatory. 'I am not growing younger, and I had hoped to count on the aid of my only son as I embark on what is likely to be the final stage of my life. You are now proposing to take him away from me.'

'You would condemn your entire lineage to obscurity?' Edward asked with a shake of his head. 'I have no reason to risk the ire of the king by taking on your son. I ask only that you make the most of your house's dissolution by ensuring some remnant of the Ducas line remains at the seat of power, here in Heidel.'

Frederick sighed, and looked squarely at Jordine as he replied.

'The final decision belongs to my son. The gods know, he will make up his own mind anyway, and damn any instruction he receives from me.'

Jordine stood, rooted to the spot, caught between the crushing weight of two irreconcilable fates. Leaving Heidel's comforts, pleasures and familiarities was unthinkable. This was more than his home; it was his life. He couldn't imagine the Western Marches would offer anything other than misery and drudgery, assigned to some crumbling garrison amidst the windy, rain-swept hills. Never being able to return to the capital of Serendia, never seeing the likes of Alfonso or Jarette again – it was more than he could bear, greater even than the pain that came with the thought of parting from his mother and father.

After what felt like an age, he spoke.

'I wish to remain in Heidel. If that means being adopted by Edward Rhundi, then so be it.'

'You will break your mother's heart,' Frederick warned. Jordine bowed his head briefly, trying to master his emotions.

'I will see her again, and you likewise, Father,' he said. 'I will not abandon either of you to an unrecorded end on the frontier. I will work within the court to convince the king to reverse his decision, even if it takes years!'

Frederick's expression didn't give away whether he believed his son or not – Jordine wasn't sure if he believed it himself.

'You… must do what you think is right,' he said eventually. 'And if the gods are good, we may yet see each other again, one day.'

FIVE

Two Years Later

Roxanne Domongatt placed her hand over her wine goblet and smiled at the servant who had approached her – he bowed and withdrew back to the edge of the hall with his pitcher.

'I hear the Escoties are raising rents again,' Sir Gabrielo said, taking a sip from his goblet. 'And there is talk of the Marchants and the Altarios doing the same. The harvest looks set to be poor throughout the eastern holdings this year, but none of the noble families in that part of the kingdom have handled their estates well since the drought.'

'A matter worthy of concern,' Roxanne said non-committally. 'And we must be sure, if the harvest does indeed fail, that there are contingencies in place to assist the common folk, and those most in need.'

'You are thoughtful and gracious as ever, Your Majesty,' Gabrielo said, clearly trying to mask the fact that he had been angling to have the Escoties or their neighbors stripped of the lands they were failing to maintain, rather than trying to prompt charitable inclinations towards the peasantry.

'I will speak to my husband and see what can be done about a relief for the poor,' Roxanne said sweetly, knowing that she had outmaneuvered Gabrielo – there was no way he could pursue a vendetta against the nobility in Serendia's eastern regions, not while the focus of the royal household was on ensuring the commoners of that part of the kingdom had enough to survive the coming winter.

'I hope you enjoy the rest of the feast, Your Majesty,' Gabrielo said, accepting defeat and slinking away.

Your Majesty, Roxanne thought to herself. Even after a year and a half, the words still sounded strange, and yet they were entirely true. After all, was she not now Roxanne Domongatt, wife to King Antonio Domongatt and Queen of Serendia?

She walked through the great hall of Heidel Castle, gracefully accepting the bows and greetings of the great and the good of the land, the evening light glimmering through the high windows glinting upon her crown. The long table dominating the space was being weighed down by the first courses of the traditional Fires of Elion banquet, but it was customary for the nobility to mingle and talk while the servants laid the thick bowls of pottage out. Roxanne was taking the chance to do just that – she considered it a vital activity, and despite her serene appearance and slow, stately progress, her mind was razor keen, always watching, always listening, always assessing.

It was only through such means that she had risen to this, the highest station in the land. The court of Serendia was as much a battlefield as the bloodiest of clashes between Valencia and the Western Alliance, and those nobles who did not appreciate that were doomed to floundering in the shifting tides of influence and patronage. Times like these, when almost the whole court was gathered in one place, were not only vital opportunities to display the king's largess, but also allowed Roxanne to test friends and foes alike, all in preparation for what she knew was to come.

One attendee in particular had caught her gaze that evening, and she sought him now with a keen eye, even as she made her progress through the clusters of chattering nobles appear random and unconcerned. She accepted the passing platitudes of Lady Marillo and Sir Gelbert Nistario with a charming smile, brushed off another servant's offer of wine, and then caught sight of what she sought – thick, tousled, platinum-blond hair, catching the light of the torches just being lit upon the walls as night crept in from outside.

She stood off, assessing her prey from afar. Jordine Rhundi, though everyone called him by his old name, Jordine Ducas. Some things were hard to shake, even after adoption – Roxanne could empathize with that. He was a rare sight around court, preferring to spend his time in youthful pursuits – hunting and drinking, gambling and womanizing. Most of the nobility thought him nothing more than a wastrel, and considered Edward Rhundi's decision to adopt him a mistake. Certainly, he had done little to enhance the Rhundi family's standing, and the sight of him on the rare occasions when he did make an appearance never failed to annoy Crucio.

The old king's opinions were less and less Roxanne's concern. Two years had passed since she had convinced him to announce his abdication, and in that time it was his eldest son, Antonio – Roxanne's husband – who had won the crown. His plan to annex Balenos had proven altogether more realistic and achievable than Prince Sergio's mooted invasion of Mediah, and despite the fact that Serendian forces had only laid claim to about half the northern territories, Antonio had come out with the support of the vast majority of the nobility, in no small part thanks to Roxanne's efforts.

In the year and a half since, she had worked tirelessly to secure her and her husband's new position. The most obvious threat, Sergio, had been temporarily placated by the gift of Fort Eindhovein, to the south – he spent much of his time there, and while there were rumors he was gathering warriors to his banner, Roxanne had expected nothing less. His presence at the banquet tonight indicated he was not yet ready to make a move, and he would play the part Roxanne had prepared for him only when the time was right. As for the last of Crucio's sons, rumor had it that Vittorio was now nothing more than a common farmer laboring in Glish. Like Sergio, he would have his uses.

She slipped closer to Jordine, getting a proper view of him through the crowd. He was dressed in a red doublet – regardless of whether it was the royal banquet or the raucous festival currently being held in Heidel's central market, it was tradition for all those attending a feast for the Fires of Elion to wear something red. That was the color of that particular deity, and for her own part Roxanne had tied a scarf of crimson silk around her slender, pale neck.

It came as no surprise to realize that Jordine was deep in conversation with Lady Elysia, Sergio's wife and the younger sister of King Seric of Calpheon. After Roxanne, she was the most powerful woman in the land, yet here was Jordine enjoying her undivided attention, in the midst of the gathered court. Roxanne was experienced enough to read their body language, the small, knowing smiles they exchanged, the way he leant in to her, and she in to him. She was now certain of what she had previously suspected.

The abandoned scion of House Ducas was sleeping with Prince Sergio's wife.

None of that came as a surprise. Jordine was the most handsome young man at court, and everyone knew of his appetites. That Lady Elysia had allowed herself to become enamored, that she would risk her high station for carnal delight, reassured Roxanne that she was no threat. It was just one more weapon she could use as she continued to work towards her ultimate ambition.

Jordine could well prove to be another such weapon. Roxanne had seduced a number of men since coming to the throne – the first had been a lowly servant, just to test that she was capable of it. Since then, several prominent nobles had been beguiled, and while their public allegiances were to King Antonio first and foremost, in truth they now served Roxanne and no other.

Adding Jordine to their ranks would undoubtedly be beneficial. Pillow-talk could prove as useful coming from the women of the court as it did from their husbands, and there was no doubt Jordine had plentiful access to that. Roxanne knew for a fact that Lady Elysia wasn't his only conquest amongst the upper reaches of the nobility. Knowing what he knew would be beneficial.

And besides, seducing Jordine would be a good, and likely very enjoyable, test of her abilities.

Roxanne was just about to move to his side and interrupt his conversation with Elysia when a shout rang through the hall. Her blood ran cold as she turned, fearing some danger she had failed to account for. An assassin? A coup by Sergio? She caught sight of the king, the front of his fine white doublet awash with crimson, and her horror redoubled.

That was, until Antonio let out another exclamation – anger rather than pain – and struck the servant standing next to him. Only then did Roxanne realize that the foolish youth had spilled his pitcher across the king's front – it was wine she was looking at, not blood.

'You clumsy little rat,' Antonio barked, his face rapidly turning as red as his ruined clothing. 'I'll have your head for this, boy!'

Gasps ran through the hall. Jordine momentarily forgotten, Roxanne strode purposefully through the shocked crowd to her husband's side, and caught his wrist before he could strike the cowering servant a second time.

'A mere mistake, my dearest husband,' she said, smile still fixed. 'Such things happen.'

Antonio didn't deign to respond, his fury focused on the servant. 'Do you have any idea how much this doublet costs! It's made from Valencian silkweave! It's more valuable than every damn servant in the citadel!'

He bellowed for Captain Malchevo, who was already nearby and ready to act, hand on the hilt of his sword.

'Kill him,' Antonio demanded.

Even Malchevo, used to obeying royal commands instantly and without question, hesitated.

'Now,' Antonio said.

Malchevo's sword sprang from his scabbard, eliciting louder gasps from the crowd.

The servant was weeping, begging incoherently for his life. For a brief, rare moment, Roxanne felt helpless, not knowing what to do. She watched as the captain swung up his sword to end the poor wretch.

'Stay your blade, Malchevo,' said another voice. The crowd parted hastily, and Crucio emerged. The aged former king's expression was fierce, and he moved to the other side of Antonio from Roxanne.

'Do you want to ruin everyone's appetite, just as the first course is being served?' he demanded. 'This is no place for bloodshed, Antonio. Let the boy live.'

'I will take no lectures in clemency from you, Father,' Antonio declared. 'Just yesterday you flew into a rage at the mere mention that I might reconsider Frederick Ducas's banishment!'

'Undoing the rulings of the past king is another matter entirely,' Crucio said sternly. 'The insolence of Frederick Ducas was far beyond a mistake made by some stupid serving boy. I will never permit his return to Heidel.'

'It is not your place to permit or deny. I am the king now, Father,' Antonio snapped, but Roxanne knew her husband well enough to see that the worst of his fury had burned itself out. She looked past Crucio and the servant at Malchevo, and shook her head slowly. The captain of the guard returned his sword to its sheath.

'Banish the boy from the citadel,' Crucio advised his son. 'His family too. Penury is as ill a fate as a swift death. I simply do not wish my son to become known for hasty, bloodthirsty judgments.'

'You should be thanking the boy, not killing him.' Sergio spoke up drolly from where he was seated at the banquet table, not having bothered to rise despite the commotion. 'You weren't wearing red, brother. He was only trying to ensure you received Elion's full blessings tonight.'

There were a few nervous laughs. Antonio's wrathful expression grew more guarded, as he seemed to become aware of the entire court staring at him. Roxanne offered a silent prayer to all the gods that he would pick the right choice, and not escalate this any further. For all his own brutal and impulsive decisions over the years, Crucio was right. Roxanne had no wish for her husband to be known as a butcher, at least not for the time being.

Finally, Antonio relented. He snapped at another set

of servants to go upstairs and prepare his wardrobe, then demanded that Malchevo march the youth who had spilled the wine out of his sight. He and his family were never to show their faces in Heidel again, under pain of death.

The court seemed to let loose a collective sigh of relief. Cautious conversation resumed, slowly rising back to its previous height. Without speaking to either his wife or his father, Antonio swept from the hall.

'I thought you had learned to temper his mood better than that, my dear,' Crucio said quietly to Roxanne. She gave the slightest shrug.

'Would you have acted any differently?' she asked.

'But I am not the king, not anymore. You must be watchful, Roxanne. He will have need of your guidance in the coming months and years.'

'You honor me,' Roxanne said. 'You know that I will never cease working to repay you and your family. I am here today only because of your good graces.'

'Sweet child,' Crucio said with a smile, patting Roxanne's shoulder affectionately. The former king moved to his place at the banquet table, which was slowly filling as the nobility took their seats.

Roxanne went in the opposite direction, stepping away, hunting for any sign of Jordine. She saw Elysia, but she was now at Sergio's side, once again the loyal and attentive wife.

She scanned the seats, and then the edge of the hall, but of the disgraced Ducas there was no sign. He had used the commotion caused by the spilled wine to slip away.

Roxanne felt a rare surge of frustration, yet outwardly her smile never wavered.

There would be time aplenty to ensnare Jordine Ducas, of that she had no doubt.

SIX

Jordine slipped from the citadel and made his way to Gallows Street, treading familiar back alleys. It was one of the less reputable parts of Heidel, but he was familiar enough with the dregs and scum of the area to know he wouldn't be troubled. He certainly felt more comfortable beneath their gaze than that of King Antonio's guards, or the scheming, plotting courtiers.

He came to the rear entrance of the Rhundi residence and let himself in using the key he had been given. The family's sole servant, Mikos, met him inside the door, and directed him to the dining room upstairs.

Edward Rhundi was just sitting down to eat. Jordine hesitated on the threshold of the small, simple chamber, until Edward spoke up.

'He isn't here. He's gone to the Lilly Valley. You can join him there – but first, sit, and eat. You must be hungry, if you left the feast early.'

Jordine stepped inside and took his place on Edward's right. Mikos began to serve them both – it was humble fare compared to the banquet Jordine had turned down, but that was no surprise. The Rhundis were too poor to afford an invitation to the king's Fires of Elion feast, too poor to dine regularly on venison and wild boar, too poor to afford a townhouse anywhere but the likes of Gallows Street. But thanks to Jordine, they weren't too poor to exert their influence among the great and the good of Serendia.

'I take it the feast was well attended?' Edward asked. Jordine took a few mouthfuls of broth before replying, knowing he had little choice other than to pass on all he had learned that evening. Or almost all, anyway.

'Only the Adolfinos were absent. Rumor is that Lord Adolfino is ill, possibly dying. There was no sign of his son.'

'Interesting,' Edward said, picking at his own meal. 'Were the Rossies and the Volpes talking, or does their feud continue? And what of the Carpagios? Were they received by the king despite their previous disagreements?'

'From what I could see, the Rossies and Volpes still want nothing to do with each other, and according to Sir Ulbert the latter are attempting to find allies in the south to help with their territorial disputes. As for the Carpagios, they were received and seated in a prominent position just below the high table, so I can only assume they are once more in Antonio's good graces.'

'Assumption is dangerous,' Edward pointed out. 'But continue. What of the Meldachies and their adoption of the Polovi boy?'

Jordine kept relating what he had discovered at the royal gathering, holding only one thing back – his liaisons with Lady Elysia. He was more than tired of divulging everything he learned to Edward, and that particular hidden scandal was one he would rather keep to himself. If nothing else, it gave him a sense of control, not to mention an advantage when it came to the unpredictable politics of the Serendian court. As much as Edward had rehabilitated Jordine's presence among the nobility in the immediate aftermath of his family's banishment, he knew relying solely on the Rhundis would leave him vulnerable if they, in turn, ever fell afoul of the new king's wrath.

'Why did you leave early?' Edward asked abruptly, interrupting Jordine's report. 'The hour is not late, and the banquet is still under way, surely? So why didn't you stay?'

'I was coming to that,' Jordine lied. 'There was an accident. One of the servants spilled wine all across the king's doublet. He was so furious he tried to have the boy cut down where he stood, in front of the whole court. He had to be talked down by the queen and Crucio.'

'Is that so?' Edward mused, smiling faintly. 'Truly, Antonio has his father's anger.'

'I heard word of a deeper dispute between them.' Jordine would have preferred to conceal that particular piece of information, but Edward would become suspicious if he heard the news elsewhere. And he would definitely hear this news elsewhere.

'It is said that Antonio is considering recalling Frederick… my father. Ending his banishment.'

Jordine kept his expression neutral as Edward carefully regarded him, seemingly attempting to gauge Jordine's own thoughts at such information.

'I take it Crucio is not receptive to such an idea?' Edward said.

'Far from it. From what others have said, and from what I overheard between the king and his father during the incident with the servant, it sounds as though it is driving a wedge between them.'

'That is dangerous news,' Edward warned. 'Dangerous, but valuable. We must do what we can to find out more, in case matters escalate.'

'You think Vittorio's prediction could come true?' Jordine asked. 'War between Crucio and his sons?'

'Perhaps. Where was Sergio amidst all this?'

'He could barely bring himself to intervene,' Jordine said. 'I do not know where he stands.'

More lies. Jordine had no intention of telling his adopted father that he had learned all manner of things about Sergio from the prince's own wife. Sergio and Lady Elysia spent much of their time in the south, at Fort Eindhovein, which Sergio was turning into his own private stronghold. There he brooded, and while he did not admit his intentions even to Elysia, she had concerns that he was gathering his strength for some future conflict.

'So, the king had to be restrained by his wife and father from gutting some stupid servant boy,' Edward mused after eating more. 'But that still does not explain why you came here early…'

Jordine had hoped Edward had overlooked that, but the master of House Rhundi was too sharp. In truth, Jordine had sensed that he was being too open with Elysia, and had decided the incident with the wine was a good opportunity to make himself scarce. He couldn't fully admit that reasoning to Edward, however.

'The king and his father were both in ill moods, and I had no wish to risk my presence souring Crucio further,' Jordine said. That, at least, was half true.

'Has Princess Jarette returned from Balenos?' Edward asked, and Jordine realized he was trying to gauge whether he had been spending time with her instead of doing as instructed and scouring the court for news and information. That suspicion, at least, was easily disabused.

'She has not,' he said. 'Though word is she is desperate to return to Heidel.'

'That appears to be a reoccurring theme,' Edward mused. 'I wonder what your reaction would be, should Crucio relent or the king overrule his wishes, and permit Frederick to return to the capital?'

'He is my father,' Jordine said, wondering how best to approach his response. 'But he abandoned me. Two years, and barely a letter from him or my mother. You took me in when the Ducas name was at its lowest. You risked your own reputation by shielding one who had defied the then-king. I owe more to you than I do to Frederick Ducas.'

Of course, none of that mentioned the less altruistic side of Edward's decision to adopt: how he had employed Jordine as a veritable spy in the Serendian court. The

Rhundis might still be one of the poorest noble houses, but they were not without influence, and that was in no small part thanks to Jordine's efforts. They both knew that, but neither would admit it to the other.

'We shall see,' Edward said eventually, as he finished his broth. 'Hopefully I can still count Frederick as a friend, should he return. And if he does, I'm sure you will inform him of how I have looked after you these past few years. The greater concern is Antonio's desire to drive this through in defiance of Crucio's wishes. He didn't stand up for your father when Crucio first banished him, so why now, years later?'

'There is likely more at play than meets the eye,' Jordine said.

'As always,' Edward replied. 'Very well. Finish your food, and you may go and hunt down my son. Tell him he isn't to waste the whole night in his cups. Marshal Cliff is in town, and he has sword instructions with him tomorrow morning. I thought you would consider joining them both. We might all have need of skill with a blade before too long.'

Jordine found Alfonso where his father had said he would be, drinking in the Lilly Valley. He was with a gaggle of so-called friends, all of them louts and grifters trying to gain influence with the Rhundis, or simply get Alfonso into more debt, but they made themselves scarce when Jordine appeared.

'I thought you were dining with the high and mighty tonight,' Alfonso said, barely glancing up from his tankard.

'I didn't find their company agreeable,' Jordine said, sitting down opposite him with his own ale. 'And you know I'd much rather be here with you than playing politics at court. I was hoping we'd go to the festival in the marketplace before the night is up.'

'I take it you've finished delivering your latest report to my father, then,' Alfonso said, not bothering to keep the bitterness from his voice. He was drunk, and Jordine was intent on joining him in that state, but his old friend's attitude stung him.

'I only pass on what I hear around the great hall,' he said. 'Your father expects it.'

'He also expects that I will grow up to be an upstanding knight of the realm and a worthy inheritor of the vast riches and prestige of the mighty House Rhundi, yet here we are,' Alfonso pointed out, taking a draft from his tankard.

'You don't understand,' Jordine said, knowing he shouldn't be drawn in like this; a public quarrel with his inebriated friend was the last thing he needed. But his temper had been worn thin, and he had restrained himself from having this conversation with Alfonso too many times. He was tired of allowing his best friend to assume he was competing for his father's favor.

'You're more a Rhundi than I am now, Joe,' Alfonso said, refusing to let it lie. 'Edward doesn't give two damns about me, not now that he has the handsome, charismatic

Jordine to carry the family name. It wouldn't surprise me if he chooses you to receive the inheritance!'

Jordine was tempted to ask what damned inheritance he could expect from such a poor family, but managed to restrain himself once again.

'I don't do any of this to earn favor from your father, Al,' he said. 'I do it because I owe him a debt. He took me in when no one else would. Without him, I'd be going mad, somewhere out on the Western Marches. I'd likely never see you again.'

'Spare me the thought of so dreadful a fate,' Alfonso said mockingly. 'You had a choice, Joe. You didn't have to abandon your family. You didn't have to leave your mother and father to go into exile without you, just so you could keep coming here to drink and rut your life away. And you didn't have to accept my father's offer, and usurp me as his sole heir.'

'I've usurped nothing,' Jordine said, patience at an end. 'You think I enjoy acting as Edward Rhundi's little spy at court? Do you think I embrace the legacy Crucio left me with? The last, disgraced Ducas, clinging onto the vestiges of his life of luxury. I see how they all look at me. Pity or disgust, that's all I receive.'

'It's all you deserve,' Rhundi snarled back. 'If you had any honor, you would have accepted banishment with your parents.'

Jordine stood without meaning to, his chair clattering back, ale spilling across the table. For a moment, he wanted nothing more than to lunge across the table at his friend. And from his startled expression, Alfonso expected him to.

Instead, he looked around at the inn's silent patrons, meeting their shocked gazes fiercely, before slowly looking back at his friend.

'You're drunk,' he said bluntly. 'So I'm going to pretend you didn't say any of that. When you crawl home, make sure you wake *your* father, and tell him Jordine Ducas won't be able to help you with your swordplay tomorrow morning. Tell him I wouldn't want someone without honor helping to teach his only son how to fight.'

SEVEN

'The old fool has gone too far this time,' Antonio said as he swept into the royal bedchamber, not even acknowledging his wife's presence. She was standing by the cage holding Mnemosyne, her prized falcon, and had been feeding it slender strips of meat.

'He is as stubborn as a Mediah mule,' he continued, striding over to the silken bed and banging a fist against one of the four carved posts supporting its canopy. 'It's a miracle you were ever able to convince him to relinquish the throne!'

Roxanne composed herself and shut the small wire door to Mnemosyne's cage before turning to face her husband. A month had passed since the Fires of Elion feast, and in that time the relationships between the Domongatts had only continued to deteriorate. Antonio and Crucio were locked in perpetual, petty strife, and Sergio had withdrawn from the capital back to his fastness at Fort Eindhovein the day after the banquet. He had not communicated with his brother or father since. It was all moving too quickly for Roxanne's liking, driven by factors she was struggling to control, and if there was one thing she detested, it was not being in control.

'The years have worn your father down,' she said, wondering what Antonio and Crucio had clashed over this time, and whether discussing it really couldn't have waited until the morning. 'He could not in all conscience deny my claim that he no longer had the drive and energy required to rule. He stepped down for the greater good of our family, and Serendia.'

'Did he?' Antonio asked rhetorically. 'Because it seems like he still rules, at least in his own head! As though it isn't enough that he questions my tax levy on the nobility or my expansion of the Black Stone mineworks and the imp labor forces in the north and west, he makes new demands daily, each more vexing than the last. Now he wishes to be solely responsible for dispensing knighthoods. He acts as though I am still a naive child, who does not grasp what that means. He would control the kingdom's greatest patronage, as well as deciding the composition of Serendia's war host. If I permit that alongside his other excesses, I will be king in name only! I did not conquer Balenos only to become my father's puppet ruler!'

Roxanne decided it would be prudent not to mention that the conquest of Balenos was still only half complete, or that he was using his own younger sister as a puppet ruler in the region.

'Giving up the reins of power is difficult,' she said, wondering where she might find compromise between father and son. Despite her best efforts, it seemed as though the middle ground between them narrowed every day.

'Your father needs time,' she went on, before Antonio could manage another outburst. 'My advice, if you wish for it, dear husband, would be to concede the smaller matters. Do not grant him the sole right to dispense knighthoods, but relinquish the little things. Your determination to absolve Frederick Ducas, for example.'

'Everyone from the court to the beggars on Soot Row knows banishing Frederick was a mistake,' Antonio said. 'And the decision to allow his boy to remain around the court like a lecherous stench only undermines it further. Reinstating Frederick would be seen as righting one of my father's wrongs, and besides, I have need of a strong and loyal high constable. If Sergio truly is preparing a military coup, having Frederick Ducas on our side could be the difference between victory and defeat.'

'You are getting ahead of yourself, husband,' Roxanne said. 'Do not create enemies where none yet exist. Your father is still popular among the people, especially in Heidel, but he is without allies where it counts. There is hardly a noble who would declare for him in the event that this dispute… gets out of hand. As for your brother, he may well harbor thoughts of usurpation, but he is in no position to do so anytime soon. We granted him Fort Eindhovein for a reason – it is a potent stronghold, but it also leaves him removed from the center of power here, in Heidel. He cannot build support while he remains far to the south.'

Antonio grunted noncommittally, pacing across the room to fling open the shutters and look down on the city below. Heidel's spires and chimneys stretched away beneath the citadel's western tower, smoke rising steadily into the clear, autumnal night air, the glow of fires and candles flickering in the windows. More ruddy light spilled from Soot Row, where the foundries were still at work, and glimmered from the steeple of the Church of Elion, where the high priest was holding the traditional autumn Vigil of the Dying Embers. Antonio took it all in, and Roxanne could feel his anger ebbing.

'As long as your father and brother do nothing foolish, all will be well,' she said, rising and going to join him, placing a hand on his shoulder. 'And if one of them does, we will be in an ideal position to deal with them.'

An hour after the king and queen had retired to bed, the guards manning the citadel's gatehouse permitted two masked and cloaked riders to pass out into the streets beyond. They cantered across the East Bridge over the Demi and on into the vineyards of the Moretti estate, where they joined another dozen figures.

Crucio was among them. He dismounted beneath the vines, the darkness shot through with sudden firelight as one of his retainers lit a torch.

The small assembly bowed, but Crucio told them to stand straight.

'You do not bow to me, friends,' he said, spreading his arms as though in benediction. 'Not until I am again wearing the crown of Serendia. Make no mistake, it saddens me beyond measure that it has come to this, but everyone knows it, from the highest offices of the court to the common rabble in the taverns – my decision to yield the throne to Antonio was misguided, and his refusal to listen to reason or sound experience is placing the kingdom on a dark path.'

'We are with you, my king,' said one of the nobles who had heeded Crucio's secret summons. 'I know I am not alone when I say that everyone here tonight is ready to die for you, and the future of Serendia.'

'Gods willing, it will not come to that,' Crucio said. 'Hopefully, my son will yet see sense. But he is a Domongatt – I expect he will not surrender without a fight. The most important thing now is to gather our strength. The common people will support us when my intentions become known, but we will still need professional soldiery if we are to convince Antonio to abdicate. And for that, we must ride south. To Fort Eindhovein.'

News came to Antonio and Roxanne while they were still in bed the next morning, brought to them by a nervous-looking servant.

'What do you mean, "gone"?' Antonio demanded, sitting bolt upright and startling Roxanne awake.

'His servants and retainers are not in their quarters,

sire, and there is no response from your father's chambers in the east tower,' the servant said, hovering in the doorway. 'There are also reports that cloaked riders left the citadel late last night, and were seen on the streets, heading south, for the Moretti estate.'

'Order Malchevo to break down his bedroom door and search the place,' Antonio barked. 'And find me the guards who were manning the gatehouse last night! Go!'

The servant fled, and Roxanne rose, calling for her maids to attend her. She and Antonio dressed in haste, the king spitting with rage.

'Last night, while you were counseling patience and common ground, that old bastard was fleeing the roost! I pray you did not know, for your sake!'

'I did not,' Roxanne said truthfully. Her mind was racing – she had anticipated something like this, but not yet. She had imagined the feud between Antonio and Crucio would rumble on for weeks yet before one snapped, but it seemed Crucio had decided to seize the initiative.

'Where could he have gone?' Antonio said, forced to stand still while a servant laced his breeches up the back. 'I'll have that old dog Moretti questioned, immediately. This whole thing stinks of treason!'

'It does,' Roxanne agreed. 'But how far does it extend? We must establish which nobles your father has beguiled.'

'You're the one who said he has no influence!'

'Little influence, but perhaps more than we anticipated. The greatest risk is that he goes to your brother.'

'He wouldn't dare,' Antonio snapped. 'Even if he was

base enough to try and turn one son against another, Sergio wouldn't be so foolish as to throw his lot in with such a desperate gambit.'

'I agree,' Roxanne said. 'But as you've pointed out, my last predictions were not entirely accurate. We must prepare for the worst, but do so with care. A call to war will only inflame the situation.'

Antonio swatted aside the servant assisting him and finished the last strings himself.

'We need to know who is with us, and who is against,' he said. 'We'll start with my own guard. I'll have Malchevo find out who was on duty at the gatehouse last night, and interrogate them. If there are any still loyal to my father among the royal guard, they'll be rooted out! At the same time, you are to begin inquiries at court. Find out who is absent, who is whispering sedition.'

'The gathering of the alms is due to be held in two weeks,' Roxanne said, thinking. 'I can order it to be brought forward. That will be enough of an excuse to bring together a sufficient number of the nobility to make inquiries.'

'Do so,' Antonio said, flinging the bedchamber door open and ordering the two guards outside to fall into step behind him. 'I'm going to find Malchevo.'

Roxanne allowed her maids to finish dressing her before ordering them both to return to the servants' quarters and begin inquiries of their own. She was angry. How had she failed to predict this? Crucio had stolen a night's march, perhaps literally, and now they were having to scramble to catch up. What mattered was a swift but measured response. Overreact, and the kingdom could be at war before the day was out.

Jordine sat on the edge of his bed, rereading the letter and smiling despite himself.

It had been delivered that morning to Gallows Street by a messenger in royal livery. Jordine's initial concern had evaporated when he discovered who it was from – Jarette.

The Domongatt princess was returning unbidden to the capital from Balenos. It was an unannounced visit; if Antonio caught wind of it before her arrival, he would order her back to his new puppet kingdom. She was sick of life in the cold north, and was now already in Heidel and hoping to see her old friends at the Golden Frog before news of her presence reached the citadel.

Jordine folded the letter away. It had been addressed to both him and Alfonso, but he hadn't seen the other member of their triumvirate for days. According to Edward, he'd taken to sleeping in a rented room at the Lilly Valley, rather than his family home. Jordine couldn't find the strength to confront him again, and Edward seemed to have little interest in reaching out to his son.

None of which Jarette was aware of. She had been gone for too long, removed from Heidel and its gossip and power plays. Jordine had said nothing in his letters to her of his clashes with Alfonso, or how Edward was using him as a spy within the court. As far as she knew, her two best friends were still living under the same roof and still getting up to their ill-advised escapades.

But perhaps that was a good thing? Maybe this was an opportunity to be seized. Alfonso had always had something for Jarette – it had been obvious to Jordine, as much as his friend tried to hide it. He had never pressed him on it, sensing it lay beyond the realms of friendly banter and mockery. The son of the pauper knight and the daughter of a king – it was as unlikely a combination as any in the realm, worthy of old stories or bawdy tavern songs. Jordine half suspected Alfonso's current moroseness was as much due to Jarette's enforced absence as it was his relationship with his father.

If that was the case, this could be the chance to heal the divide. If nothing else, he was sure Jarette's irreverent humor – always so unbecoming for a princess – would help lift Alfonso's spirits. He would go to the Golden Frog and take Jarette to find Alfonso, and the three of them could reminisce about past adventures over a flagon or two.

His sudden good mood evaporated before he had even reached the front door. Edward caught him as he came downstairs, a letter of his own in one hand, the paper bearing the royal seal.

'Have you heard about this?' he asked, brandishing it. Jordine frowned, sudden concern taking hold. Had Jarette written a second letter to Alfonso, which his father had intercepted?

'Heard about what?' he replied.

'A formal notice from the citadel,' Edward said. 'The

queen has commanded that Alms Day be brought forward one week.'

Jordine did his best to hide his relief, making to brush by with an offhand comment that the Rhundis never had money to spare for Alms Day anyway, but Edward blocked his route to the door.

'There is more to this than the well-to-do making their yearly show of largess,' he said. 'There are all sorts of rumors on the wind this morning. While you were sleeping off your hangover, I have been hearing word of strange happenings at the citadel, and cloaked riders out on the streets in the dead of night.'

'How thrilling,' Jordine said acerbically. 'But as you've just pointed out, I'm still recovering from last night's libations, and would appreciate being left to do so in peace. I feel like someone took a mace to my skull.'

'Spare me your self-pity,' Edward snapped. 'Something is happening out there, something important. We need to find out just what, before we're left behind. Understood?'

Jordine was sorely tempted to grab hold of Edward and force him out of the way, but he took a long, slow breath, and made himself speak instead.

'What would you have me do?'

'Go to the citadel, see if you can gain entry on some pretense. If not, observe who enters and who leaves, and question your usual contacts. Someone will know something. And rouse Alfonso while you're at it. He did not return home last night.'

'He and I are no longer on speaking terms,' Jordine said.

'You are not children anymore, you should—'

'If you spent half as much time attending to your only son as you do the wiles of the court, he might not have grown to despise you,' Jordine barked, rising to his full height and facing Edward down. 'You may use me as you please, but Al deserves better. Go and find him yourself, and tell him as much!'

Edward just stared at him, lost for words. Jordine pushed past and out, into the morning light.

EIGHT

Edward was right about at least one thing – something important was occurring at the citadel. The entrances were barred, and Jordine noted a larger-than-usual number of royal guards on the battlements above, as well as outside the gatehouse, where courtiers and other visitors were being turned away.

The citadel had been locked down.

As interesting as that was, Jordine had no intention of doing as Edward had instructed and wasting a morning lingering in side-streets watching those who approached the portcullis. He was about to turn and make for the Golden Frog when a familiar voice caused him to pause.

'Going looking for someone, Jordine Ducas?'

Jordine smiled at the cloaked figure who had addressed him, standing in the doorway to a closed tanner's shop.

'I go to seek the fairest princess in all of Serendia,'

he replied, feigning a puzzled look. 'I don't suppose you've seen her, have you, traveler?'

'It's easy to be the fairest when you're also the only one,' Jarette said, grinning at him from beneath her hood. 'Didn't you get my letter?'

'I did,' Jordine said, glancing up and down the street to make sure they weren't being observed. Thankfully, the shut gates were holding the attention of the steadily growing crowd in the street. 'I was just about to make for the Golden Frog. Why aren't you there?'

'Rumors,' Jarette said conspiratorially. 'I came home to find Heidel awash with them. I heard the castle is shut up, so decided rather than sit and wait on the last of the mighty Ducases to make his appearance, I would take a look at what's happening for myself.'

'You left your entourage at the inn?'

'I did. One of the perks of being the glorious ruler of Balenos – people actually have to do what I say now. Or at least some of them do, occasionally. Where's Al?'

'Probably at the Lilly Valley,' Jordine said. 'But your guess is as good as mine.'

'Isn't it a little early for that, even for you two?'

'I wasn't with him. We… aren't on speaking terms.'

Jarette let loose a short, wicked laugh.

'Oh, you two! What was it this time? Did you try to drink each other under the table, and end up getting thrown out? Or did he leave the tab for you to pick up, again? Or did you both fall in love with the same bar wench?'

'It's not like that,' Jordine said, feeling mild annoyance at Jarette's cheerful indifference. 'Things haven't been the same since the adoption. Or since you left.'

'Who would have thought?' Jarette said. 'The only one with any brains between the three of us. No wonder everything's been going to shit since I was banished – sorry, *enthroned* – in the north!'

Jordine couldn't help but laugh again at his friend's aggressive tone. Time away had not dulled her edge one bit.

'Well, I for one am glad to have you back, oh great queen of Balenos. I suspect your family might be less delighted though. Won't your brother just send you away again?'

'He can try,' Jarette growled. 'But something tells me he has more on his mind right now.'

'You have any idea what's happening in there?' Jordine asked, nodding back towards the citadel looming above them.

'A servant probably spilled more wine over my brother, and he's ordering mass murder in recompense,' Jarette said with only a hint of humor.

'You heard about that, then?'

'Half the continent has heard about it. The gods know, we Domongatts have our tempers, all of us, but when you start ordering summary executions in your own feasting hall, it suggests perhaps you don't have the right temperament for kingship.'

'Careful, your brother might consider that treasonous,' Jordine warned. Jarette simply scoffed and began to walk away.

'Where are you going?' Jordine asked, hurrying to catch up.

'You said Al was in the Lilly Valley, didn't you?' she demanded without breaking stride. 'I'm going to find him. Sorry to disappoint, Ducas, but I didn't come all this way to see your handsome face alone.'

Jordine roused Alfonso from the musty darkness of his commandeered tavern bedroom. It seemed at first that his adopted brother would lash out at him for the intrusion, but then his eyes fixed on Jarette.

Jordine had never seen his friend change so quickly. Color began to return to his deathly pale cheeks, and he gave the first proper smile Jordine had seen in weeks.

'Your brother won't be pleased with a surprise visit,' he warned as he got properly dressed behind the room's blanket screen, while Jordine prized open the shutters and allowed some light and air into the stinking, fetid chamber.

'So everyone keeps telling me,' Jarette responded, allowing her hood down now that she was temporarily hidden inside. Her red hair shone in the light streaming through the window, and Jordine had to look away hastily, for fear the princess would notice that he had been admiring her. Nothing but merciless mockery would follow something like that.

'She has picked a fine day to return to us,' Jordine said, addressing Alfonso through the screen. 'Have you heard the rumors?'

'I've known nothing but a pounding headache since I slipped into unconsciousness in the arms of some wench last night, Joe,' Alfonso said tersely, still out of sight. 'No, I haven't heard any of your damned rumors.'

'The citadel is shut, and the guard have been called out,' Jordine went on, sensing that Alfonso wasn't willing to let the rift between them heal just yet, whether Jarette was with them or not. 'There are reports of strange figures riding the streets last night. Something has happened, but nobody is sure exactly what.'

'Maybe someone's murdered my brother,' Jarette said lightly, then shrugged when Jordine looked at her in alarm.

'None of us have any shortage of enemies, Joe,' she said defensively.

'If that were the case, then you truly would have picked a bad time to come home,' Alfonso said, stepping out from behind the screen, still looking disheveled but at least now fully dressed. 'As a direct claimant to the throne, your own life would be in danger.'

'Well, whoever's responsible would have to bump off Sergio as well, and good luck reaching him while he's tucked up with Elysia in Fort Eindhovein,' Jarette said. 'Unless it's Sergio's doing.'

'This is idle speculation,' Jordine complained. 'If we're going to get to the bottom of this, we need to gain entry to the citadel.'

'Is that what we're doing now?' Alfonso asked. '"Getting to the bottom of this"? Did my father order you to investigate, Jordine? His faithful, blond-haired hound. For my own part, I'd rather get a head start on the ale.'

'Don't be so petulant,' Jarette ordered. 'Whatever happened between you two, you need to fix it. You were supposed to be looking out for each other while I was gone. And don't act like you aren't intrigued by all this, Al. It's lucky I'm with you both.'

'Why?' Jordine asked, causing Jarette to look at him as though he was a complete imbecile.

'My name is Jarette Domongatt, princess of the blood,' she exclaimed. 'If anyone in Serendia can get you into the citadel, it's me!'

Jarette was as good as her word. Hood down, she walked Jordine and Alfonso right up to the front gate, where the guards in their plate armor and red and yellow liveries intercepted them.

'Have I been gone so long that you do not recognize your princess?' Jarette demanded tartly as she cast back her hood. Their commander, a sergeant Jordine vaguely recognized, exchanged alarmed glances with his immediate subordinate before attempting to placate the princess.

'My orders come direct from the king, Your Highness. No one is to leave, nor enter, not until I am instructed otherwise.'

'Why? What could possibly have upset my dear brother to such an extent that he has locked himself away in his own castle?'

'I am not at liberty to say, Your Highness.'

'Ridiculous,' Jarette snapped. 'Do you know how far I have traveled? All the way from the far north, from Balenos! Spending day and night on rutted tracks, through the autumn rains! Come to see my brother, *the king*, with news so urgent I must deliver it in person! You serve Antonio, so you must know his temper. You must know what fate awaits you when I inform him that you delayed my entry into my own family's citadel, and forced me to wait outside with the common muck. If the information I carry is not delivered by me *in person* and *immediately*, it won't only be your life at stake. The entire kingdom will stand on the brink!'

Jordine did his best not to laugh as he watched the sergeant wither beneath the bombardment, shriveling like a cursed fig tree. By the time Jarette finished, he was snapping at his men to stand aside and calling up to the guards manning the portcullis to unbar the gate.

'What of your companions?' he managed, one last token attempt at defiance as Jordine and Alfonso made to stride past him in Jarette's wake.

'You mean my guards?' Jarette demanded. 'You would have me walk the halls and corridors alone in these most dangerous of times?'

'My own men can provide an escort of—'

'Your own men have done quite enough already, wouldn't you say? Be thankful I am not reporting your insubordination, sergeant. Not *yet*.'

No further attempt was made to impede the trio as

they walked in. The citadel's cobbled courtyard, usually busy with servants, dignitaries and guards hurrying to and fro, was almost deserted. Part of the reason became rapidly apparent.

There were two bodies hanging from a gibbet erected in the courtyard's center. Their heads were still hooded, and while they had been stripped of their armor, it was obvious from their uniform underclothes that they had both once been members of the royal guard. Crows had already started to gather on the crossbeam holding up the two limp corpses, and one cawed viciously at Jarette, Jordine and Alfonso as they emerged from the gatehouse.

'For the love of Elion,' Jarette hissed under her breath. 'What is my brother up to now?'

They carried on past the grisly sight, into the keep. There were guards everywhere, but none tried to stop the trio. Jarette demanded to know the king's whereabouts from one, and he directed them to a private audience chamber within the north wall.

They heard raised voices as they drew nearer, ringing down through the spiral staircase leading to the room. Moments later, Roxanne appeared, the queen descending in the opposite direction.

Jordine and Alfonso hastily bowed and made way, as much as the tight stone spiral would permit, but Jarette stood gazing up at the queen. Jordine caught a flash of surprise on Roxanne's face before she composed herself.

'Princess,' she said, smiling at Jarette, who did not return the expression.

'Roxanne,' she replied tersely.

'We did not receive word that you were returning to the capital,' Roxanne said, showing no sign of disapproval at the younger woman's tone.

'Because I did not send any,' Jarette said. 'I thought my brother and father might enjoy a surprise visit, but I see at least one of them is in a hanging mood.'

'That would be the former,' Roxanne said, glancing back up the stairway. 'I would advise against seeing him at this precise moment.'

'I've come a long way,' Jarette responded. 'And I want to know what's going on. Why are members of the royal guard being strung up in the courtyard? Why are the gates barred?'

'If you are set on seeing him, you can ask him yourself,' Roxanne said. Her gaze moved from Jarette to Jordine and Alfonso, as though she was about to demand to know the reason the pair were accompanying the princess within the citadel. But instead of speaking, she collected the skirts of her voluminous green dress and resumed her descent, brushing close to Jordine as she passed. Jarette finally moved to make way for her.

'Pity,' Jarette muttered as they began to climb once more. 'I was hoping she was the one they'd assassinated.'

NINE

They found King Antonio with Captain Malchevo in the audience chamber, conversing in low tones. Talk stopped when the trio entered, and Antonio let out a curse.

'For the love of all the gods! Jarette, what are you doing here?'

'It's good to see you too, big brother,' Jarette exclaimed with false joy. 'I see your rule is as stable and benevolent as it was before you banished me to the edge of the continent.'

Antonio's expression was dark, and grew even more so as he took in the presence of Jordine and Alfonso at Jarette's back.

'Why are they here?' he demanded.

'They are my gallant protectors,' Jarette said. 'I have need of them in such fraught times. Are there assassins stalking the corridors? Is a coup bubbling up among the nobles? Surely those are the only explanations for your current state of anxiety, dear brother.'

Antonio exchanged a glance with the ever-stoic Malchevo, before addressing Jarette again.

'What do you know of what happened here last night?'

'Nothing,' Jarette exclaimed. 'I only arrived in Heidel this morning! If you won't simply tell me what is causing such a fuss, I will go and find Father and have it from him.'

'You will do well to find him,' Antonio said, glancing briefly at Jordine and Alfonso before deciding to continue. 'He is gone. He left last night, with his retinue. A few servants and several members of my guard accompanied him. The two you saw swinging down in the courtyard were the ones who permitted him to leave without raising the alarm.'

'I wasn't aware Father was under house arrest,' Jarette said.

'Nor was he, but his actions recently have been… concerning. He has been making increasingly unreasonable demands. Just yesterday he asked to bear the sole right to the dispensation of knighthoods, and oversight of the Serendian host – and when I refused, he flew into a rage.'

'How unlike him to do that,' Jarette said sarcastically. 'And I'm sure you, on the other hand, were the model of diplomacy and restraint?'

'I don't have time for your razor tongue, sister,' Antonio snarled. 'We have to assume my father is planning to dethrone me and trying to raise a coup. Serendia stands on the brink of war.'

'The ironies are endless,' Jarette said, striding over to the chamber's arrow slit and gazing down onto the autumnal vista stretching away to the north. 'He was the one who threw everything into turmoil by abdicating, and the one who chose you to rule over Sergio. Yet now he wants his throne back. And you really think he would go to war against his chosen heir to recover it?'

'I do not know what he is thinking,' Antonio admitted. 'Only that he has let his arrogance and his need for aggrandizement take control. I cannot tell where he has ridden to. My fear is it may be south, to Fort Eindhovein.'

'Sergio,' Jarette said, looking back at her eldest brother. 'You think they would conspire against you?'

'For Father, it is the shortest, straightest path back to the throne,' Antonio said. 'For Sergio… well, we have hardly been on good terms since my ascension.'

'I really was born into the most loving and stable of families,' Jarette said with a sigh. 'It sounds as though I would be best served by heading back north and letting you boys fight it out. I should be thanking you, actually. If you hadn't sent me away to that miserable place, I might well have been caught up in all this.'

'It would be best if you stayed,' Antonio said. 'It is much easier to guarantee your safety here. If there is a faction, or factions, seeking to usurp the throne, they will likely view you as an obstacle to be removed.'

'How thoughtful,' Jarette said. 'Or is this just a cover to shut me away, as it seems you wish you had done with Father? If so, you might as well cast me into the citadel's dungeons. I will not become my older brother's glorified prisoner.'

'You will never be my prisoner, Jarette,' Antonio snapped. 'You are free to go whenever you like. But consider what I have said. This is currently the safest place in Serendia, for either of us.'

Jordine expected Jarette to argue further, but she did not. He supposed she was considering her options, and did not fancy the thought of returning north to the barren, windswept hills of Balenos, with winter looming.

'I will stay for now,' she told her brother. 'And hopefully help the rest of you come to your senses, before it's too late. You see conspiracies everywhere, and I doubt your noble queen helps ease your mind in that regard.'

'Roxanne is as surprised by my father's disappearance as anyone,' Antonio said. Jarette scoffed but didn't press her point.

The king looked suddenly tired. He joined Jarette at the window.

'Eat with me tonight,' he said. 'Just the two of us. Help me clear my mind. I'll even ask Roxanne to dine elsewhere, if you won't sit with her.'

Jarette cast a lingering look back at Jordine and Alfonso, and Antonio followed her gaze.

'I'm sure you both have missed my sister's company,' he said to them. 'And I have no doubt you wish to speak with her of all that has since passed, but I must ask that you allow me to enjoy her company this evening. If not as a king, then as her brother, currently in his hour of need.'

Jordine was taken aback by Antonio's display of civility. He looked to Jarette, who nodded.

'Of course, sire,' Jordine said, bowing, knowing they had little choice other than to grant Antonio his request. He sensed Alfonso might argue against losing Jarette's company even for one evening, regardless of whether he was addressing his king or not. Jordine put a firm hand on his shoulder and steered him towards the stairs.

'We wish you both a pleasant eve, Your Majesties,' he said as they departed.

To Jordine's surprise, he and Alfonso were stopped by the guards at the gate.

'Her Royal Highness wishes to speak with you,' one of the men in the red lion livery said, gesturing to the guardhouse. Alfonso made to enter with Jordine, but the guard checked him with his halberd.

'Just him,' he said, nodding at Jordine. They both hesitated, looking at one another over the lowered weapon.

'Go,' Alfonso said, his tone still edged with bitterness. 'Real Rhundis don't get private royal audiences.'

'Go home, Al,' Jordine advised, refusing to be drawn by the barbed comment. 'I'll see you there.'

Within the guardhouse he found the queen of Serendia standing alone, her regal emerald dress and the diamond necklace that glittered at her throat a sharp contrast to the cramped, dingy space, unfurnished but for a table and a few chairs. A half-eaten hunk of bread and cheese lay on a pewter platter, alongside a spread of playing cards – the guards had been in the midst of their luncheon when the queen had evicted them for her impromptu audience.

'Your Highness,' Jordine said, bowing low. He had seen Roxanne numerous times before, but almost always from afar, and never alone. The encounter was dredging up all kinds of nerves he normally wouldn't feel even among ladies of high station. Courtiers and the disgruntled wives of noblemen were another matter entirely compared to the queen of the land.

'It is a pleasure to meet you in person, Jordine Rhundi,' Roxanne replied. 'Or would you prefer to be addressed as Jordine Ducas?'

'Whichever pleases Your Majesty more,' Jordine said, hoping he did not sound foolish. Roxanne smiled, and walked to the table, gazing down at the playing cards left there.

'You may well be known as Ducas and nothing else before the year is out. For some months now, on my advice, the king has been considering permitting the return of your mother and father from exile.'

Jordine had not been sure what to expect from the queen's summons, but it had not been this. He inclined his head, wondering how much to admit to already knowing.

'I have heard rumors, Your Majesty, that a pardon is in consideration,' he said. 'But I have received little word from my parents since they left Heidel. I was not even entirely certain that they still lived.'

'The latest news to reach us from the Marches tells us they do,' Roxanne said. 'And your father has already risen to the rank of sergeant among the forces commanded by

Marshal Johann Cliff. His abilities remain undimmed, despite his advancing years.'

'With respect, Your Majesty, may I ask why the king is considering a pardon?' Jordine said. 'The king did not speak out when Frederick was first banished by his father. Why the change of heart, especially when it seems to be causing such a rift within the royal family?'

'Frederick is one of the most able warriors in this kingdom,' Roxanne said. 'Not just as a combatant, but as a strategist and a leader of men. Being stripped of his rank and banished to the Western Marches at his age would have broken most others, but it is clear your father is made of sterner mettle. The king has noticed that and is mindful of the need for strong leadership in these troubled times. With enemies on all sides, it would be the height of foolishness to leave such an asset to waste away on our western border. At least, that is what I have advised in the past. Thankfully, the king seems minded to heed my words.'

'And if there is trouble between His Majesty and Crucio, he trusts that Frederick's close comradeship with the old king would not cause him to question his loyalties?' Jordine pressed.

'Do you not think the nature of your father's banishment would have turned him forever against the former king?'

Jordine took a breath, wondering whether he was undermining his father's chance at a return from exile.

'Unlike me, Frederick is a man of honor,' he said. 'I believe if Crucio was contrite, he would forgive him. But he is sworn to serve the king of Serendia, and that is Antonio

Domongatt. He would never hesitate to do his duty.'

'And Crucio is too stubborn to ever willingly end his banishment,' Roxanne finished. 'Which is why a pardon makes eminent sense. I wonder, when you next write to him, would you make mention of these rumors you have heard about the king's intentions? I would never presume to speak for him myself, of course, but it would be good if Frederick knew he will always have a welcome in Heidel so long as Antonio is on the throne, ahead of any formal pronouncements that may come.'

'I will mention it, Your Majesty,' Jordine said. He had not planned to write to Frederick anytime soon, but given the speed of events occurring in the capital, it would be for the best if he did.

'You have my thanks, Jordine,' Roxanne said, putting a hand briefly on his arm. 'It is difficult to know who to trust in times such as these, but I believe we will know soon enough just who is friend, and who is foe. I am sure you will stand with us against the latter.'

'Always, Your Majesty,' Jordine said, and bowed.

Jordine had little desire to return immediately to Gallows Street and report all he had discovered to Edward. Instead, he ate lunch in the marketplace, dallying on his way back along Soot Row, wasting some coppers on a necklace for one of the barmaids at the Lilly Valley he had taken a liking to. By the time he had returned to his erstwhile home, the hour was growing late.

Edward was still up. He told Jordine that Alfonso had returned home earlier and was already abed. He had seemingly made up with his father, at least enough to pass on all he had learned, including the alarm gripping the citadel and Crucio Domongatt's nighttime disappearance.

'What did the queen want with you?' Edward asked.

'She confirmed the rumors I have already relayed,' Jordine said wearily. 'Antonio is giving strong consideration to pardoning my father. He believes he would be an asset, should the situation deteriorate any further.'

'He would,' Edward agreed thoughtfully.

'Do you wish to see him returned as well?' Jordine asked, his tone almost accusatory.

'Of course I would welcome back my old comrade,' Edward said. 'You know I have always stood by him, and his family.'

'It will be interesting to see if he views things the same way.'

'And what of you?' Edward countered. 'You play your cards close to your chest, boy. I can see that you have been avoiding giving any opinion on your father's return. You do not wish to seem weak, or to lose what you currently have. You do not even call him Father.'

'I see no point in speculating,' Jordine said, knowing the answer was a poor one, but unwilling to give Edward any more than he already had. 'But whether Frederick returns, or whether I am one day chosen for knighthood, a time is coming when I will no longer be beholden to you, Edward Rhundi.'

'Perhaps,' Edward allowed. 'But that time has not come yet, and you would do well to remember that, Jordine *Rhundi*.'

Jordine climbed the stairs to his bedchamber. He passed Alfonso's room on the way, and hesitated, about to knock. Then, instead, he carried on.

As he was washing his face in the bowl set before the window, he heard the clatter of hooves, and opened the shutter ajar. To his surprise he spotted Mikos, riding for the far end of the street, headed off into the night on some unknown errand.

Jordine sighed and closed the shutters, making sure they were latched tight. All was change, and the night air was heavy with threat.

A storm was coming to Heidel, and part of Jordine knew that no matter where he sought shelter, he would be swept up in it along with everyone else.

TEN

'My father is bound here,' Prince Sergio told Elysia, slamming the letter he had just read down onto the empty banquet table. 'He will likely arrive before nightfall.'

Elysia showed no immediate reaction but drew the letter to her, read it, then reread it.

'Who is this from?' she asked. 'It bears no sign nor seal?'

'Edward Rhundi,' Sergio said. 'It was his man who delivered it. He rode day and night to reach us before Crucio.'

'And we are sure this news he brings is accurate?' Elysia asked. 'Do you think Crucio would really be so bold as to depose his own son, just two years after abdicating in his favor?'

'The old fool made a mistake, and he knows it,' Sergio said. 'He should have chosen me. Instead, he would rather try to reclaim his lost glories.'

'He will turn you and Antonio against one another,' Elysia cautioned, but Sergio merely laughed.

'He will try. But he is weak. He won't have the stomach to do what must be done. Antonio was always his favorite. He will hope I'll be the one to move against him. Sergio and Antonio, squabbling like spoiled brats, and then he can play the peacemaker. The idiot peasantry still speak of him as the true king. He will use his popularity to retake the throne, regardless of the outcome of any conflict between me and my brother.'

'Then what is to be done?' Elysia asked, pushing the letter away from her, as though it might be incriminating. 'We must tread carefully, if we are not to be caught on the wrong side of all this.'

'Do not fear, my beloved wife,' Sergio said sardonically. 'All is in hand. I have already composed a reply to our friend, Sir Rhundi.'

'I did not know you were so closely aligned with the pauper knight,' Elysia said.

'Few do,' Sergio responded. 'Whether they are commoners or so-called nobles, those without wealth are easily bought. Edward Rhundi has represented our interests covertly in the capital for some time. My influence cannot be banished the way my younger sister was. Edward keeps me regularly informed through the Ducas boy, Jordine.'

Elysia blanched, but Sergio was too busy pondering his own schemes to notice.

'I think I have noticed him around court,' she said

casually, recovering herself. 'I did not know he was feeding you information through Edward.'

'It was a clever stroke, adopting him,' Sergio admitted. 'Even without the Ducas name, he is better connected than a penniless house like the Rhundis will ever be, and the ladies at court seem idiotically infatuated with him. Of course, if anything were to go wrong, if there was any hint of foul play or treason, an adoptee with no other noble family is easily disavowed. And he knows nothing of the connection between Edward and me.'

'Of course,' Elysia echoed, feigning disinterested agreement before attempting to change the subject. 'Should I prepare the guest chambers for Crucio's arrival?'

Sergio let out a short, humorless bark of laughter.

'Oh no, Elysia. I was planning on calling out the guard instead.'

Fort Eindhovein lay close to the border with Drieghan. It was the strongest fastness outside of Heidel, rivaled only by the Watchtower of the Western Marches, and after days on the road, it was a welcome sight to Crucio.

The journey south from Heidel had taken longer than he had hoped, the tracks turned to mud by autumn rains. One of his retinue's horses had gone lame, and time had to be spent haggling for a fresh one at the roadside, all while attempting not to give away the identity of the party, or where they were bound.

Crucio had no doubt that Antonio had guessed his

intentions by now. He could only hope that he was still one step ahead of the factions in Heidel. Speed was the most essential element; speed and momentum. He had to keep going, refuse to give in to the doubts that had started as they had carried on south from the Moretti estate. He had chosen to act. Now, he had no choice other than to see it through. The small, loyal band of courtiers and nobles who had followed him reassured him. What he was doing was not for personal gain or glory, but for the good of Serendia. The kingdom needed a new ruler, before its current one did irreparable damage.

They rode through Eindhovein village, towards the towering fortress gates. Sergio's banner – the crimson Domongatt lion set against a white field – was fluttering above the ramparts, and the keep that towered beyond.

The gates were shut. Crucio spurred to the front of his entourage as they curbed their horses in its shadow, and threw back his hood before calling up at the bare stone parapets.

'Hail! I am Crucio Domongatt, and I have come to speak with my son!'

He expected a respectful response, and for the gates to part before him, but there was nothing, no sound but the moaning of the bitter wind and the snapping of the standard overhead.

He looked to his chief retainer, Luchevo, and the commander of his bodyguard, Belcaro. Both appeared concerned, glancing from Crucio to the strangely deserted parapets.

'Perhaps we should turn back, Your Majesty,' Belcaro suggested quietly. 'Something feels wrong here. Ride back beyond the village, and I will return with whatever message you desire for the prince.'

Crucio was about to agree when a voice finally answered him from above.

'And what is it my father wishes to speak with me about?'

Crucio looked back up, a hand raised to help shield his face from the wind, and saw his second son now standing at one of the crenels between the merlons, leaning forward to address him over the parapet's edge.

'You will know once we are able to speak face-to-face, my son,' Crucio responded. 'I pray, open the gates for your father!'

'How easy you make it sound,' Sergio responded, his voice as cold as the wind. 'Open the gates to my citadel and admit just a few dozen weary travelers. Yet what else do I allow inside when I do? Sedition? Treason? War?'

'I have only come to talk,' Crucio urged. 'And to bring you news from Heidel.'

'It's a long way to come in person carrying nothing but court gossip, Father,' Sergio said. 'And how much of it concerns my brother's misrule? That is the truth behind this unannounced visit, isn't it? You come here to agitate against our king.'

'Someone reached him before us,' Luchevo warned Crucio in a low voice. 'He knew we were coming.'

That was the only way to explain the closed gate, and

Sergio waiting for them atop the ramparts. Crucio felt a plunging sense of despair. Had he really misjudged his second son so badly?

'I have placed myself at your mercy, Sergio,' he called out. 'I am not alone in feeling aggrieved at your brother's actions. Choosing him over you was a mistake. If he continues unchecked, he will be the ruination of our royal line, and the whole of Serendia.'

'Then you admit it?' Sergio demanded. 'You admit I would have made a better king than Antonio?'

'I believe so, yes.'

'And you come now to beg my aid in overthrowing him? Do you really believe I would raise my host and make war on my own blood?'

'No,' Crucio responded, his voice firm. 'I am no warmonger. My desire is that you may lend your voice to mine, and help convince Antonio to change course.'

'Lend my voice, and my men-at-arms,' Sergio said.

'You know as well as I that Antonio respects strength,' Crucio said. 'But once he sees the people—'

Sergio interrupted him.

'Since when did any of us care for the opinions of the people? They will bless you to the highest heavens one day, and damn you to the choking deeps the next, depending on how whim and fancy move them. Use the mob to enthrone you, and that same mob will dethrone you as soon as the harvests fail and the taxes rise. That is as certain as the turning seasons.'

'You are wise, my son,' Crucio admitted. 'Too wise to

spend the rest of your days rotting in Eindhovein. I will ask one last time – open the gates, and let us talk properly, father to son.'

'I have nothing more to say to you,' Sergio replied. 'You will leave Eindhovein, immediately. If you have any honor left, you will ride back to Heidel and seek to mend the breach with Antonio, before it is too late. But I will have no part in your plotting. Let the common people you revere so much know that Sergio did not open his gates to treason. You will not turn brother against brother, my father.'

'It is no use, sire,' Luchevo said urgently, placing a hand on Crucio's wrist. 'We must away, before the prince does something rash. If he were to seize us, and deliver us back to Antonio under guard…'

Crucio prevaricated, his heart riven. Had he really fallen so low that his own son would not offer him succor? And if Sergio refused to support him, where could he go now? Not back to Heidel – surely Antonio would expect the worst, and would already be raising forces against him. But if not there, then where? Into exile? He had been no friend to Mediah during his reign. Would Guy Seric remember their old campaigns together against Valencia, and accept him into Calpheon?

'Your Highness, please,' Luchevo urged, shifting his grip to the bridle of Crucio's mount, making to pull on it. 'We must not linger!'

There was one other option, Crucio thought. One other wrong that he might yet right, before it was too late. In doing so, the son he had spurned might yet prove to be the one to carry on his legacy.

'We make for Glish,' he said to his retainers, trying to avoid letting them see the tears in his eyes as he turned his back on Sergio. 'Pray that Vittorio still resides there.'

'You are sure that was the correct decision, my love?' Elysia asked as she joined Sergio on the ramparts, wrapped against the wind in thick Drieghan wildcat furs. Crucio and his entourage were still visible, passing through Eindhovein village, taking the road northwest.

'Without a doubt,' Sergio said. 'Everything is proceeding as I intend. Father has played his part, and now it is time for Antonio to do the same.'

Striding down from the gatehouse, Sergio called for his fastest rider.

ELEVEN

Not long after Jarette's return to Heidel, Jordine was called upon by his adoptive father to visit Soot Row.

He had seen little of Alfonso, and nothing of Jarette, since the latter had gotten them into the royal citadel. The princess had sent word that she would be spending the next few days with her brother, but that they were welcome to visit. Jordine was dubious about how willing a guest Jarette was, but his desire to avoid Antonio outweighed his desire to see his old friend. For his part, Alfonso remained intent on not interacting with Jordine, speaking to him only when they encountered one another at home.

Jordine had grown accustomed to spying for Edward Rhundi, but running his errands was another matter. He told him as much after Edward demanded he go to Soot Row late one night, to pick up a delivery from one of the blacksmiths.

'It is not some trinket I am asking you to collect,'

he said when Jordine initially refused. 'I would have Mikos bring it, but he is already absent on an errand.'

'Carrying another message for you?' Jordine asked. He had seen Mikos return early the previous morning, then depart again that same day. Whoever Edward was in communication with, they had much to write back and forth.

'That is none of your business,' Edward said. 'But it will be, if you go to Soot Row for me. It is a matter of great importance.'

'So you wish to embroil me further in your schemes?' Jordine asked. Edward sighed heavily.

'Everything I do, I do for the good of the kingdom,' he said. 'I wish both you, and my son, would accept that. I have few enough allies as it is, but the ones I do are powerful, and they have called upon me to play my part.'

'And that part involves collecting... *what* from Soot Row? Arms and armor?'

'Go and bring it to me, and I will let you know. You should take the handcart Mikos usually pushes to market. It will be heavy.'

'I will do so, but only this once,' Jordine said. 'I am your adopted son, not some common servant. If you are doing your part for this powerful ally you speak of, you should be able to afford more than just Mikos to do your bidding.'

Jordine went as instructed, pushing Mikos's handcart ahead of him through Heidel's back streets. Edward had advised him to wear one of the servant's plain cloaks to avoid being recognized, and Jordine had readily agreed – he had no wish to be seen running errands like a common servant for House Rhundi.

Despite his defiance, a part of him was intrigued. What had Edward ordered from Soot Row? The blacksmiths that labored in the forges which ran along that particular street were the best in Serendia, and any noble of any kind of standing ensured his arms and armor bore the engravings of the Row's finest. Yet as far as Jordine knew, the Rhundis were too poor to purchase equipment from those particular forges.

A brief set of written instructions from Edward had him wait in an alleyway behind one of the smithing shops, where the waste was discarded. Jordine covered his nose, but it did little to mask the stench. He focused his mind on the pounding of hammers that echoed along the street as he waited. Even this late, the forges were still busy. Every day, more and more orders for blades and battle plate came in. Someone somewhere certainly seemed to be preparing for war.

Several dwarfs in grubby leather smocks passed by, sparing Jordine a curious glance as they went. Eventually a bellows girl emerged from the back door of one of the workshops, the ruddy glow of the furnaces briefly falling across Jordine.

'I'm Ornella,' she said by way of introduction, glancing furtively up at Jordine. 'My father asked me to bring this out to you.'

Jordine moved to help her heave two sacks from the doorway onto the cart, their contents scraping and clattering. It had to be armor of some kind. Ornella had seemingly already been paid on behalf of her father and had instructions not to linger, as she disappeared back into the workshop as soon as the cart was full, the slam of the door and the scrape of its lock bolt announcing that Jordine's presence was no longer welcome.

He decided it would be unwise to remain and rifle through the sacks. Instead, he made his way back to Gallows Street as swiftly as he could, laboring with the cart's weight, looking about himself furtively for fear that he was being followed, either by back-alley vagabonds, or something worse.

It was with some relief that he arrived back at the Rhundi residence. Edward himself emerged from the back door and helped him lug the sacks inside.

'What in the name of the gods is all this?' Jordine demanded breathlessly as soon as the door was shut and locked. The sacks had been deposited on the dining room table.

When Edward did not respond, he moved to one and untied it, reaching inside.

The first item he drew out was a helmet. It was a bascinet, its plate metal gleaming in the candlelight, as yet unsullied by any blade or blow. At first glance it looked not dissimilar to the one Jordine owned, but he noted the gilt filigree decorating the visor, and the lion-head crest embossed atop the forehead. He had seen those markings before, numerous times.

He set the weighty piece of protective war gear to one side, and drew out more of the sack's contents – another piece of plate armor, a breastplate, once again engraved with the roaring royal lion of Serendia.

'This is the armor worn by the royal guard,' he said to Edward, still inspecting the cuirass. 'But they are new. You've intercepted part of a new shipment for Antonio's defenders.'

'Not quite,' Edward said. 'I contracted the smith who forges the armor of the royal guards for two extra sets.'

'Why?' Jordine asked, trying to fathom Edward's reasoning.

'Before I tell you, you must swear an oath to me here and now that none of this leaves this chamber,' Edward said earnestly. 'Not even Alfonso must know.'

'It's treason, isn't it?' Jordine said, feeling mounting panic. 'You are planning to betray the king.'

'Quite the opposite,' Edward said. 'I hope we may yet intervene to save him.'

'How?'

'First, make your oath.'

'I swear on all the gods I will say nothing of what you are about to tell me, unless I deem it treasonous against the king,' Jordine said, wondering what kind of damnation he was bringing upon himself with such words. Edward was silent, as though trying to judge whether he believed Jordine was sincere, but eventually he spoke.

'I have received word about Crucio's whereabouts. After he vanished from the citadel, he rode south, to Fort Eindhovein. He sought out Prince Sergio and attempted to convince him to raise his host against the king. Sergio refused. By all reports, Crucio is now traveling to Glish, hoping he can convince Vittorio to support him where Sergio will not.'

'How do you know all this?' Jordine demanded. 'You are better informed than the royal household itself.'

'I have the backing of a number of prominent nobles,' Edward said, 'the names of whom will remain anonymous. The important thing is that Crucio is bent on civil war. He must be stopped. To that end, I am asking you to write to Jarette and inform her of the rumors you have heard abounding in the taverns of Heidel. Tell her Crucio seeks to usurp the throne but has been rejected by Sergio and is now riding to Glish. If the gods are good, it will rouse Antonio into going to oppose him, before it is too late and the people rise up in support of his father.'

'Surely this news can be delivered to the king directly, if it is this urgent?' Jordine asked.

'Would you be the one to deliver it?' Edward said. 'You know the depths of his wrath. As much as he has broken with his father, there is a danger he will refuse to believe Crucio is openly leading a coup against him. In that case, his rage may fall on those spreading such rumors. That is why my allies and I have no wish to go to him directly.'

'So you would send me to suffer his fury instead?'

'No. You are only passing on the rumors you have heard to Jarette. He will listen to her.'

'Why not tell the queen? She is more keenly aware of affairs of state than anyone.'

'We are not yet certain where her loyalties lie,' Edward responded.

Jordine stepped away from Edward, pacing to one end of the room and then the other, trying to straighten the tangle his adoptive father was weaving. He had no wish to see Serendia consumed by civil war, and no reason to want Crucio back on the throne. Yet the effort Edward was going to in order to preserve Antonio's rule seemed so oblique, so underhanded. It was clear by his own admission that the pauper knight was himself being used by individuals more powerful than he, but who? Who wished to maintain Antonio's rule, yet was too afraid to publicly support the king? Perhaps they feared what would happen if Crucio ultimately emerged triumphant? Then they could leave Edward to face his wrath, and Edward could in turn use Jordine as his shield.

'None of this explains the armor,' he said eventually, stopping by the table and placing a hand on the bascinet he had removed from the sacking. 'What has the apparel of the royal guards got to do with any of this?'

'It is preparation for the next phase,' Edward said. 'All being well, Antonio will be convinced to travel to Glish and confront Crucio. And you and I will accompany him, as part of his guard.'

'What fresh madness is this?' Jordine demanded, even more taken aback by Edward's newest revelation. 'You wish for the two of us to infiltrate the royal guard? In Elion's name, why?'

'To make sure that the threat of usurpation can never

raise its head again,' Edward said, his voice cold and determined as he held Jordine's gaze. 'I told you there is a danger Antonio may not choose to take a stand against his father. At the end, he may not be willing to do what must be done. If that is the case, those loyal to him, those who would see stability for Serendia, must act. We must kill the king's father.'

'Kill Crucio Domongatt?' Jordine asked incredulously.

'Yes. I do not believe he will cease trying to retake the throne, either covertly or by force. We must end forever the threat of civil strife. The only way we can do that is by slaying Crucio.'

Jordine felt sick. He drew out a chair and sat heavily next to the table heaped with armor, his head buried in his hands.

'I will do the deed,' Edward said, placing a hand tentatively on Jordine's shoulder. 'But I would feel more assured if you were at my side.'

'So you can blame me when the king demands to know why his father has been murdered by one of his guards?' Jordine demanded harshly, knocking away Edward's hand.

'All being well, none will know about the involvement of either of us,' Edward said. 'That is the purpose of this armor.'

'You seek to turn me into an assassin. To drench my hands in royal blood!'

'I seek the peace and security of Serendia,' Edward snarled, his patience at an end. 'We have been offered an opportunity, you and I, to play our part in guaranteeing that. It is an act of courage I am calling upon you to perform. Or did you really think there was nothing more to life than whoring and drinking and gambling? That you would see out the rest of your days under my roof in idle pursuits? No, you serve House Rhundi, Jordine, and this is how you will perform that service.'

'And what of your trueborn son?' Jordine snapped, looking up at Edward fiercely. 'You do not call upon him to serve. To perform this "act of courage." You will not sully him by making him spill royal blood. By enrolling him in treachery and murder.'

'I do not call upon him because I know he does not have the stomach for it,' Edward snapped back. 'He is a disappointment to me. You at least act boldly, with the confidence that comes with high station. That is what I wish for this house, but Alfonso is too cautious, too thoughtful.'

'You have made him so with your neglect,' Jordine said. 'He yearns for your approval, Edward. He has grown to despise me, because he thinks you hold me in higher regard.'

'Perhaps I do,' Edward responded. 'Regardless, he is not fit for a duty such as this. You know he would not go through with it.'

Jordine couldn't deny that. Edward strode to the heavy, carved timber cabinet that dominated one wall of the dining chamber, and unlatched its front, drawing out a sheaf of parchment and an inkpot and quill from within, before clearing space on the table and placing them down in front of Jordine, next to the bascinet.

'Write,' he ordered. 'Write to your friend, Princess Jarette, and tell her of all you have heard over the past few days. Crucio has beseeched the king's brother for aid in overthrowing him, but Sergio has refused to be part of his devious scheme. Crucio now rides for Glish, hoping against hope that the last of his sons will support his treacherous coup.'

He banged his fist on the table for emphasis, making the armor clatter.

'Write,' he hissed.

Jordine gripped the quill, head bowed, hand shaking. Then, slowly, he began to pen the words he had been instructed to.

TWELVE

'You believe this?' Roxanne asked, raising the note and fixing her eyes on Jarette, sitting across the dining table from her.

'I believe Jordine is passing on what he has heard, yes,' Jarette replied. 'How accurate it is, I do not know. I have not yet been back in Heidel a month.'

'It is treason,' Antonio said from the head of the table, casting his knife back down on his plate with a clatter. 'Nothing less. We can at least be thankful Sergio was not drawn into Father's plans. I feared he would go to him, but to demand he raise his host against me…'

'We should not react with—' Roxanne began to say, but Antonio cut her off.

'We feared all along that he was going to Eindhovein. Now Glish is all that remains to him. He must be stopped, before he can raise the peasant rabble against us.'

Roxanne had to concede there was truth in that, but

she again felt as though matters were escalating too swiftly. She had her own people taking note of rumor and gossip throughout Heidel, and none had yet come to her with such firm and certain news.

'It is strange that these accounts Jordine repeats are so detailed,' she said, looking once more at Jarette. 'I would speak to him about where he heard them in person.'

'There is no time for that,' Antonio exclaimed, his short temper fraying. 'As soon as the sun rises, I must march on Glish, and end this madness before it roots itself any deeper!'

'If that is what you deem best, then by all means, it shall be so,' Roxanne said, battling to keep her demeanor in check in the face of Antonio's constant desire to meet every new problem head-on. 'But if so, I would urge you, do not raise the host to meet your father. A strong contingent of the royal guard will surely be sufficient. If Sergio has not joined him, Crucio can have no more than several dozen followers, few of them armed and armored. By meeting him with only the royal guard, you show yourself to be confident and in control. Your father will have no choice but to acknowledge you as the one true king, once his attempts to rabble-rouse with Vittorio come to nothing.'

'And what of Vittorio himself?' Jarette spoke up. 'Our brother has done nothing but live a quiet, simple life since Father sent him away.'

'You still exchange letters with him, I take it?' Antonio demanded. Jarette nodded defiantly.

'You know the way Father treated him was abhorrent.

He predicted the abdication would lead to bloodshed between us all, and for that he was banished. And now look who seeks him out, as though intent on fulfilling that same prophecy. If the rumors are true, Father should be ashamed. He is no longer the man who once raised us.'

Roxanne knew that as the two youngest siblings, Vittorio and Jarette had been the closest growing up. As an adopted child, she had been on the sharp end of their teasing and games, youthful exuberance that, in Jarette's case, had sometimes blossomed into full-blown spitefulness. She had no love for the banished prince, but what Jarette had claimed seemed to have been true – until now, the youth had appeared content living a pastoral life in Glish. This was no time to make further enemies, especially if targeting Vittorio might turn Jarette against Antonio.

'If Sergio rejected your father's advances, I'm certain Vittorio will as well,' Roxanne said to Jarette and Antonio. 'There is no need for him to become embroiled in any of this.'

'We shall see when I reach Glish,' Antonio said, scraping his chair back and rising, the ladies doing likewise as servants scurried forward to remove the king's napkin and pull his chair fully out of the way.

'I believe you are correct, my beloved,' he said to Roxanne. 'I have neither the time nor the inclination to call out the host and raise the war banners above the parapets. I will ride at dawn tomorrow with a troop of the guard, and Captain Malchevo. Will you both feel secure here with the rest of the guard cohort under Sergeant Hogali?'

'I'm sure we'll survive,' Jarette said.

Roxanne moved round the table and squeezed her husband's hand, looking him in the eye. 'Be careful, my king,' she told him earnestly. 'These are the most uncertain of times, and I cannot afford to lose you. Serendia cannot afford to lose you.'

Jordine and Edward had already set out before the king and his guards departed Heidel. They rode with their new armor stowed, spending two days in a country tavern on the outskirts of Glish. The place was quiet, harvest season now passed and the onset of winter combining with the recent rains to mean there were few travelers on the roads. That suited Edward's purposes.

Ever since picking up the armor, Jordine had been wrestling with his conscience. He wanted desperately to speak to Alfonso, to tell him that his father was deeply involved in a conspiracy, but he feared doing so would inevitably draw his friend into it as well. The same went for Jarette – he was haunted by what she would think of him if she ever found out that the letter he had sent her, the letter now setting Antonio on the road to a lethal confrontation with his father, had been invented on Edward's orders.

The problem was, Edward's claims all made sense. It did seem Crucio was intent on snatching back the kingdom he had gifted to his eldest son, and that the only reason Serendia was not at war with itself yet was because Sergio had done the unexpected, and refused to help his father dethrone his older brother.

It was hard to imagine Sergio doing that out of love for Antonio. From what he had seen, the middle of the three Domongatt sons was just as ambitious as his older sibling, maybe more so. Lady Elysia had more or less confirmed to Jordine, during their illicit encounters, that Sergio was building his forces in Eindhovein, though for what exactly she either did not know, or would not say.

The idea that someone would discover his dalliances with Elysia only made everything more fraught. In such dangerous times, the last thing he needed was for an affair with the wife of a Domongatt prince to become public knowledge. He now regretted pursuing Elysia – it had been foolishness born out of the vices of lust and idleness, a young man's act of arrogance, taking her just because he could. Elysia was a kind and earnest woman, and he had encouraged the folly between them. If knowledge of their affair became public, he had already decided to take all blame, claiming – not unfairly – that he had enticed her. Hopefully her status as a sister of King Seric of Calpheon would at least protect her from the harshest of punishments, and then Jordine could look to himself with a clearer conscience.

Each trouble seemed to be mounting one atop another, and he had no time to unmake them. He tried to convince Edward not to go through with his plan, that they would surely be discovered, but the pauper knight refused to turn back to Heidel, and Jordine knew he was now implicated as well. Whoever was controlling the Rhundis, they had Edward wholly at their beck and call.

During the third day at the inn, King Antonio passed

by on the road to Heidel. As Edward had predicted, he was accompanied only by a small retinue and a cohort of royal guards, led by Captain Malchevo. They watched the royal passage from one of the inn's upper windows and, afterwards, helped armor each other. Clad in full plate and with their visors lowered, they would be indistinguishable from the other guards.

'Here,' Edward said, drawing something more from the sacks they had brought. Cloaks, Jordine realized, the same royal purple ones the guards wore.

Disguises complete, they departed the inn and rode after the king.

Antonio led his retinue to the southeastern road into Glish, and there halted them and barred the way.

The town represented a miserable prospect at this time of year. The streets were quiet and the surrounding patchwork of fields little more than a morass of mud, stripped bare several months earlier. The busy work of harvest-tide was long complete, and Glish's main export, the produce from its farms, was mostly already on its way to Heidel and beyond.

Glish's inhabitants were simple, hard-working folk, and royal visits were few and far between – the last time Antonio had been to the town had been before his coronation. It was little surprise, then, that as they waited, people started to gather, made curious by the presence of the armored warriors on the edge of town.

'Perhaps you should address them, sire?' Malchevo wondered, gesturing at the nearest embankment. Short slopes ran up on either side of the rutted roadway, providing the perfect elevation for the growing crowd of peasants.

'No,' Antonio snapped, in no mood for oratory. 'I came here to speak to my father, not some common muck.'

He was tempted to order his guards to disperse them, but didn't want his entourage to be busy when Crucio arrived. Besides, it would be good for the ordinary people to bear witness to what was about to happen. If the common belief that Crucio was well-liked among the peasantry was true, they must be the ones to see him submit to Antonio. His father would bow and renew his oaths of allegiance, or he would die. By nightfall, Antonio would have regained total control over the kingdom.

Time passed interminably, until a commotion from the embankment to the right drew Antonio's attention. The farmhands and laborers there were parting, allowing someone to descend onto the roadway and approach the royal entourage.

At first, he took it to be nothing more than some youthful rustic, dressed in dirty garb, with a straw hat and a stick to aid his traipsing through boggy fields. As he drew nearer, however, he recognized the face beneath the hat's broad brim.

'I was wondering if you would show yourself,' he said dispassionately.

'I didn't believe the stable boy when he told me,'

Vittorio said. 'The great king and master of all Serendia, come to visit our humble town.'

Antonio scowled at his younger brother's mockery. As Vittorio drew nearer, Malchevo stepped between them both, sword whispering from its scabbard.

'That's close enough,' the captain of the guard growled. Vittorio halted and laughed.

'What, afraid I'm going to beat your king to death with a stick?' he asked, brandishing the length of wood in both hands like a broadsword.

'Be thankful I have not come here for you, little Vittorio,' Antonio said before Malchevo could respond.

'Then why have you come? To enjoy the country air?'

'I am here because our father is also bound for this place. He comes seeking you.'

'Come to make his apology after all these years? Is he going to reinstate me? If so, I must disappoint him. I have a life here, a better one than I could ever hope for as the third son of the royal line.'

'What if you were the first son?' Antonio demanded. Vittorio laughed.

'I believe you have that role well wrapped up, big brother.'

'Not if Crucio has his way. He seeks to dethrone me. He has already ridden to Sergio in Eindhovein, to beg for his assistance, but he was turned away. Now word has it he rides for Glish. You are his last hope.'

'And you have come to snuff out that hope?' Vittorio asked, opening his arms wide and glancing at Malchevo, who was still glaring at him. 'Well, here I am. Cut me down, and you will have one less potential rival for your throne.'

'I told you, I am not here for you,' Antonio snapped. 'Nor do I plan on slaughtering my own family. Not even our father. He is misguided. Once he sees there is no hope of usurping me, I pray he will finally accept his fate. He will never be king again.'

'So you bring your royal guard to convince him of that,' Vittorio noted.

'Yes. None but a small retinue have joined him.'

'And what will you do to him once he has submitted?'

'That remains to be seen. Banishment, or living out his last days on some estate in the eastern regions.'

'Our family has quite the predilection for exiling people.'

'Would you rather I killed him?' Antonio snarled. 'You are living proof of Domongatt mercy at work.'

'Mercy? What was my crime? Speaking the truth?' Vittorio asked, giving Antonio that mocking smirk that had infuriated him so when they were children.

'Well, you certainly seem to have made a new life for yourself, milking cows and grubbing in the dirt,' Antonio responded. 'You should thank the rest of us for helping you to discover the simpler joys in life.'

'I would thank you to leave this place, and not bring war and death to these people,' Vittorio said. 'They have done nothing to deserve it. They are loyal subjects.'

'But of whom?' Antonio demanded. 'There will be no death here, unless our father wills it. Now, stand aside.'

Vittorio hesitated, as though preparing to contest Antonio's presence further, but he was interrupted by the drumming of hoofbeats in the muck. One of the guards Malchevo had posted farther down the road as a lookout was returning, with haste.

'They are coming, sire,' he reported breathlessly.

'How many?' Antonio demanded. 'Are they armed?'

'Around two dozen, my liege, and some but not all.'

'Stand ready,' Antonio snapped at his guards, and they closed in on his flanks and rear, one unfurling the royal standard, the Domongatt crimson lion fluttering on its yellow field. Some of the onlooking peasantry gasped at the regal sight.

'Do not do this, brother,' Vittorio urged. 'There is still time for you to depart. I will send Father on his way. I have no intention of helping him start a civil war. You have my word on it.'

'Be silent, and clear the road,' Antonio snapped, having no time for his little brother any longer. Vittorio finally obeyed, rejoining the commoners lining the roadway's embankments.

The sound of more hoofbeats reached Antonio in the expectant silence that followed, before the riders in question came galloping around the nearest bend, a gaggle of horsemen, most of them cloaked, coming surging up the road to Glish. They eased off as they found their route barred, slowing to a trot and then a full halt a dozen yards away.

Antonio searched for his father among the horsemen,

and not immediately seeing him, stepped forward and called out to the group as a whole.

'Your king stands before you. I ask you to dismount, and make yourselves known!'

There were muttered conversations among the mounted ranks, and Antonio was gratified to find they had not expected this confrontation. Their advantage of surprise was long lost.

At length, a familiar voice barked at the others to move aside, and Crucio Domongatt spurred forward, halting his mount just short of Antonio. He looked bedraggled and worn from the road, his royal cloak mud-stained, his beard white and unkempt. He appeared older and more exhausted than Antonio had ever seen him before, but there was still pride in his gaze, the kindling light of defiance.

'Get down off your horse, Father,' Antonio ordered, in no mood for recalcitrance. 'And speak to me, as family.'

'Not as a subject to his king?' Crucio demanded. Antonio let out a short, cold laugh.

'If you expect me to kneel, you will be sorely disappointed. There is only one king here, and it is not you.'

Crucio glanced back towards his retainers, before kicking a foot from his stirrup and dismounting. Most of those behind him did likewise, and the small coterie of armored knights with him closed in protectively. Antonio's royal guard did the same.

'You have taken quite the circuitous route just to visit this cow-shit collection of farms,' Antonio said, spreading his arms to encompass the rude settlement behind him, as well as the peasantry packed on the embankments.

'Do I need written permission to leave Heidel, or travel to any part of the kingdom I love so well?' Crucio said.

'Do not take me for a child, Father,' Antonio growled, taking a step nearer. 'I know what you are about. In your mounting senility, you seek to depose me, your eldest son, the very man you chose above all others to inherit this kingdom you claim to love.'

'I would know by whose account you make such accusations,' Crucio said.

'Every account from here to the border with Mediah,' Antonio exclaimed. 'Did you really think it would not be obvious? Or that Sergio would join you in this madness?'

'I seek only the betterment of Serendia, as I always have,' Crucio said, his own tone beginning to burn with the infamous Domongatt anger. 'I am not mounting a coup against you, my son, no matter what your advisors, or your wife, might have told you. I wish simply to address the rift between us.'

'By raising a host against me?' Antonio said. 'That is why you are here, is it not? To convince Vittorio to join you in your schemes, and rouse the common folk in rebellion against their liege lords? You would reduce Serendia to rack and ruin, a place of lawlessness and civil war.'

'I have come here seeking only the strength to make you reconsider your rule,' Crucio said. 'These past two years you have placed Serendia on a path to the very chaos you claim to abhor. You overtax the lords and pay no heed when they overtax their tenants in turn. You have abandoned any pretense of good relations with Calpheon. The peace which I secured at great danger and cost during my reign has not borne fruit. And you will heed no advice that may turn you towards a better path.'

'The only advice I have ever received from you was to further your own authority and control,' Antonio countered, voice rising. 'Your wars emptied the kingdom's coffers, and they are not easily refilled. You have no idea how difficult it is, attempting to match your legacy and win the respect of lord and peasant alike when you remain, forever at my shoulder, forever casting your shadow over my efforts!'

'Everything I do, I do for the good of our family, and Serendia,' Crucio argued. 'They are one and the same.'

'Then kneel now, and renew your oaths to me,' Antonio snapped. 'Or do you think that would not be for "the good of our family, and Serendia"?'

'I cannot do so in good conscience, knowing that you would reign without any recourse to your brothers and me. Without sound advice, without trust, the throne you sit upon would have no foundation.'

'Yet you were the one who chose me to sit upon it,' Antonio raged. 'Do you not see the hypocrisy! The way your impulsiveness has brought this family to the brink of ruin?'

'Everyone makes mistakes, even kings,' Crucio said. 'The sin lies in not rectifying those mistakes.'

Antonio tried to find the words to answer, and could

not, at least not immediately. He found his sword in his hand, and did not remember drawing it.

More weapons rasped from their scabbards, on both sides. He shouted at his father, fury the likes of which he had never known burning away his thoughts and sending fire through his limbs, making them tremble.

'Father, today is the day I cut all ties between us. You shamed me, your own son and king, in front of my men. And now you seek to reclaim the crown? Perhaps you will respect me as king when I rid you of your head, thus having nowhere to place a crown.'

With a scream, he flung himself at Crucio.

THIRTEEN

It all happened so fast.

The royal guards and Crucio's retinue clashed. Steel met steel, the sounds of combat ringing back from the embankments on either side, while the onlooking people of Glish scattered in panic.

Antonio made directly for Crucio, in the middle of the road. At first the king's father seemed frozen, but then the instincts of an old warrior kicked in, and he drew his sword just in time to meet the blade of his son.

Only a single blow landed before someone crashed into Antonio from the side, knocking him away from his father. Crucio likewise found himself dragged back, trying to turn and strike his assailant before realizing it was the captain of his own small bodyguard, Belcaro.

'Save yourself, sire,' the man shouted, forcing his body between Crucio and more of the royal guards. Crucio was torn between knowing that he had moments before the superior numbers and equipment of Antonio's men overwhelmed his retinue, and the old, instinctive desire to stand and fight. As he hesitated, he saw blood spilling, turning the churned mud of the roadway dark, and an object – a severed head – coming to a halt in the midst of the melee.

Crucio simply stared at it, unmoving in the middle of the carnage, a sense of utter horror overwhelming him as his mind tried to deny what his eyes saw.

The head belonged to his son.

Antonio was dead.

'You killed him,' Jordine exclaimed, coming to a halt on the far side of the road's embankment. 'You killed the king!'

'And unless you want to die too, you'll keep moving,' Edward snarled from behind his lowered visor. He snatched Jordine by the pauldron and heaved him into the small copse of trees where they had tied their horses.

It had been a simple enough thing to dismount and join the rear ranks of the royal guard once Crucio and his retinue had arrived. All attention had been on the confrontation between the king and his father, and the two interlopers had been indistinguishable from the rest of Antonio's protectors, wearing identical armor and cloaks and with the visors of their bascinets lowered.

Jordine had steeled himself, knowing that speed was key. He had hoped that Crucio would attempt to strike at Antonio, which would presumably have given Edward the opportunity to cut him down. But it was Antonio who had lost his temper and charged, with Jordine and Edward driving forward in haste to stay at his side.

After that, things were a blur of pushing, shoving and clashing blades, but Jordine had distinctly seen the figure he knew to be Edward slash along the backs of Antonio's legs, dropping him to his knees in front of his stunned father, before delivering a stroke that had cleaved the king's head from his shoulders. Jordine had been as shocked as everyone else, but as both sides had continued to grapple and Crucio's bodyguards attempted to drag him away, Edward had snatched Jordine and pulled him in the opposite direction, heaving him out of the melee.

By that point the peasantry on the embankments had descended into panicked chaos, and the pair were able to force their way through, out of sight of the roadway.

They paused as they reached the trees, panting after the sprint across the muddy, harvested fields. Before he could untie his horse's bridle, Jordine grabbed onto Edward by both shoulders and rammed him up against the nearest tree.

'What in the name of all the gods have you done?' he shouted. Edward pushed back against him, and they grappled, before Jordine lost his footing and slipped onto one knee.

Briefly, he was convinced Edward was about to cut him down the way he had Antonio. The king's blood was still running, dark and red, from the blade of his bared sword.

Then, Edward wiped it on his stolen cloak, and sheathed it.

'Get up,' he snapped dispassionately at Jordine, who surged back to his feet, but this time managed to restrain himself from lunging at his adoptive father.

'You are a traitor,' he snarled instead, voice riven with venomous fury. 'And you would turn me into one too.'

'I have only done what needed to be done,' Edward exclaimed, pointing back across the field to where a commotion could still be heard emanating from the roadway. 'Antonio was not fit to be king, and neither is his father! Antonio's misrule is at an end, and Crucio will now be remembered as a son-slayer. No one will support his bid for the throne. With one blow, I have averted civil war.'

'This is Sergio's doing, isn't it?' Jordine demanded, refusing to back down. 'He is the one you serve. What has he promised you? New estates? A high station when he is king? Constable, or chamberlain? Or is the pauper knight bought by simple bags of gold?'

'You do not know of what you speak, so for that, I will forgive you, just this once,' Edward retorted. 'Antonio was in thrall to his wife, and could see no enemy beyond his own father. Crucio should have chosen Sergio to succeed him. He is the strongest of the Domongatt line, and the one most unafraid to advance the glory of Serendia. There will be no more internal squabbling, no more plotting. Within the month, this kingdom will have returned to strong and stable governance under a worthy monarch.'

'But why involve me, when you knew you could not

even tell me the real reason for coming here? You need me as a scapegoat, is that it? You would leave me to take the blame for this cold murder?'

'If I wanted to place the blame on you, Jordine, I would simply have abandoned you standing back there in the roadway, with Antonio's headless corpse at your feet,' Edward snapped. 'I was not sure I could get out on my own. And as much as you seem to hate me, what I said about you and Alfonso is true. I truly hoped you would embrace the Rhundi name, and prove to be the best of my sons. Once Sergio is crowned, he will reward us. Not only me, but you as well. And so he should. We have secured the kingdom's future here today.'

'Do not include me in your crimes,' Jordine hissed. 'I am no assassin.'

'But you will be called one, if you speak of this to anyone,' Edward warned. 'Now, cease this damnable foolishness, and ride with me. We must find a place to dispose of this armor. Then, we make for Heidel, to prepare the city for the arrival of its true king.'

Jordine hesitated. He wanted to strike at Edward again, to vent his shame and frustration. He had been used, manipulated with casual ease. Yet there was no undoing what had been done. He was now as involved in Sergio's coup as Edward was. And he had no doubt that, regardless of the claims he had made about wishing the best for him, if Edward's act was exposed he would surely blame Jordine.

Edward had turned away from him, and was mounting his horse. Jordine briefly considered returning to the road and telling of all that had happened. It would surely mean his own death, but at least he would face it with a clearer conscience. Yet instead, he found himself untying and mounting his own horse, and turning after Edward as the king-killer rode from the copse and made for the northeastern road, to Heidel.

FOURTEEN

Jarette strode into the throne room and made to strike Roxanne.

The guards' hands were on their sword hilts in an instant, but the queen caught the princess's arm by the wrist before the blow could land. They stood locked together, eyes fixed on one another in furious passion.

'No matter what has happened at Glish, I am still your queen,' Roxanne said, slow and firm. 'Hit me, and I shall have you cut down where you stand.'

'As you had my brother cut down?' Jarette snapped, yanking her arm free. 'Your own husband!'

'I have no hand in any of this, and to claim I do is treason,' Roxanne replied, her expression like ice, her cheeks ashen. For all her distrust of the queen, Jarette knew in that moment that, despite her own suspicions, she was just as shocked by the reports.

Word had only just reached the capital of Antonio's

death, sent by Captain Malchevo. According to the succinct report – delivered to both Roxanne and Jarette – the king had been beheaded during an altercation between the royal party and Crucio's retinue. Exactly who had struck the murderous blow, Malchevo seemed to be deliberately avoiding, though the implication that it was Crucio's followers, or the elder Domongatt himself, was obvious. Afterwards Crucio had fled. Where? Malchevo did not know. The guards were now returning with all haste to Heidel, bearing the king's body.

Jarette felt sick to the pit of her stomach. She had clashed more times with Antonio than she cared count, especially since he had sent her to Balenos. Yet she had always felt closer to him than Sergio, and the idea that he was dead, by the hand of their own father, was unbearable, like being trapped in a waking nightmare, a surreal place of terror from which she could not escape.

'What are we going to do?' she found herself asking Roxanne, suddenly regretting her impulsive attempt at striking the queen.

'We must find who is responsible,' Roxanne said, crumpling Malchevo's letter in her hand. 'Swift, summary justice is the only answer. And if that means ordering Crucio Domongatt to be hunted down like a dog, then so be it.'

'What about the succession?' Jarette said, struggling to bring order to the chaos of her own thoughts. 'Antonio had no named heir. As soon as word of this reaches the rest of the court, we will be in the midst of a crisis. And that's before considering how the common people will react.'

'I will order the citadel to be sealed once again,' Roxanne said. 'You must send messengers to those you trust within the court. I will do likewise. If our allies are informed prior to anyone else, we can ensure the response to this is properly coordinated.'

Jarette thought about just who she could personally count as allies within the ranks of Serendia's nobility – precious few came to mind, even more so given how long she had spent in the north. But she at least knew she could count on her friends.

'I will send word to the Rhundis,' she said. 'At the very least, Jordine and Alfonso will be able to act as trusted eyes on the streets.'

'It's a start,' Roxanne said. 'I suspect we will know friend from foe sooner rather than later.'

Jordine booked a room at the Golden Frog as soon as he and Edward made it back to Heidel, arriving in the middle of the night. He couldn't stomach the idea of remaining under the same roof as Edward, and was even more afraid that he would run into Alfonso, and be unable to keep the reality of what had happened from him. The only good thing Edward had done was avoid implicating his trueborn son, and Jordine would not be responsible for dragging Alfonso down with him.

He spent the night alone, unable to sleep, unwilling to even descend to the taproom and attempt to drown himself in ale. There was too great a danger of getting drunk and speaking of everything he had witnessed to the likes of the innkeeper, Constante; and besides, it felt wholly unnatural to be down amongst the merrymaking crowd below, knowing all of them were oblivious to the storm that was coming.

He contemplated fleeing. He could travel to Calpheon, or perhaps even Valencia. Rip himself free from this web he had become entangled in and start anew. He had made up his mind to do just that, but when morning came, he could not find the strength to rise from his bed and leave the room.

Jarette's message reached him around midday – the princess had presumably instructed its courier to search Heidel's inns and taverns for him. The youth who delivered it claimed he had been told nothing of its contents, and had not been instructed to wait for his reply.

He opened it, and found a terse note from Jarette, requesting his presence at the citadel immediately. It didn't say why, and a renewed sense of dread filled him. Surely word had reached the castle of Antonio's death. Yet did they know anything of his involvement, or Edward Rhundi's? Surely, if that had been the case, it would have been armed guards beating down the door, and not a mere messenger?

The guilt made Jordine want to weep, but he fought to compose himself. Not answering Jarette's summons would raise suspicion. As detestable as it would be to lie to one of his oldest friends, what choice did he have?

It was raining outside, a miserable drizzle that turned the streets to cloying muck and drained the world down to shades of grey. Jordine drew his cloak tight, and was about to step off in the direction of the citadel, looming over the thatch and timber roofs, when the drumbeat of hooves in the muck forced him to pause.

Two riders approached the Golden Frog's front door. Jordine's heart sank even further as he recognized Edward and Alfonso. The father was leading the way, and gestured curtly to Jordine as soon as he saw him.

'It is well that you are ready to leave, boy. I feared I would find you stewing in a drunken stupor. We make for the west bridge.'

'Why?' Jordine asked, finding there was still defiance in his voice.

'Because we have been ordered to meet with the king,' Edward responded.

'Why would King Antonio want to meet us south of the river?' Alfonso called out, his tone suggesting it wasn't the first time he had asked his father as much since setting out from Gallows Street.

'You still haven't told him?' Jordine demanded. Edward glared down at him in silence.

'Told me what?' Alfonso snapped. 'For the love of Elion, will someone explain what is happening?'

'You will both see soon enough,' Edward snapped, before spurring off along the street, leaving Jordine to clamber up behind Alfonso.

'Where did you two go?' Alfonso asked as he rode after his father, his tone equal parts angry and concerned. 'I know you were both absent this past week.'

'It is better if you don't ask,' Jordine said, knowing the claim would only infuriate his friend more.

'If only Father would share his secrets with someone other than his adopted son,' Alfonso said bitterly.

They cantered through the rain-sodden streets, to the southernmost gate over the Demi. There they found a gaggle of bedraggled town guardsmen, sheltering from the rain in doorways and under the masonry arch. The gate itself was open to permit the flow of traffic into and out of Heidel's southern extent, though at the moment nothing was passing through.

The Rhundis dismounted and stood beneath the arch, rainwater cascading down past them, watching the southern road through the worsening torrent.

'What are we waiting for?' Alfonso asked.

'I told you,' Edward said. 'The king.'

Jordine understood what was coming. Yet again, he found himself wondering if he should speak up. This could be his last chance. The final opportunity to avert the fate that otherwise must befall his home.

But then a voice cried from the top of the gatehouse. One of the sentries there had seen something. There came the sound of running footsteps as more of the town guard hurried up onto the ramparts.

Jordine saw what those above had already spotted. Figures emerged through the curtain of rain, riders crossing the west bridge over the seething Demi, at full gallop, their iron-shod hooves striking sparks from the cobblestones. They were men-at-arms, armored and carrying lances.

Several of the town guards hurried to turn the gate's closing mechanism, but Edward moved to interpose himself before they could begin closing it.

'Hold fast,' he commanded. 'Or would you shut the gates of Heidel in the face of your monarch?'

The guards exchanged confused, nervous glances, but none attempted to defy the knight. Jordine and Alfonso moved to the side of the gateway as the first horsemen came surging through into the town, the thunder of their hooves reverberating beneath the archway.

None of the town guards attempted to stop them. Jordine knew he had just been complicit in ensuring Heidel fell without so much as a word being raised in protest.

One of the horsemen pulled off to one side, pausing in the gateway in front of Jordine, Edward and Alfonso. It was Prince Sergio, armored but with his helmet hanging from his saddle's pommel. His surcoat was not its usual red and white, but bore instead the red and yellow of the king's heraldry.

Edward knelt before him. Jordine refused to do likewise.

'Is Heidel prepared for my arrival?' Sergio demanded over the sound of his men-at-arms continuing to pass by.

'I cannot speak for the citadel, sire,' Edward said. 'But you will meet no resistance in the town.'

'You have done well, Rhundi,' Sergio said, ignoring Jordine and Alfonso. 'Remain here for now, and keep the gates open. Ensure none challenge the Eindhovein host.

Once they are across the river in their entirety, come and find me at the castle.'

'As you will it, my liege,' Edward said. Sergio rode on.

'Why does Sergio wear the king's livery?' Alfonso asked, as the last of the horsemen galloped by. Infantry were following, rain-sodden spearmen and archers tramping in under the gateway.

'Antonio is dead,' Jordine said, unable to endure it any longer. 'And your father serves Sergio, as he has done for many months. Today, he will claim his reward.'

'Is this true?' Alfonso asked, turning on his father.

'Antonio is slain, yes,' Edward said, looking at the passing soldiery rather than his son. 'Of Crucio's fate, I do not know. But Sergio is king now. He is the next in line. And he has brought his host from Eindhovein to make sure of that.'

'Why didn't you tell me?' Alfonso demanded. 'Why wouldn't you inform your son of any of this?'

'Because it was Edward who slew Antonio,' Jordine said.

Jarette rushed up onto the ramparts, ignoring the stinging rain that struck her pale skin and instantly began to soak her fur cloak.

Roxanne was already present on the citadel walls, alongside Malchevo. The retinue that had accompanied Antonio had returned with his remains just hours earlier. Jarette had not been able to bring herself to look upon her brother, but had heard Malchevo's grim report – he had not personally witnessed the killing blow, but it seemed certain Crucio was responsible, despite the despair he had displayed when he had realized what he had done. After the murderous act, Crucio and his small band of followers had fled, none knew where.

Jarette had been pacing her chambers, waiting anxiously on the arrival of Jordine and Alfonso, when the sound of a commotion on the streets outside had drawn her up onto the citadel's walls.

She saw now what was causing it. The road leading from the castle gate was filled with soldiers, marching up through the town from the south. What few people there were on the streets had fled indoors, barring entrances and banging shutters closed.

An army had entered Heidel, and no one in the citadel seemed to have known about its approach until now.

She tried to make out the crests and sigils on display in the rain, recognizing a few minor lords and knights, but the largest retinue appeared to be displaying the royal livery.

'It is Sergio,' Roxanne said, anticipating Jarette's first question. 'He has brought his host to Heidel. He comes to claim the throne.'

'He knew,' Jarette said, realization striking as cold and stinging as the rain. 'It isn't possible that word of Antonio's death reached him in Eindhovein and he was able to march a host this far north so quickly. He already knew Antonio was dead, or soon would be. He must have set out over a week ago.'

'I agree,' Roxanne said, not taking her eyes off the approaching host. 'But there is nothing we can do about that now.'

'We must resist,' Jarette snapped. 'This is usurpation! He has some hand in Antonio's death, he must have!'

'We have no means of resisting a force like this,' Roxanne said. 'The citadel is garrisoned by the royal guard alone, without the stockpiles necessary to weather a siege. There is no time to raise more extensive forces or make the proper preparations. And the town is already taken. If we attempt to keep Sergio out, Heidel will inevitably suffer. He may even order it to be sacked if we do not open the gates immediately.'

'Surely he would not sack the town he seeks to become king of?' Jarette said, a part of her still trying to come to terms with what was happening.

'I suspect Sergio would resort to many actions we might not previously have thought him capable of,' Roxanne replied darkly. 'And ultimately, defying him will do no good, not in the short term. Without a named successor, Sergio is next in line to the throne.'

'How can you say that?' Jarette shouted, turning fully on Roxanne. 'Are you in league with him? Did you send my brother away to be murdered, to pave the way for Sergio's coup?'

'Why in the names of all the gods would I do that?' Roxanne demanded in turn, finally looking at Jarette, glaring from under her raised hood. 'I am the queen! Do you think Sergio plans on allowing me to remain as such once he has installed himself here? If I stand in his way, I will be the first to be executed!'

'Not if you have already made a deal with him,' Jarette pointed out, still trying to work through how Sergio had brought such a powerful force to the very gates of the citadel without anyone guessing his intentions.

'You will see soon enough that I have not,' Roxanne said, her tone riven between bitterness and despair. 'I am a fool, not to have predicted something like this. It was never Crucio who was the true threat. Sergio has been playing a long game, and today he is making his final move.'

The gates to the citadel opened, and Sergio's retinue swept inside, securing the courtyard and then the keep beyond it, barring doors and taking post at windows and arrow slits. Only when the entirety of the castle's guards, servants and staff had been brought out in the yard did Sergio himself enter, followed by Elysia.

He did not pause to address the assembly, not even looking at Roxanne or Jarette as he rode past and dismounted before striding up the steps and into the keep. There was no one to stop him from entering the throne room.

He stood for a while, surveying the empty chamber, watching how the light shining in through the high arches caught the dancing dust and gleamed from the fine old timber of the two thrones upon their flagstone dais. How often had he stood among the court, humbly hearing the royal decrees, or knelt before these very thrones, while in his heart he yearned to be the one seated upon them?

The captain of his retinue, Hildara, approached and bowed.

'The keep is secured, my liege, and with it the citadel. Heidel is yours.'

'May I be the first to congratulate you, my king,' Elysia said, leaning in to kiss his cheek. 'Now, at last, Serendia will be free from the disunity that has undermined it for so long.'

'And with you as my queen, we shall be united in peace and prosperity with noble Calpheon,' Sergio said, not looking at his wife as he stepped towards the thrones, mounting the dais. Slowly, he turned and sat, Elysia moving to take her place at his side.

'Hail, Sergio Domongatt,' Hildara called out, a lone voice ringing from the throne room's high rafters. 'Hail, the king of Serendia!'

PART TWO

FIFTEEN

Roxanne rode south alone, disguised as her handmaid, Carolin.

A month had passed since Sergio's arrival at Heidel. Roxanne had known as soon as she had seen his standards within the town that defiance would be met with death. The two individuals who had most guaranteed her own safety and security in Serendia – Antonio and Crucio – were now dead or gone, and she had to look to her own survival.

That had meant placating Sergio, initially. She had ordered the citadel to be opened and had feigned relief at her brother-in-law's arrival, pretending she hadn't even considered his role in Antonio's death. He was, she freely admitted, the rightful heir now that her husband lay treacherously slain by his father's hand.

She had knelt and sworn fealty to Sergio, and had even signed a declaration abdicating her own position to Elysia, who now reigned as queen. Yet all the while, she had worked to identify just how Sergio had betrayed his brother, and who was involved in the latticework of alliances and deals that had led to his uncontested seizure of the throne.

Others had chosen a less wise series of responses to Sergio's ascension. Against Roxanne's private advice, Jarette had raged at her older brother, accusing him of treachery and usurpation. Roxanne suspected the only reason Sergio had not had her killed was his knowledge that to do so immediately after his hasty coronation would only have lent credence to the princess's claims. That, and the fact that Jarette had no means of following through with her accusations, no evidence and no notable allies among the nobility, meant Sergio could afford to appear lenient. Some were not so fortunate – Captain Malchevo, chosen as the scapegoat for Antonio's death, was hung from gallows erected in Heidel's town square.

Sergio had permitted Roxanne to reside at a townhouse on Westbow, near the Church of Elion. He had 'advised' that she not leave Heidel, ostensibly for her own safety – Crucio was still at large, and the new king had put a bounty on his head. Roxanne suspected instructions to remain within the town were born more out of a desire to stop her meddling elsewhere than any true concern for her safety.

She would only follow Sergio's orders for as long as they suited her. He had refused to call the court to meet in its entirety, allowing the nobility to come and swear fealty to their new king only as individuals or in small groups.

Doing so ensured there was no concentration of power, at least not one Sergio could not control. He was far more cunning than Roxanne had ever given him credit for, yet she was determined to outwit him. She blamed herself for failing to predict his schemes, and had sworn a private oath that, for all her public acceptance of her fate, she would not rest until her vengeance was complete. And for that reason, not long after the first winter snows had blanketed the land to the north of the town, she fled Heidel.

She assumed the guards at the gates had instructions to stop her leaving, so she went disguised as her handmaid, claiming she had been instructed to take a delivery of firewood from one of the winter markets that had sprung up just south of the river, where traders could sell their wares without having to pay the merchant tax that was enforced as soon as they passed through Heidel's town gates. She had also brought her falcon, Mnemosyne, hooded and caged, stating the bird needed exercise.

Roxanne's true purpose lay farther south. She rode for Eindhovein, trusting that the information she had received from her few remaining informants would prove to be correct. Trusting that Jordine Ducas was wiling away his days there in bitter exile.

His was a name that had come up repeatedly whenever Roxanne had pursued more information on just how Sergio had orchestrated his brother's death. He had been spotted taking delivery of something from Soot Row, and no one could remember seeing him in his usual haunts in the days preceding Antonio's death. It seemed hard to imagine such a dissolute youth partaking in so ambitious a scheme, yet Roxanne recalled how clearly he had been enamored with Elysia the last time she had spotted him attending a royal feast. It was less of a stretch to imagine Sergio's wife seducing him into treasonous acts.

After Sergio's coronation, the Rhundis – including Jordine – had departed from Heidel. Word was they had been provided with a new residence in lands granted by Sergio near his old powerbase at Eindhovein. That in itself was suspicious. Such a reversal of fortunes for the pauper knight pointed to services rendered before Sergio had even claimed his crown.

So it was to Eindhovein that Roxanne rode, knowing that once she had passed beyond the Demi there would be no turning back. Once he discovered her absence, Sergio would put a bounty on her capture, just as he had with his own father. She could not return to Heidel, not unless she had something to bargain with. She was gambling it all on her instincts.

That handsome, blond youth knew something, and she was staking her life on finding out exactly what.

Jordine turned his steed, Greybolt, for home.

He had been riding the moorlands for most of the morning, fantasizing about freedom. Edward had organized a hunt through the estate, the third in the month since their arrival, but Jordine had refused to participate. He could not stomach Edward's presence, or Alfonso's accusing looks.

Instead, he had taken Greybolt – the only gift to the family from Sergio he had actually accepted – and ridden alone, his thoughts as bleak and morose as the grey winter landscape of southern Serendia.

There was a certain irony to his current fate, he supposed. He had accepted the Rhundis' offer of adoption so he did not have to depart Heidel, yet here he was, far now from the kingdom's capital. Not that he had wished to stay there. By all accounts the town was in a virtual state of lockdown as Sergio slowly sifted the nobility, establishing just who could be trusted, and who still harbored secret dissatisfaction towards the new regime. In a sense, the fact that the Rhundis' reward had taken them away from the capital was a blessing. He doubted he could have knelt before Sergio and sworn public fealty to him, the way so many others were being required to.

He had received no word from Jarette, and could only hope she was safe. Alfonso had pleaded to be allowed to return to Heidel to see her, but Edward had refused. House Rhundi had received its reward, and the wisest thing to do now was to lie low. Their new estate, formerly one of the crown's private holdings, was relatively poor compared to the lands and properties of the kingdom's most powerful lords, but it was a regal property compared to the poor townhouse that until recently had been the Rhundis' sole property. Edward was the pauper knight no more, and he was relishing his newfound standing. He had already hosted a banquet at the main hall for the local Eindhovein gentry, and the boar hunts were interminable.

Jordine couldn't stomach any of it, and he was strongly considering just continuing to ride south, over the border with Drieghan. He would find his own way, maybe as a sellsword, freelance or adventurer-for-hire. If he rode back to the house and retrieved a few belongings and some food for the road, he could be in Drieghan by nightfall.

He turned Greybolt back towards the estate, wondering if he could actually muster the courage to follow through with the idea. For all its uncertainties, it still felt preferable to spending another night with the Rhundis.

The new home in question was a stout timber structure, built atop a low hill just southwest of the town of Eindhovein. The jagged turrets of Fort Eindhovein were visible in the distance, framed against the leaden grey sky. There was a hint of snow in the air as Jordine rode up the main road through the estate, but thoughts about securing an extra cloak and some fodder for Greybolt before he departed melted away as he heard an angry shout ring out from the yard before the main house. Feeling a sudden sense of foreboding, he urged his mare to quicken her pace.

They rounded the stable block, scattering a gaggle of geese that had been crossing the road, and found the source of the commotion. A dozen men-at-arms in the blue and white livery of one of the local lords had surrounded a mounted woman at the front doors of the house. Several of the Rhundis' new servants looked on anxiously, seeming unwilling to intervene – from the way she was dressed, Jordine thought at first that the woman was one of the household maids, and had no idea why she would be mounted, or why a wedge of soldiers were seeking to detain her. The leader of the men-at-arms, a sergeant, was mounted too, and he was driving his steed alongside that of the maid and barking at her to get down.

'What is the meaning of this?' Jordine shouted as he rode up, driving Greybolt in amongst the foot soldiers and forcing them to part for him. The sergeant turned on Jordine, red-faced with anger.

'We have apprehended a fugitive from the capital,' he declared, gesturing at the maid. 'I have orders to bring her to my liege, Squire Legano.'

Jordine looked properly at the maid, and only then did he spot that she was no maid at all. It was Roxanne Domongatt.

He stared, then turned back to the sergeant.

'This is one of the new Heidel servants, hired by my father,' he said, overcoming the distaste he felt at calling Edward Rhundi his father. 'It's impossible to get decent help out here. He will want words with your squire when he hears you've been harrying her for no good reason.'

'This is Lady Roxanne Domongatt, wife of the former king,' the sergeant said, refusing to be cowed. 'She is to be taken and returned to Heidel, for her own safety.'

'Don't be ridiculous! Why would the queen of Serendia be this far south, disguised as a common servant?'

'Roxanne is not queen any longer,' the sergeant pressed on. 'She has abdicated in favor of Lady Elysia, the king's wife.'

Jordine could tell the sergeant wasn't going to budge,

but he was spared having to continue the charade when Roxanne abruptly dug her spurs in. Her mount flung itself forward with a shriek, sending men-at-arms scattering across the yard with a clatter of armor, and almost unhorsing both the sergeant and Jordine.

'Halt,' the sergeant bellowed, making to spur after Roxanne, but Jordine punched him. The blow was a good one, catching the man-at-arms squarely on the jaw and sending him toppling from his mount.

Those other soldiers still on their feet shouted, and one made to snatch Greybolt's bridle, but Jordine lashed out with a foot and kicked him in the face before turning and spurring after Roxanne.

He had no idea why the former queen was in Eindhovein disguised as a maid, but he was determined to find out.

They sent the geese scattering for a second time, thundering along the track to the south. The recent cold had left the ground hard, a sharp contrast to the cloying mud caused by the rains in previous weeks. Jordine gave Greybolt her head, quickly closing the distance on Roxanne.

He saw her snatch a glance back, and did likewise, seeing that the sergeant had regained his own horse and was in pursuit, his foot soldiers running after him in vain.

'There's a drop in the ground after the trees ahead,' he shouted at Roxanne. 'Off to the right!'

He had no reason to expect her to trust him, but he hoped she understood he was her only chance at avoiding capture.

It seemed she had realized the same thing – she turned

sharply after riding through a stand of trees that edged the roadway, across a field and down into the dead ground that Jordine knew lay to the right of the road. The slope was gentle and deceptive, allowing a rider to remain unseen from the roadway despite the appearance of a flat, continuous field. He had already used it when trying to avoid Edward and Alfonso when he had spotted them on the road from the house.

He followed Roxanne down, and was relieved when he saw her reining in at the bottom of the depression. He did likewise with Greybolt, holding a hand up in wary greeting, half expecting her to turn away from him and continue to ride. She didn't, though, but simply watched as he held a finger to his lips.

Sure enough, there came the sound of hoofbeats from the roadway as the sergeant passed by, not realizing his quarry was only a few dozen yards away. The sound receded, followed a little while later by the thumping of feet as the men-at-arms on foot attempted to keep up. Once they had all passed, Jordine turned back to Roxanne, speaking low and urgently.

'Why are you here? Why are you being pursued?'

'Just get me to somewhere safe and quiet, and I'll tell you,' she responded tersely.

As she spoke, he took her in properly for the first time since she had appeared. It was clear from the muddy state of both her mount and her disguise that she had been on the road for days, riding hard. She appeared to have brought few belongings with her, other than an incongruous falcon, hooded and secured in a catch against her horse's flank.

Her dishevelment lent her a wild kind of beauty – Jordine had only ever previously seen her in the stultified setting of the court, where everything from her dresses to her styled hair to her smile had been set and curated to perfection. That was no longer the case, and he felt as though he was looking upon her for the first time, seeing her as he never had done before. Seeing the real person, and not the screen of formality she had always hidden behind.

'We should keep going south,' he suggested. 'The border isn't far, and that sergeant will likely make for it, but if we cut across these fields to the east and pick up the road to the old Elonian monastery, there's an inn where I doubt you'll be troubled.'

'Lead on, then,' Roxanne said.

SIXTEEN

They rode to Southwich, a poor farming settlement hard on the frontier with Drieghan. Jordine took them to the Reaver's Rest, the last inn before the border. It was a rough place, but he had scouted it on several previous occasions, knowing that someday he might make use of it, if he ever followed through with his fantasies of abandoning his life in Serendia.

He told Roxanne to remain outside and astride her horse while he went in and checked for any signs of threat, mainly the border guards who sometimes used the Rest as a waypoint. Finding none, he went back out into the inn's yard, half expecting Roxanne to have gone. She was still there though, clearly trying to hide her anxiousness as she waited for him.

'It's quiet inside,' Jordine told her. 'And I doubt those men-at-arms will venture this far east of the main road. The sun sets early at this time of year, it'll be dark in a few hours. I suggest we wait it out.'

She nodded her agreement and passed over both mounts to the inn's stable boy before following him inside, though she insisted on bringing the caged falcon. The taproom was dark and dingy, timbers blackened by a century of smoke, but there were few patrons about. Jordine secured a table in the corner and paid for ale and a platter of bread and cheese for them both.

He knew the best thing to do would be to leave her and return to the Rhundi estate. He was sure Edward would be able to smooth over his striking of Squire Legano's sergeant, but on the other hand, making off with the former queen of the land as she fled in disguise was riven with threat and danger, and that was exactly what he was craving. Anything to distract from the drudgery and self-hatred that had hounded him since Antonio's death.

He waited for the food and drink to be delivered to the table, then spoke in a quiet, guarded tone.

'Why are you here, my lady?'

'I came looking for you,' she answered, the words taking him by surprise. 'I heard the Rhundis have been given an estate near Eindhovein,' she went on, 'a reward for services to the crown.'

'Then you heard correctly,' Jordine said. 'Though I am sorry those services were not to the crown you wore. Why are you traveling disguised as a maid?'

'I fear for my life,' Roxanne said, watching Jordine as he took a bite of bread and cheese. 'It is not safe for me in Heidel.'

'Why?' Jordine asked after swallowing a mouthful. 'I understand your position has been at risk since Antonio's death, but you have surrendered the crown to Lady Elysia, have you not? Is Sergio really so insecure that he still sees you as a threat?'

'I fear he does,' Roxanne said, finally beginning to eat as well. 'Two weeks ago, several masked men sought to force entry to the townhouse I have been provided with in Heidel. I was being watched and followed everywhere I went within the capital. If I were to remain there, my time would be limited.'

'Surely you have allies in Heidel and beyond?' Jordine asked. 'Some willing to come to your aid, or shelter you?'

'Sergio's spies are everywhere, and he is making sure those he thinks may prove seditious are kept apart. I can trust no one in the town.'

'Yet you think you can trust me? We have scarce spoken, and it must be obvious enough that the Rhundis are aligned with Sergio?'

'Yet you are not a Rhundi,' Roxanne said. 'You are a Ducas. My husband opposed the banishment of your father.'

'He said nothing when Crucio sent my family away,' Jordine corrected her.

'But as we discussed when last we met, he was preparing to overturn his exile. We viewed you as an ally, a potentially vital one. Yet you turned against him.'

Jordine frowned, putting down the bread he had been eating.

'I turned against no one. I considered myself loyal to

your husband, just as my family was loyal to his father, even after he ordered our banishment.'

'Then you had no hand in his death?' Roxanne demanded.

Jordine could find no reply, and Roxanne's expression hardened.

'Your silence damns you, Jordine,' she said.

'You are in no position to make such accusations,' Jordine countered. 'Who are you to come all this way, seeking to entrap me?'

'I want only answers,' Roxanne said. 'My husband is dead, and I am alone, abandoned by all I once held dear. If you will not help me, you should turn me over to Sergio, and collect another fine reward for your adoptive parents!'

She bowed her head and began to weep. Jordine felt a pang of distress, and shifted uncomfortably in his seat, pushing the platter of food closer to her.

'You must not give in to despair, Your Majesty,' he urged. 'That is not what a queen of Serendia would do.'

'I am a queen no longer—' Roxanne began to say between rising sobs, but Jordine continued, trying to cut through her despair.

'You may no longer wear a crown, but you have a nobility none can take away from you. Unlike every past ruler of Serendia, unlike any so-called noble of the court, you earned your position. You came from nothing, from a burning ruin, and you won a place in this kingdom that will live on long after someone like me, or any other petty noble, has faded into obscurity.'

Roxanne wiped tears from her eyes and sniffed.

'You speak well, Jordine. It is no surprise you are so popular with the ladies of the court.'

Jordine scoffed. 'Elion blessed me with a handsome face and a quick tongue. Sometimes they are more trouble than they are worth.'

'Jealous husbands become dangerous when they are men of status and power,' Roxanne observed. 'You play deadly games, Jordine.'

'Yet those same husbands think nothing of taking mistresses or forcing themselves upon their wives' maids,' Jordine pointed out. 'I merely help even the odds.'

Roxanne gave a small, sad laugh, drying her eyes once more before going back to picking at the food.

'I fear I must flee Serendia,' she said at length. 'Without evidence that Sergio caused my husband's death, I have no means of resisting his usurpation.'

'Where would you go?' Jordine asked. Roxanne gave a miserable shrug.

'I cannot trust Seric not to surrender me back into Sergio's clutches, given Elysia is his daughter, so Calpheon is too dangerous. Balenos now lies mostly under Serendia's sway. That leaves Mediah. Maybe beyond, to Valencia.'

'And you intend to travel all that way alone?' Jordine wondered.

'I have survived worse,' Roxanne pointed out, a note of defiance entering her voice. 'As you just said, I worked my way from nothing to the highest station in the land. I may never be queen again, but I will survive.'

‘That is the sort of determination that befits you,’ Jordine said, nodding. ‘Do not allow despair to steal it away again, Your Majesty.’

Roxanne smiled, and raised her tankard.

‘Well said, Jordine Ducas. Will you drink with me? To defiance, and new beginnings.’

Jordine echoed her, and drank, sensing her eyes still on him as she did likewise.

‘Tell me, what news do you have of Jarette?’ he asked as he set his tankard back down. ‘I cannot imagine she reacted well to Sergio’s arrival in Heidel.’

‘She was furious,’ Roxanne said. ‘I advised her not to resist, at least not openly, but she accused him of murdering their brother. She was fortunate he did not have her seized on charges of sedition.’

‘There is nothing unexpected about that, then,’ Jordine said. ‘But she is safe? Is he holding her as he tried to do with you?’

‘She is in the citadel, and I have not seen her,’ Roxanne admitted. ‘You care for her, do you not? Perhaps more than a friend might?’

Jordine laughed. ‘Do you think so little of me that you do not believe I can have female friends? I am not some stallion in heat, Your Majesty. I have never considered Jarette in that way.’

‘You understand she is too fierce for you to tame,’ Roxanne said, almost teasingly. ‘Many men would find that alluring.’

‘And I wish them all the best,’ Jordine said. ‘She has

certainly never had a lack of suitors to reject. Including our friend Alfonso.'

'Oh?' Roxanne asked. 'Does she know of his affections?'

'She is touchingly oblivious, and I would not dare tell her,' Jordine said. 'One day he will work up the courage to share his true feelings.'

He trailed off, unwilling to speak of how his friendship with Alfonso had cracked and fractured over the past year. The thought saddened him.

'I suppose you have many such tales from the court,' Roxanne said, finishing the last of the bread and cheese. 'Beneath the formality, the place is a hotbed of illicit relations and gossip.'

'It certainly was,' Jordine said. 'But out here I am privy to none of it. Things haven't been the same.'

'Then why not relive past glories by telling me of some of it?' Roxanne asked, a hint of mischief in her voice. 'Am I right in thinking you have bedded Lady Elysia?'

Jordine was taken aback by the forwardness of the question, so much so that Roxanne laughed.

'Do not worry, I am in no position to out either of you to the king or the court. I don't suppose you anticipated at the time that your tryst was with the future queen of Serendia.'

'That I did not,' Jordine admitted ruefully, finding himself smiling as well. 'But for what it's worth, Lady Elysia is a fine woman. I seduced her on a whim, and I regret it. It is a sorry thing, that she ended up with a man like Sergio.'

'Which is likely why she permitted herself to fall for

your charms,' Roxanne observed. 'Ladies of noble birth have little say in who they end up tied to. Elysia was used by her own father to secure Calpheon's alliance with Serendia. Lying with you was an act of defiance and an assertion of her own agency, even if it was done in secret.'

'You speak as one experienced in such things,' Jordine said. Roxanne looked at him sharply, but then offered him another smile.

'We all play the game, Jordine. I never once complained of my husband's dalliances with other women. And I made sure he never knew when my own eyes wandered.'

Jordine went up and ordered more ale, and paid for a room for Roxanne upstairs, then carried her small collection of belongings, including the caged falcon, up to the room. Back at the table, they returned to talking about the scandals of the court, their conversation becoming increasingly carefree.

For Jordine, it was a relief, almost an unburdening. He had not spoken freely about such trivialities since he, Alfonso and Jarette had last enjoyed a drink together in the Lilly Valley, and that had been well over a year ago. For a little while, he found himself forgetting all that had happened in recent months, the pains of lost friendship and lost family.

The hour grew late. Eventually Jordine dragged himself away from the table, and finding only a few coins left in his purse, told Roxanne that it was well past time he was leaving. There was no one else in the taproom other than one tired-looking dwarf barman.

He rose unsteadily and she accompanied him to the door, arm in arm, still laughing at a comment about the kirtle dress that Lady Yazmina had made for her little lapdog on her first day at court.

'Are you sure you're in a fit state to ride all the way back to Eindhovein?' she asked as they went. Jordine waved his free hand dismissively.

'I've been in the saddle in worse states,' he said, fumbling slightly with the handle to the inn's door. He flung it open and stepped outside, about to roust the stable boy and call for Greybolt, but the blast of cold air that hit him stole his breath.

Night had well and truly fallen, gripping the countryside in frigid darkness. Snow blanketed the ground, presumably having started not long after they had arrived at the inn, and more of it was still coming down, a slow, lazy cascade caught in the firelight spilling from the door.

Jordine and Roxanne stood, still arm-in-arm, taking in the silence. For a moment, they felt like the only people left in the world.

They kissed. Jordine didn't know who began it, only that they found themselves pressed against each other, finding warmth in more than just their embrace. He lost himself in it for a time, until she pulled back, and he felt a jolt of fear, realizing what he had just done.

'Come back inside with me,' she whispered. The words soothed him. He took her hand and allowed himself to be led in, up the creaking staircase to the small bedroom on the first floor. She stopped outside the door.

'Tell me the truth,' she demanded fiercely, a hand upon his chest. 'Am I about to lie with my husband's killer?'

'Upon my life, with every god of the firmament as my witness, I did not kill Antonio Domongatt,' Jordine said. Roxanne nodded.

'Then let us forget all that grim business. Forget that I was once your queen, just for one night.'

Jordine nodded, and followed her into the bedroom.

The sound of empty bottles being discarded onto the rubbish heap outside the inn's back door woke Jordine.

He stirred groggily, his head thumping, feeling the warmth of the bedsheets then a patch of coldness beside him.

Slowly, he opened his eyes.

Roxanne was already up and almost fully dressed, finishing the laces on the back of her maid's dress. The shutters were open, and a white, wintery light was spilling into the room.

'Good morning,' she said when she noticed Jordine stirring.

'So it wasn't a dream,' he murmured, throat dry. Roxanne scoffed.

'Please, you can spare me the lines you usually used on the ladies of the court the morning after,' she said, tying up the last lace. She opened one of her saddlebags and, to Jordine's surprise, produced a thin strip of meat, before proceeding to undo the gate to the falcon's cage. As she began to feed it, she glanced back at him on the bed.

'Thank you for yesterday,' she said. 'Not just for paying for this room, but for seeing me safe from those men-at-arms. I owe you debts I fear I may not be able to repay.'

'I did not help you with the intention of leaving you indebted,' Jordine said.

'Your character does you credit, lion of Serendia,' Roxanne responded.

Jordine thought about how untrue that was, about all the misdeeds he was responsible for, how they weighed on him. It had felt good to share just a few of them last night. But why should he stop there? Why should he carry the heaviest weight any longer?

'Edward killed your husband,' he said unbidden, almost spitting the words, like poison he was desperate to purge from his body. 'Edward Rhundi killed King Antonio.'

Roxanne stared at him in shock, frozen beside the cage, and Jordine felt the need to hastily exonerate himself, knowing he could not now go back on what he was saying.

'I was with him when he did it, but I did not know of his intentions beforehand. He managed to make it look as though it was Crucio's doing.'

'Why?' Roxanne asked, a slight tremble visible in her slender shoulders now as she stared at Jordine. 'Why would Edward Rhundi kill the king?'

'Sergio commanded it,' Jordine said. 'The Rhundis are in his thrall, and are now enjoying their rewards. But I regret it. I swear upon my life and my honor, or what remains of it, that I did not know Edward's intent before he struck the blow that slew Antonio.'

Roxanne looked at him hard, then, to his surprise, leaned over and kissed him tenderly on the brow.

'I believe you, Jordine,' she said. 'And you have my thanks, for speaking these truths to me. It would have been easy to stay silent, but again you prove the quality of your character. Do not allow yourself to become burdened by the misdeeds of others. Their shame is not yours.'

Jordine felt a soaring sense of relief. He tried to hide how much the former queen's words meant to him.

'Where will you go now?' he asked.

'Mediah, I suppose,' she said, shutting the falcon's cage. 'I don't know if I will go further. I must admit, I have always had a hankering for adventure. The circumstances leading to it aren't exactly ideal, but I intend to make the most of it.'

'Will I see you again?' Jordine asked. He had not really meant to speak the words, and felt like a fool the moment they left his lips. There was no reason to imagine this goodbye would be anything other than permanent, but Roxanne seemed to have a talent for drawing out his innermost thoughts.

She looked at him again, and smiled sadly.

'I certainly hope so, Jordine Ducas.'

Roxanne bade farewell to Jordine and rode east, crossing over the main southern road and carrying on. At one point she saw what she took to be a patrol skirting one of the ridgelines to the north, possibly sent out by one of the local lords to hunt for her, but she lost them in the next valley, cutting across country.

The whole time, Jordine weighed upon her mind. She had expected to find a dissolute youth, arrogant and overconfident, happy to make use of a fallen queen before discarding her. That was the role she had prepared herself to play, but instead she had found him to be thoughtful, gallant and loyal. It made doing what she now intended harder, but that could not be helped. She could not afford to hesitate.

She was only doing what had to be done. Jordine had spoken of survival, and the determination to overcome all odds. And he had been right. Roxanne would always survive, regardless of what it took. Not for her own self-preservation, but for that thing that had driven her for as long as she could remember – the desire for vengeance, smoldering deep inside her, the embers of a burned home that had never been fully extinguished.

Rather than carry on east, she turned north, keeping to country lanes and spending her nights in dingy rural inns and taverns. By such routes, she came eventually back to Heidel. She rode directly across the East Bridge as the sun was starting to set, and called upon the town guards manning the gate there.

'I am Roxanne Domongatt, and I believe the king has a bounty on my head.'

SEVENTEEN

'You are bold to return here,' Sergio said, eyeing Roxanne with contempt from where he was lounging atop the throne. 'Bold, or foolish.'

'As bold as you were, when you commanded Edward Rhundi to murder your older brother?' Roxanne demanded, holding Sergio's gaze.

The new captain of the royal guard, Hildara, sprang forward, her sword rasping from its scabbard, but Roxanne raised a single hand and spoke, the words warding off the blow.

'Strike me down and every commoner in Heidel and every servant in this citadel will know of this usurpation. There will be a mob in the streets within a few hours, and they'll have both your heads on spikes by dawn.'

'How dare you—' Hildara started to say, but Roxanne spoke over her, continuing to look at Sergio while ignoring the blade poised to cut her head from her shoulders.

'Dismiss your guards,' she instructed. 'And let us discuss how we might ensure an outcome where all of us live to see another day.'

'Sire, surely you cannot permit this?' Hildara exclaimed, still outraged on behalf of her monarch, but Sergio snapped at her.

'You are dismissed! Wait outside.'

Hildara looked like she was actually going to argue with a direct order, before finally mastering herself and sweeping past Roxanne, accompanied by the other guards in the throne room.

Roxanne waited until she heard the doors bang shut behind them, the echo reverberating through the cavernous hall. She was still dressed as a maidservant, still muddy and disheveled from her travels. In truth she was exhausted, and her heart was pounding in her breast, but she allowed none of that to show. Displaying the slightest weakness could give Sergio an opening, and seal her fate.

'Let us not dissemble, Your Highness,' she said, her voice calm and clear. 'We are both too clever to try to play the other for a fool. I know that you killed my husband.'

'Give me one reason,' Sergio said, 'one convincing, cast-iron reason, why I shouldn't call for Hildara and have her cut you down where you stand? The gods know, she is eager enough to slay you.'

'I do not need to make a case against you, Sergio,' Roxanne said. 'I have irrefutable evidence to hand.'

She whistled, a long, ululating note, reaching such a pitch that it made Sergio grimace.

For a short while, nothing happened. Then there was a flurry of beating wings, before Mnemosyne alighted in one of the arrow slits in the lower section of the throne room's outer-facing wall. The bird ruffled its feathers, and seemed to look at Roxanne expectantly.

'A falcon,' Sergio said, beginning to laugh. 'Is it a magical bird? Is it going to squawk accusations against me in the streets if I refuse to give an airing to your tripe?'

'Your Highness is as perceptive as ever,' Roxanne said acidly. 'It is indeed more than a mere falcon, but its power lies not in speech. It lies in knowledge, absolute knowledge of past events that it can share, at my command.'

Sergio's laughter ceased abruptly.

'A memory falcon,' he breathed. 'Impossible. Where did you—'

'You seem to have doubts, Your Majesty, so allow me the pleasure of disabusing them,' Roxanne pressed on, permitting herself a slender smile. She spoke the arcane words of command, and the falcon emitted a piercing cry. The throne room dissolved around them both.

The miserable little bedroom above the taproom of the Reaver's Rest replaced it. Roxanne found herself watching through what appeared to be the bars of a cage, knowing Sergio was currently experiencing the same shared vision. She could see herself, or rather the memory of herself, standing beside the cage, and Jordine beyond her, still in bed, gazing up at her intently.

Jordine spoke, the words sounding distant, yet still audible.

'Edward killed your husband. Edward Rhundi killed King Antonio. I was with him when he did it, but I did not know of his intentions beforehand. He managed to make it look as though it was Crucio's doing.'

Roxanne spoke the next phrase of command, and the vision conjured by Mnemosyne dissolved like running wax, until she was back in the throne room of Heidel citadel once more.

Sergio's face had turned ashen grey. Roxanne experienced one final flurry of doubts. This was a betrayal, and not only of Jordine. If she carried on, there would be bloody, brutal consequences.

Yet she had come too far to stop now. She stepped closer to Sergio, driving her words home like a dagger.

'Heidel is still full of people loyal to Crucio. All I need to do is open my mouth, and your fate shall be sealed. There's only one way out of this. Take me as your queen. Dwell on this as long as you need. I'm sure you'll make the right choice.'

EIGHTEEN

The Rhundis were summoned back to the capital.

After Roxanne's departure, Jordine had managed to dismiss claims that he had even encountered the former queen, successfully arguing to Edward that the sergeant who had attempted to apprehend her had been mistaken. In the following days he had slipped back into the drudgery of life at Eindhovein, and so returning to Heidel proved to be an unexpected relief.

Guilt still haunted him, but the familiar streets and bustle brought him a degree of comfort. It felt like coming home from exile. The pall of fear and suspicion that had fallen over the capital in the first weeks of Sergio's reign seemed to have lifted – traders again hawked their wares in the marketplace, the subjects of note attended the Church of Elion for the bi-weekly sermons, while revelers drank and caroused in the Lilly Valley and Golden Frog. Few, if any, seemed to have changed their ways just because a new head wore the crown.

Edward was called upon by one of Sergio's messengers almost as soon as they arrived back at Gallows Street, but there seemed to be no requirement for Jordine to follow him. That evening, he came to a decision. With Edward still absent, he knocked on Alfonso's door.

His former friend answered it, his face unreadable.

'I was going to try to meet with Jarette,' Jordine said. 'And I was wondering if you wanted to come with me?'

Alfonso's expression didn't change as he replied.

'You know where she is?'

'Still in the citadel, I'm assuming. But Sergio can't keep her locked away for the rest of her life.'

'He's the kind of man that would try.'

'Regardless, at worst we're turned away at the gate. I've missed her, and I'd wager you have as well. So come with me.'

Alfonso looked pained.

'You speak as though we can just go back to our old lives,' he said. 'As though the world around us hasn't changed irrevocably. As though *we* haven't changed. But we have, Jordine. You are a king-killer. You, and my father.'

The words stung harder than any blow. Jordine looked away for a moment before replying, knowing that this reckoning had been coming.

'I did not kill the king,' Jordine said.

'But you helped my father kill him.'

'I did not know that was Edward's purpose, going to Glish,' Jordine said. 'He lied to me! He told me we were there to protect Antonio from Crucio, not kill him! It was all the work of Sergio, and I was a fool for not realizing it sooner.'

'Then why not speak out?' Alfonso pressed. 'Why not tell all of Serendia what kind of man their new monarch really is?'

'You think it would make a difference?' Jordine asked. 'You think anyone would listen? Sergio has planned this all too well. The court is fragmented, and there is no hope any noble of sufficiently high rank would be willing to risk himself making a stand with us. And your father would immediately discredit me.'

'I will speak to him—' Alfonso began to say, but Jordine put a hand on his shoulder, trying to cut through the anger and frustration they both felt.

'It will do neither of us any good. Antonio is dead. With Crucio gone and Vittorio plowing fields in Glish, there are none to take up the crown other than Jarette, and I think she'd rather become an Elion Valkyrie than be anointed queen and sole ruler of Serendia. But…'

He mustered a smile before continuing.

'…maybe we should ask her that in person.'

Alfonso frowned. 'You're going to tell her you conspired in the death of her brother?'

'Well, if I don't tell her my side of the story, I suspect you will. And from what the servants are saying and how Sergio's had her shut away, I suspect she hasn't been shy in making her own accusations. So no, I don't think the world can go back to the way it was, my friend. But I think it's about time I started doing something to repair the damage. And that starts by bringing you, myself and Jarette together again. Will you come and help me?'

Alfonso hesitated, before finally nodding.

'I'll hear what you have to say to her. Maybe, just maybe, there is a way back for the Rhundis.'

'I want her dead by dawn,' Sergio said.

Edward remained silent, praying to all the gods that he had misunderstood his king.

'Did you not hear me?' Sergio snapped, his voice ringing coldly around the throne room.

'You… you wish me to poison your wife?' Edward repeated, feeling sick just uttering the words. 'You wish me to murder the queen?'

'Elysia is conspiring against me,' Sergio snapped, pacing before his throne, hands clamped behind his back. 'I have intercepted letters to her brother, urging that Calpheon use our current instability to annex Balenos!'

'May I see said letters?' Edward asked. Sergio stopped and looked at him furiously.

'Do you doubt your king?'

'I have never heard tell of duplicitous dealings by Queen Elysia,' Edward said, knowing what he was saying was foolish, but unable to stomach the raw, blatant lie he was being fed.

'She is not your damned wife, Edward! She is a treasonous witch, and she cannot be allowed to live!'

'*If* she has committed treason, then surely she should

be tried, as per the laws of the land,' Edward maintained, refusing to wilt before Sergio's anger. 'The high court must be convened and evidence presented.'

'Damn your courts and evidence, Edward Rhundi,' Sergio barked, shaking with rage as he stopped and glared at him. 'You forget yourself! Without me you would still be the pauper knight, with little more standing than some merchant or yeoman farmer. Remember what you owe me!'

'My services have been repaid,' Edward said. It was madness to defy the king, especially in his current mood, but he could not stop himself. He could not bow and scrape and scurry away to do Sergio's will, not when it meant yet more bloodshed.

'I did not aid you in the past because I craved wealth or higher status,' he went on, knowing that if he did not speak his mind now, he never would. 'I did it because I genuinely believed you would be a stronger ruler than Antonio, that you would end the friction between him and your father and restore order to the court. I fear now that I was foolish to hope for such a thing.'

Sergio had gone still and silent, and Edward found this even more alarming than his overt rage. The king glared at him a while longer, as though expecting him to recant and obey, but Edward stood his ground, though it took all his courage and willpower to do so.

He had known pain enough these past months, though he had been careful to hide it, even from the likes of Jordine and Alfonso. The truth was, since the sword stroke that had cut off Antonio's head, he had known in his heart that he was damned.

At last, Sergio smiled, the expression as cold and unwelcoming as the impending midwinter.

'It seems your usefulness to the crown has run its course, Sir Rhundi,' he said. 'If you do not see the worthiness of my reign, I will make sure you will not see anything at all.'

Jordine and Alfonso were walking up Arrow Street towards the main gate of the citadel when they heard a bell tolling inside the walls ahead. They exchanged a glance and began to lengthen their pace, but hadn't yet managed to reach the gates when a commotion off to their right made them pause.

There was shouting and a scream from the narrow lane between the last of Heidel's buildings and the citadel's western walls. Jordine and Alfonso exchanged a glance, then turned down the passage.

Torchlight illuminated a crowd of people, ashen-faced with shock and fear. Jordine couldn't see what they were looking at, and began to push through with Alfonso, demanding they make way.

There was a man crouched at the center of the gathering. He was shaking and appeared to be weeping, his head in his hands. Alfonso rushed to his side, and Jordine realized why.

'Father,' Alfonso exclaimed, gripping the bowed man

by the shoulders. It was Edward Rhundi. But what was he doing alone, outside the citadel's walls? Jordine was about to ask as much when Alfonso, who had been trying to peer at his father's face, let out a cry of horror that matched those they'd heard earlier from the crowd.

'M-My boy, is that you?' Edward stammered, lowering his hands from his face and looking about. Except he could not look, because Edward Rhundi no longer had any eyes.

Jordine recoiled. His adoptive father's eyes had been ripped out, now nothing but bloody pits. More blood drenched his cheeks and hands, glistening black in the torchlight.

'Please,' Edward went on, voice trembling with pain. 'Please, please forgive me.'

NINETEEN

The call came to Marshal Cliff in the dead of night.

He was awake in an instant, knife in hand. He hadn't slept well since the Valencian campaigns, and never went to bed without a blade, even in the supposed security of the Watchtower, Serendia's great stronghold in the Western Marches.

The sergeant who had woken him backed off, his voice a rasping whisper in the candle-lit shadows of the simple stone chamber that acted as his living quarters.

'Only me, sire. Sorry to wake you, but we've had word from Captain Armstrong. They've found him.'

Cliff rode north through the night, accompanied by his personal retinue. He found Armstrong's post, a lesser watchtower overlooking the northern end of the Marches, near to where the borders of Calpheon and Balenos met with that of Serendia.

Despite there being nobles of higher standing in the Western Marches, Cliff considered Armstrong his immediate subordinate on the border – the two had served together in the Serendian host since the days of their youth, and there was none he trusted more. The veteran knight welcomed him, torch held aloft, and led him down into the tower's dungeon. There the flames illuminated the cold darkness, and a bedraggled figure, recoiling from the light.

'Stand straight,' Armstrong ordered, moving closer so the prisoner could no longer avoid the torchlight. 'Look at us.'

He did so, and Marshal Johann Cliff recognized the man who had once been his king. He was starved and bedraggled, his grey hair and beard grown out, his eyes hollowed by grief and despair – but in that moment, as Armstrong snapped at him, a defiance reignited in his gaze, and a familiar, formal bearing reasserted itself in his shoulders.

'My lord,' Cliff said, his tone neutral. 'You are a long way from home.'

'I have no home, not any longer,' Crucio replied, his voice a dull, dry croak. 'And no family to call my own. I am not your lord anymore. Just a beggar of the hills.'

'If that is so, you will not survive the coming winter,' Cliff said.

'Perhaps that is for the best,' Crucio countered.

Instructions had arrived from Heidel that the former

king, if found, was to be seized and taken immediately under armed escort to the capital. It was hard to accept that the monarch who had knighted Cliff when he had been a young man, the veteran campaigner he had fought alongside in a dozen battles, had been reduced to living like a raggedy vagrant, abandoned by all, without even a servant to tend to him. It was clear his situation was beyond desperate. Unless Cliff disobeyed his orders.

'You know your son has commanded you be taken to Heidel, to stand trial for the murder of Antonio?' he asked. Crucio flinched visibly.

'I did not kill him,' he said loudly. 'I would never... He came at me with sword drawn! It... it was one of his own guards who slew him! You must believe me!'

Cliff wanted to placate his former king, but he understood exactly how dangerous this situation was, and not just for Crucio. He excused himself and spoke to Armstrong outside the tower, the light of the torch flickering across their grave countenances.

'By rights, I should send him back to Heidel under guard,' Cliff said.

'By rights, we should already be in Heidel, kneeling in front of Sergio Domongatt,' Armstrong pointed out. Cliff grimaced but said nothing.

'You know as well as I what the men are saying,' Armstrong went on, his voice dropping to a whisper. 'Sergio orchestrated his brother's death. How else was he able to occupy Heidel so quickly? He knew when Antonio would perish. Crucio was just his pawn.'

'We have no evidence of that, and such claims are treason,' Cliff said swiftly, glancing over Armstrong's shoulder to ensure none of their men-at-arms were near enough to hear them.

'Yet you know them to be true,' Armstrong said. 'The game has ended. We need only look at how the pieces have fallen to know who has been moving them this whole time.'

Armstrong was correct, of course. Cliff had felt it in his bones, ever since the surprise word of Antonio's death followed by Sergio's arrival in the capital had reached the Western Marches. There were grumblings among the garrison forces Cliff oversaw, dissatisfaction with the change in regime. Despite shocking accounts of Crucio murdering his own son in a failed coup, many still seemed to harbor lingering support for the former king, especially the old campaigners among the ranks.

The situation was compounded by Sergio's demand that Cliff and his subordinates ride immediately for Heidel to swear their allegiance. Cliff had sent a messenger back inquiring who the command of the border force should be left under if all of its leadership was being summoned to the capital – there had not yet been a response, and he was using that as sufficient excuse to remain in the Marches.

He knew he couldn't do so forever. A choice had to be made.

'If we delay going to Heidel with Crucio, and word reaches Sergio…' Armstrong trailed off, knowing he did not have to finish the sentence. Sergio would declare them all traitors, and muster the main body of the Serendian host against them.

'Tell no one of Crucio's presence here,' he told Armstrong. 'I am returning to the Watchtower, but you will likely see me again, come tomorrow.'

Armstrong nodded, though he seemed unhappy.

'Trust me to choose the right path, as you always have, my friend,' Cliff urged him. 'I will see you before the next sunset.'

Cliff returned to the Watchtower with the dawn, but he did not summon his immediate subordinates in the garrison. Instead, he called for a single sergeant. The guard at the door showed him into Cliff's chamber, and the sergeant bowed.

'You wished to see me, my liege?' asked Frederick Ducas.

Cliff had been standing, gazing down at the maps and markers spread across the table that dominated the room, but at length he looked up and acknowledged Frederick with a nod.

'A vital matter has presented itself,' he said. 'And right now, I trust no one else to choose the correct course.'

'What does it concern, sire?' Frederick asked, but Cliff waved a hand.

'Before we continue, I would have you stop addressing me as your superior. For as long as you are in this chamber, treat me as you once did. As a friend, and comrade-in-arms.'

Surprise crossed Frederick's face. It had been almost

two years since he had first arrived at the Watchtower with his wife, Martha, and nothing more than the clothes on their backs and the belongings they were carrying in their saddlebags. Word of King Crucio's banishment of the Ducases from Heidel had shocked Cliff – like Crucio himself, Cliff had spent years fighting alongside Frederick during the campaigns against Valencia. To see his old friend brought so low by the decree of one they had spent much of their lives fighting for had been a bitter blow.

Cliff had done what he could to ensure Frederick and his wife were spared the worst hardships of the frontier in those early months, but the instructions from Heidel had been ruthlessly clear – the Ducases were not to be shown any particular kindness or favor. Frederick was now a common man-at-arms in the garrison force of the Western Marches.

Fortunately, Antonio had seemed less intent on maintaining the persecution of the Ducases, and Cliff had met with no resistance when he had Frederick promoted to the rank of sergeant in his own personal retinue. It was not mere favoritism – despite his steadily advancing years, Frederick was still an excellent soldier and a natural-born leader. Within six months of having joined the garrison, he had successfully hunted down and destroyed a force of imp bandits that had been plaguing the border regions. The last two years had not been easy on the fallen scion of House Ducas, yet he still held himself with the proud bearing of a warrior. There was no other he would trust more, except perhaps Armstrong.

'Crucio has been found,' he told Frederick simply. 'Armstrong found him wandering in the hills to the north. A few more days in this weather and he would have frozen, or starved.'

Frederick betrayed no emotion at the news.

'Armstrong still has him under guard?' he asked.

'He does. I have just returned from seeing him.'

'And now you must decide whether or not to send him to Heidel, to be executed,' Frederick surmised.

'Those are my orders,' Cliff said. 'It could certainly be considered fortuitous timing, if my goal was to ingratiate myself with the new regime. I have already been instructed to attend Heidel and swear my oaths to Sergio. If I did so, while also delivering his wayward father to him…'

'There would certainly be no questions about your loyalty, at least in the short term,' Frederick finished. 'And yet you are in two minds.'

Cliff cleared his throat, knowing he could edge around the matter no more. Better to do what he always preferred, and attack head-on.

'There is no one in this garrison that Crucio has wronged more than you and your family, Frederick,' he said. 'By rights, knowing that our former king has been reduced to abject destitution could be viewed as a divine, righteous punishment. But I know you to be a man of honor. You are not someone who would relish seeing the king we once fought and bled alongside laid low, even after he has treated you so cruelly. You are also much liked within the garrison. Everyone in the Western Marches knows your qualities. For those reasons, I wanted to ask you plainly – do you think the men would support Crucio, if I declared that I believe him to be the true king of Serendia? And do you think they would follow me in a march on Heidel?'

Cliff knew he had just put his life in Frederick's hands, yet he found that he was unafraid – he trusted his old friend. For his own part, Frederick allowed the stoic appearance of a dutiful soldier to drop. He looked troubled, and suddenly older and more tired than Cliff had realized. He leaned against the table, looking down at the maps and their markers for what felt like an age. Eventually, he spoke.

'It could be done,' he said. 'But it would need to be fast. A forced march east. Reach the capital before it becomes obvious what's happening. Much as Sergio did.'

'And you think the men would stand with me?' Cliff asked. 'And with Crucio?'

'I suppose that depends in part on Crucio's state of mind,' Frederick said, clearly choosing his words carefully. 'He has been on a downward spiral for years now, Cliff. I'm not sure how much of the warrior-king we once fought alongside is left. Does he even still wish to rule?'

'He seemed broken when I met with him,' Cliff admitted. 'But I suspect there was still a fire in there, deep down. Do you really think he murdered Antonio?'

'Whether he did or not no longer truly matters. Sergio used his brother's death to claim the throne. And I think the majority of the garrison here has no time for that. If you declared you will not swear fealty to Sergio, I vouch the vast majority will support you. Whether they would be willing to march on the capital though…'

He trailed off again, picking up the piece on the map representing Sergio and the royal guard in Heidel, turning it over.

'It is no different from any other campaign we have fought,' Cliff said eventually, thinking aloud. 'If this were some foreign city we were in a position to take, would we hesitate?'

'You speak as though you, I and Crucio were still in our primes,' Frederick responded, smiling sadly. 'At my age, I'm not even sure I could maintain the pace of a forced march, let alone in winter.'

'I promise you a horse,' Cliff said, smiling too, feeling an infectious enthusiasm growing. 'You and your noble wife. Gods willing, we will see out the rest of the winter in Heidel keep.'

'I want to speak with him,' Frederick said, cutting through Cliff's mounting confidence. 'Before you address the garrison, or tell any others of what has transpired here. I want to speak to Crucio, in person.'

'As do I,' Cliff said. 'We must be sure, if we are to stake our lives on this attempt, that it is not doomed to fail from the beginning. That some madness or treachery from our old king does not unmake us.'

'We should go now,' Frederick urged, but Cliff dismissed his words with a wave.

'I am bone weary from a night in the saddle, and as

you have so cruelly pointed out, I am not as young as I once was. Let us eat breakfast together, and discuss these matters some more. Then, when the sun is fully up and has burned off the worst of the frost, I will ride north again with you.'

Cliff was as good as his word, taking Frederick north to meet the man who had banished him to the farthest reaches of the kingdom.

They found Crucio still in the care of Captain Armstrong. As per the instructions Cliff had left before his departure, he had been permitted up into the tower proper, where he had been wrapped in blankets and was eating soup and bread as Cliff and Frederick arrived. Cliff noted the nervous, uncertain expressions of the men-at-arms he passed – clearly they were now aware of the identity of their prisoner-turned-guest. It would only be a matter of time before rumors began to spread like a pox. The old king of Serendia had been found.

Cliff dismissed the guards, and even Armstrong, from the main chamber of the tower, leaving only himself, Frederick and Crucio present. The former king put down his hunk of bread and looked between the two. Cliff watched for any hint of anger as he recognized Frederick, but there appeared to be only concern. Did he think Cliff had brought Frederick here to enact vengeance?

'My liege,' Cliff said. 'I have returned with Frederick Ducas. In the two years since he joined the garrison here in the Western Marches, he has risen to become the most trusted sergeant in my own personal retinue.'

'Is that so?' Crucio said guardedly, still watching Frederick like an old silver fox eyeing the huntsman. For his own part, Frederick's expression gave nothing away.

'Frederick and I have been discussing matters,' Cliff continued. 'And we are of one mind. The kingdom is in a parlous state. By fair means or foul, Sergio has taken the crown without the express, unified consent of the court. And while we would never challenge the royal lineage of House Domongatt, we believe current circumstances do not do your noble family justice.'

Crucio frowned, then let out an unexpected, gruff laugh.

'You were always better at fighting than talking, Johann. Do an old man the courtesy of speaking plainly.'

'Sergio does not deserve to wear the crown,' Frederick cut in, speaking for the first time. 'Cliff is prepared to lead the garrison host of the Western Marches to Heidel, and remove him from the throne. But he will only do it if you are prepared to sit as king once again, and if you swear to rule by the majority consent of the court.'

Hearing it spoken aloud brought home the danger of what Cliff was proposing. He watched Crucio, wondering if the king would fly into one of his infamous rages. Would he reject outright the thought of leading an army against his own son? Would he rage at the idea that he would only be permitted to reign again if he adhered to the wishes of the court? Or was the opposite true? Was he a broken man, no longer fit to take on the rulership of Serendia?

Crucio scraped his chair back and stood, slowly and not without difficulty. He paced around the table until he was standing in front of Frederick.

The former high constable held the gaze of the former king, neither flinching. Then, Crucio placed a hand on Frederick's shoulder.

'I have had months to consider my own failures,' he said. 'And the way I treated you was one of them, Frederick Ducas. It was no coincidence that my banishment of you coincided with the beginning of my… decline, into this present state, this punishing existence of loss and failure. I am a king, and I do not believe kings ask for forgiveness from any outside their own family, but what I would request is that you find it in yourself to render me a second chance.'

'I would not be here if I had not resolved to do so,' Frederick said, and though his tone and expression were still hard as stone, he inclined his head fractionally in a sign of respect.

Crucio released him and looked at Cliff.

'I take it you think the garrison will follow us, if we march on Heidel?' he asked.

'They will follow you,' Cliff clarified. 'If you declare your intention to retake the throne, and return the kingdom to a degree of stability.'

'That is all I have ever wished to do,' Crucio said. 'I was… misled into abdicating. None of my sons were ready to bear the crown. I see that now. But you have made demands of me this day, and I must make one of you, if we are to proceed with this venture.'

Cliff steeled himself, expecting Crucio to require some brutal measure to secure his authority – perhaps the purging of the court of those who had sworn fealty to Sergio, or the execution of those warriors of the garrison who would not follow him to Heidel. Yet as Crucio spoke, Cliff understood he had misjudged the man he was intent on staking his life on.

'I did not kill Antonio. It was an act of treachery that saw him slain. It haunts my every waking moment and conjures nightmares every time I close my eyes to sleep. There is no greater pain than the loss of a son.'

'I know,' Frederick said, to Cliff's surprise. Crucio nodded, and went on.

'Sergio has treated me with disdain and has stolen the crown from his own brother by having him killed. And yet, he is still my son. Cut off his limbs, if you must. But, for my sake, I pray you spare his life.'

Cliff looked at Frederick. What Crucio had asked would only make matters more difficult. Even if they were able to depose Sergio without killing him, it was hard to imagine that he would accept defeat. As long as he lived, there would be a danger that he would seek to retake the crown. But Cliff knew he did not need to explain as much to Crucio. He would be well aware of the dangers involved in what he was asking. The fact that he still wished to show mercy caused a great sense of relief in Cliff. Despite the weight of years and the burden of loss, something of the noble king he had served long ago still remained.

'You have my oath that I will do all in my power to see that Sergio is not slain when we retake Heidel,' he said.

'Then you may count on me, my loyal and faithful marshal,' Crucio said. 'As I shall count on you. Simply tell me what you need from me.'

'I will send orders to the outposts to muster the garrison at the Watchtower,' Cliff said, his mind already starting to race ahead. 'You will need to address them, as will I. All being well, we can be on the march within the week. We will bring in what supplies we can, but more will need to be taken on the road. We all know the difficulties of campaigning in this season. Above all, we must be swift. We need to reach the capital before the snows, and before Sergio realizes our intentions. We are good for one more campaign together, my king. It may well be our most important yet.'

TWENTY

'I'm going to find who is responsible for this,' Alfonso snarled, 'and I'm going to kill them.'

Jordine was standing with his friend outside Edward's bedchamber, in the townhouse on Gallows Street. Edward was within, being tended to by Dr del Mattio, one of the best chirurgeons in Heidel.

Since his pleas for forgiveness, Edward hadn't spoken, and Jordine had feared for a while that the blood loss would kill him. The doctor had assured them both now that his condition had become stable, though there was little besides balms, herbs and prayer that could safeguard against the threat of infection. The wounds had apparently been dealt swiftly and cruelly.

'He was not robbed,' Jordine pointed out. 'So he was not attacked by some common thieves in a back alley.'

'There must be witnesses,' Alfonso said. 'We should

head back towards the citadel and start questioning people. Someone will have seen something.'

Jordine agreed, and they left the house in the care of Mikos, with instructions to unbar the door to no one except them.

The sun was not long up as they left Gallows Street, yet despite the lingering darkness and the bitter chill in the air, the streets seemed busy. People were flocking in the direction of Heidel's center, and it didn't take long to find out why – a royal proclamation was about to be announced at the market lion.

'This must have something to do with last night,' Alfonso muttered. 'You heard the bell tolling inside the citadel as we approached? It sounded like the alarm. It's no coincidence Father was found just outside the walls.'

Jordine kept silent, and they began to hurry, making it to the square just as the royal herald was clambering up before the lion. It was a weathered statue of the rampant Serendian lion, mounted atop a series of stone steps at the center of the square. Whenever an announcement was to be made before the people, it was done in front of the great feline by one of the town's criers or, if it came from the king or queen, by the royal herald.

Today it was the demibeast herald in his regal livery of red and yellow who began speaking as the crowd thickened, stamping a hoof on the steps to silence the crowd.

'It is with the utmost sorrow that His Majesty, Sergio

Domongatt, wishes to make known that late last night, at an exact time yet to be determined, Her Majesty Queen Elysia Domongatt, formerly of Calpheon, ended her own life by jumping from the west tower of the royal citadel. A letter detailing her reasons for this grave and tragic act was discovered within her bedchamber. His Majesty this morning lies stricken with grief, as the love of his life, and the queen of this noble kingdom, is no more. He has no doubt that you, the good and honest people of Heidel, share in his dismay and his sorrow. He now decrees a period of mourning and reflection. The citadel will be closed until further notice, and the queen will be interred in a private ceremony within the castle crypt. Long live Serendia, long live the king!'

Some people echoed the loyal cry, but most of the crowd immediately fell to discord. A few shouted at the herald, demanding more information, but he was escorted away by a small troop of the royal guard.

Jordine felt a sick sense of dismay. Elysia, dead? And by her own hand? What demons could have caused her to fling herself from one of the tallest towers in the citadel? For an awful moment, he imagined their affair might have something to do with it. Had she been overcome by remorse, or feared Sergio was about to discover what had happened?

Alfonso brought him back, gripping his arm.

'My father attacked and blinded and the queen dead, within an hour or so of each other,' he muttered darkly. 'They have to be connected. Something dark is at work in the castle. Some malignancy that must be exposed, before it claims any more lives!'

'But how?' Jordine asked, wondering what they could have missed. 'The citadel is once again to be shut to all except the royal household. We have no means of getting to the root of any of this, not unless your father begins to speak, and tells us what happened.'

'It's not Father I'm worried about, not anymore,' Alfonso admitted, sounding almost reluctant as he looked from the castle towers and walls framing the rooftops of the buildings on the east side of the square. 'It's Jarette. She's still in there. That's even assuming she's still alive.'

'What are you proposing?' Jordine asked, hoping his friend had something resembling a plan.

'I don't know,' Alfonso hissed, clearly frustrated. 'But there must be something!'

'We should still ask if anyone saw what happened to your father,' Jordine prompted. 'At least we can do that outside the walls. And finding the identity of his attacker might help us discover what's happened within. It may even give us the pretense we need to get inside.'

Jordine was accustomed to collecting gossip from the taverns and brothels of Heidel, but a veil of silence had been drawn over whatever had happened to Edward Rhundi. Those he expected to know about the incident either claimed ignorance, or simply advised Jordine not to ask questions.

He returned to Gallows Street and found Alfonso emerging from his father's bedroom.

'How is he?' he asked.

'Sleeping.'

'Has he said anything, to you or del Mattio or Mikos? Anything about his attacker?'

'No. He is still in a great deal of pain.'

Jordine didn't push the matter – he could see from Alfonso's drawn expression that he was struggling with what had happened to his father. Jordine understood his friend's suffering. For all that he abhorred what Edward had made him do, how he had manipulated him and created a rift between him and Alfonso, to see a man he knew well so brutally treated was a hard blow to take. The thought of Elysia's untimely death only made matters worse. Alfonso was surely correct – there had to be a connection there, one they were missing.

That evening, Jordine was preparing for bed when he heard movement from the front of the house. He picked up his sword in its scabbard and slipped downstairs.

It was no intruder. He found Alfonso, finishing tying one of Mikos's servant cloaks around his shoulders.

'What are you doing?' Jordine demanded, keeping his voice low in an effort not to wake the rest of the household. Alfonso looked startled, but quickly became defiant.

'Nothing, Joe. Go back to bed.'

'You're going to the castle, aren't you?'

'This doesn't need to concern you!'

'You know it does, Al. What in the name of the crimson

lion are you thinking? That you can talk your way inside, pretending to be a servant?'

The brief look of embarrassment that crossed Alfonso's face was confirmation that Jordine was on the right track. He shook his head.

'It won't work. At best, you'll be turned away at the gates. At worst, you'll be seized as a spy. The Rhundis might have a good reputation with Sergio, but with everything that's happening, there's no guarantee you'll be released unharmed.'

'Which is exactly why I need to get inside,' Alfonso exclaimed, failing to keep his voice down. 'Jarette isn't safe!'

Jordine stepped forward and grasped his friend by the wrist, making him look into his eyes.

'Listen to me. I know you care for her. But getting yourself arrested by the royal guards isn't going to help her. I have a contact I can use in the citadel. Martyn, the cook's boy. He comes to the marketplace to buy ingredients for the king's feasts. There's a market tomorrow, the last one of the season. I'll speak to Martyn about Jarette, and if you really wish, see if he can get us inside. That's our best bet. In fact, I'd say it's our only one.'

'You were always a better gambler than me,' Alfonso muttered, pulling his arm free from Jordine's grip, but nodding. 'Very well. We go tomorrow. But if you can't find Martyn, or he won't help us, I'll go alone. Promise you won't try to stop me.'

'I promise,' Jordine said, wondering if it was yet another oath he was going to have to break.

As Jordine had hoped, Martyn and a few other servants were present at the Heidel market the next day, purchasing vegetables and firewood. Though hesitant to share at first, he confirmed that Jarette was confined to the castle but was unharmed and not being held in the dungeon. He also said that Elysia had indeed been found dead at the foot of the west tower, near the main gatehouse. He refused to elaborate on the rumors seemingly going around the citadel's servants and the royal household.

He also refused to smuggle both Jordine and Alfonso inside. After a great deal of negotiating, smoothed by every coin Jordine was carrying in his purse, he agreed to try to get Jordine in, but would not allow Alfonso to go as well. The discovery of both within the walls could be deemed an incursion. Jordine's antics were well enough known among the servants and guards that, if caught, he could believably claim to just be involved in some tryst with a handmaiden.

Alfonso, though relieved to hear that Jarette was unharmed, was less than enthusiastic about staying behind while Jordine infiltrated the castle, but Martyn was adamant – it would be his neck in the noose if they were caught. Reluctantly, Alfonso agreed to let Jordine go alone. He promised to return to Gallows Street by the next morning.

Martyn smuggled him through the gatehouse on the produce cart, concealed beneath sacks full of gnarlroot vegetables. From there he hustled him into one of the castle kitchen's pantries, where he gave him a servant's livery, told him to get changed, and then to wait until the evening meal had been served and the royal household was bedded down for the night.

'This is where I leave you, Joe. Good luck. If this fails...'

'I won't breathe a word about you, Martyn.'

Jordine followed his instructions to the letter, waiting until nightfall and stealing a meal for himself from the pantry supplies. He then slipped out, into the main kitchen block.

The last of the day's meals had been eaten several hours earlier, and all was quiet and still. The fire in the deep hearth at the far end of the chamber had been quenched, and the old hound who subsided off the kitchen's scraps was dozing peacefully by the embers.

Jordine slipped between the preparation tables and the herbs hanging from the rafters, and up the spiral staircase that he estimated would take him to the chambers and corridors along the castle's east side, where Jarette's bedchamber was located.

Being unarmed felt strange, but for all the danger involved, it was the most excitement he had experienced since helping Roxanne escape from Squire Legano's men-at-arms. His love of risk remained undimmed.

He crouched in the stairwell while waiting for a pair of royal guards to pass by in the corridor above, then moved up in their wake. Their armor and heavy treads made them easy to hear approaching, a fact he used to dodge a second patrol one level further up, hiding in a latrine closet until they were gone. If his memories of the citadel's interior were correct, Jarette's chamber was in the southeast tower, just one more floor up.

Just before the stairwell, his good fortune ran out. He caught the sound of someone descending at the last moment, a lighter, quieter tread than those of the guards. He began to double back, but it was too far to the nearest door or the other end of the corridor. He had nowhere to go.

He remained where he was, ready to flee, fight or lie his way out, depending on who he was confronted with. In the end, he did none of those things.

Roxanne stepped out into the corridor, her features illuminated by the candle she was carrying. She went very still. They stared at one another in silence, each as surprised as the other.

'What are you doing here?' Jordine asked.

'I was about to ask you the same thing,' Roxanne responded. 'And unless you have just this night taken up new duties as a royal servant, I think I have more right to ask that question than you.'

'You rode east,' Jordine said, still wrestling with his disbelief. 'You had fled Heidel, in fear for your life. Why would you come back, to the very stronghold of the man responsible for the death of your husband? Unless what you told me in Eindhovein was a lie?'

Roxanne pursed her lips, looking past Jordine, checking that the corridor was still clear.

'There were some mistruths in our last encounter, but I did not lie to you,' she said softly. 'Sergio wanted me dead.'

'But no longer. You live here at his pleasure? And you are not confined like Jarette, so you are no royal prisoner.'

'Be careful, Jordine. I need but scream, and you will be seized. Do not imagine the Rhundis hold the same favor with Sergio that they once did.'

'Was that your doing?' Jordine demanded, his anger beginning to build. 'Edward Rhundi lies blinded and near death. And what of Elysia? Your presence here does not feel like mere coincidence.'

'This is no place for this kind of conversation,' Roxanne hissed. 'But because of your past assistance, I will humor you. Come to my chambers and I will tell you what I can, truthfully.'

'I have not come here to crawl back into your bed,' Jordine said bitterly. 'I am trying to ensure Jarette is safe.'

'She is,' Roxanne said. 'I told you, she would not heed my advice not to speak out against Sergio when he first took the crown, but he has done no more than confine her to this side of the castle.'

'Why should I believe you?'

'I will show her to you, but you must promise not to wake her,' Roxanne said. 'My own handmaid, Carolin, has taken up serving her, and she told me not half an hour ago she is abed.'

Jordine agreed, still wary. He followed Roxanne upstairs, to a doorway that she unlatched softly, just wide enough for Jordine to peer into. All was darkness, but Roxanne raised her candle and its faint, flickering light spilled onto a four-poster bed, and the person lying atop it. Jordine saw that familiar red hair, and the pale face it framed, fast asleep.

He withdrew. Roxanne shut the door and turned, beginning to walk away. Wordlessly, Jordine followed.

One of Roxanne's handmaids was still in her bedchamber, but she dismissed her, saying she had no need of assistance, and the young woman hurried out. Jordine stood by the door, unwilling to enter further, as Roxanne paced across and closed the window shutters, then touched the flame she carried to several other candles across the room, spreading their glowing illumination.

'Tell me why you are here,' Jordine repeated.

'I am following your advice,' Roxanne said as she lit the last candle. 'I am surviving.'

'By living in a place where you claimed you were under daily threat? You sought me out purely for what I knew, didn't you? That was why you got me drunk, and lured me upstairs in that tavern.'

'You came willingly enough,' Roxanne said. 'You wanted to unburden yourself, to cast off the guilt you felt. Do not act as though it was not a relief on your part. And yes, I used the information you gave me.'

'You confronted Sergio?' Jordine asked, wondering at just how bold Roxanne was. She had carved out a place for herself in the highest reaches of Serendia's nobility, twice now. Underestimating the force of will and determination of such a woman was foolish, and a mistake he could ill afford to repeat.

'I confronted my husband's killer, yes,' she said, advancing on Jordine, then reaching past him to properly close the bedchamber door and draw its locking bolt. 'And I offered him a choice. Either he accepted me as his new queen, or I would reveal his actions to the entirety of Serendia.'

Jordine just stared, trying to comprehend how far Roxanne had gone.

'Queen?' he said. 'But Sergio is already married! Did you kill Elysia?'

'I did not,' Roxanne said firmly. 'I implied to Sergio that she had been unfaithful, which was true, though I did not mention your name. I suggested divorce. But I should have anticipated that he would prefer a quicker solution. I suspect that is how Edward Rhundi fell afoul of him. After all, he was Sergio's pawn when it came to removing Antonio. I imagine Sergio demanded Edward murder Elysia, but the pauper knight finally found his conscience.'

'Yet Elysia is still dead,' Jordine pointed out.

'By the king's own hand, no doubt,' Roxanne replied. 'But I had no involvement in it. I deplore so brutal an act.'

'No involvement, yet she would still be alive if you had not made such demands of Sergio. I wonder at your sanity, wanting to be wedded to such a man. Is the power and prestige of the crown so great that you would endure a life at his side?'

'You do not understand true power until you have tasted it,' Roxanne said. 'Sergio outwitted us all, and after Antonio, I paid the highest price. I could not rest until I had redressed that imbalance.'

'That's all this is to you, then? A game? He makes his

play, and you make yours, and you both clear the board at the end and congratulate one another?'

'The game isn't over yet,' Roxanne said.

Jordine turned away, battling his disgust.

'I take it back,' he said. 'You are well suited to each other.'

'I am not as cold-hearted as you might imagine,' Roxanne said, pacing round Jordine so she was once again standing before him. 'I once thought as little of you as you do now of me – an arrogant youth with a callous heart, too used to freely spending his wealth and his good looks. Maybe there's a ring of truth to that, but I also found a young man who is kind and chivalrous. I do not believe you helped me escape the men-at-arms at Eindhovein and sheltered me in that inn because you wished to take advantage of a former queen. You would have done the same if I had been some unknown maid or peasant. There is goodness within you, Jordine, and you cannot let the actions of others and the guilt they force upon you tarnish it. I know of what I speak – my own life has been blighted enough by misdeeds that were not my own.'

'Yet we remain accountable,' Jordine pointed out. 'What would you have me do? I remained silent about the murder of Antonio, and now you expect me to do the same about the death of Elysia, and the brutality visited upon Edward? Am I to return to Alfonso, and tell him I have no idea why his father had his eyes gouged out? If I say nothing, I am as guilty as Sergio, as Edward, as you. I am part of the rot gnawing at Serendia.'

'You must do what you think to be right,' Roxanne

said. 'There will be rumors enough when my betrothal to Sergio is announced next month. But if you speak publicly about what we have discussed tonight, I won't be able to protect you from him. Or Alfonso, for that matter. Any favors the Rhundis held with Sergio were lost the moment Edward refused to kill for him a second time.'

'So my options are bitter silence, or death with a clear conscience?' Jordine said, glaring at Roxanne.

'No,' Roxanne said. 'There is no clear conscience for you, Jordine. If you speak out against Sergio, and inspire an uprising, how many will die to keep your conscience clean?'

'You have the forked tongue of a snake,' Jordine spat.

'I speak hard truths,' Roxanne replied just as firmly.

'Whether I remain silent or not, war may still find Serendia,' Jordine pointed out. 'Elysia was the younger sister of the king of Calpheon. There will be outrage once he learns of her death. And I doubt Sergio will do much to placate it.'

'I will make sure he does enough. I have already lost my position once; I will not risk losing it again by permitting a conflict with Calpheon.'

'Yet you'd be willing to let me speak out and cause an uprising against the king? One that would likely not spare you, if it learned the full details of your involvement?'

'You keep trying to goad me into acting in a way that matches your opinion of me,' Roxanne said. 'But I will not. I will not call for the guards, nor have you imprisoned or dragged before Sergio. I will not even attempt to defend my actions any longer. I seek no guarantees from you, no promises or assurances that you will hold your tongue. I believe you to be a just man, Jordine Ducas. You must do what that conscience of yours dictates.'

Sounds from beyond the bedchamber door caused Jordine to fall silent. He heard footsteps and low voices, passing by in the corridor outside. Roxanne spoke again once they had receded.

'It will be easier to smuggle you out once the guard shift changes, but that won't be for another six hours. Until then, I recommend you remain here. We won't be disturbed.'

The last thing Jordine wanted was to spend another night with Roxanne, but her words made sense. He had intended to remain in Jarette's chamber until it was safe to slip away, yet one was no more secure than another.

'You have no ale to ply me with this time,' he pointed out.

Roxanne smiled.

'Then I suppose the charms of a queen will have to be sufficient.'

'She is safe,' Jordine told Alfonso the next morning, when he got back to Gallows Street. 'I saw her on the eastern side of the castle.'

'Did you speak with her?' he asked eagerly.

'No. I thought slipping into a princess's bedchamber at night dressed as a servant and then waking her might result in a short and lethal encounter with the royal guards. But I saw her. She was sleeping soundly. I also saw Roxanne.'

Alfonso's expression grew dark. Jordine had told him the truth of his encounter with the former queen in Eindhovein, though not exactly how intimate it had been.

'I thought you said she had ridden to Mediah?'

'So I thought, but apparently not. She returned to the citadel, and Sergio has welcomed her back.'

'You told me she feared for her life,' Alfonso said. 'And she seems too clever to believe Sergio will simply permit her back into the royal household. She must have some usefulness to him. Or some power over him.'

Jordine had intended to tell Alfonso everything, to admit that the information he had given Roxanne had now been used to reinstate her, at the cost of Elysia's life, and his father's eyes and possible sanity. Yet the words turned ashen in his throat, and he could only turn aside, composing himself.

He brushed away Alfonso's concerns and told him to look after his father. Nothing more could be done about Jarette for the time being, he claimed, and hopefully Sergio would permit contact with her soon.

Once he had withdrawn to his own bedroom, alone, he struck the bedposts in silent rage, before collapsing atop the sheets and falling into a dark and fathomless sleep.

TWENTY-ONE

The western garrison marched for Heidel.

Cliff dared hope that the gods were smiling on the expedition. The garrison had mustered at the Watchtower, where both he and Crucio had addressed the men. The mood was good. Seeing their old commanders – Crucio, Cliff and Frederick – reunited and ready for a new campaign had guaranteed the backing of the veteran warriors, and the rest had followed. The host had knelt and sworn renewed fealty to their old ruler. Afterwards, Crucio had formally absolved Frederick and knighted him once more, to cheers from the soldiery.

It had been a good start, made better by the weather. The rain and snow had held off, while the temperatures were cold enough to freeze the mud of the roads, creating firmer ground and speeding the march. Three nights after setting out, the vanguard was riding past the farms belonging to Murana Lynch.

Both Cliff and Frederick urged speed. If Sergio was given enough time, he would be able to prepare Heidel for a siege, and Crucio's force did not have the supplies to see out the winter beyond the walls of the town. Even worse, Sergio might be able to muster his nobles and the main body of the Serendian host, which could lead to a pitched battle. If that were the case, Cliff could not predict the outcome. Surprise was currently their greatest advantage, and he was determined to make full use of it.

Three days after setting out from the Watchtower, rumors began to reach Heidel of the approaching army. Sergio dismissed them at first, until accounts started mentioning that Crucio was with them. In a raging panic, Sergio ordered his own host to muster, and for the capital to prepare itself for invasion.

By then, it was too late for any realistic hope that the nobles of Serendia would rally to Sergio with their armed retinues. Yet there was time enough for the seizure of foodstuffs and the closing of the gates. By the time Crucio's host came within sight of the westernmost reaches of the town, the way into the town had been firmly shut and barred.

'We must still strike, while we can,' Crucio urged at the council of war held that night. Cliff, Frederick and the other senior knights from the Western Marches gathered in an old watermill a mile west of the town walls, sited on a small tributary that ran down to the Demi.

'An escalade,' Crucio went on, banging a palm against the maps Cliff had brought and spread on the mill-keeper's kitchen table. The motion caused the candles lighting the room to flicker.

'We do not have the equipment for a direct assault,' Sir Lugretz, the oldest knight at the gathering besides Cliff, Armstrong and Frederick, pointed out.

'But we can build what we need,' Crucio said. 'Enough timber can be taken from the Westwood, and we can pull nails from the houses of the hamlets back along the road. We can have two dozen ladders ready by tomorrow night.'

'Ladders, yes, but not proper siege equipment,' Lugretz said. 'Neither a covered battering ram, nor siege towers. We do not have enough time and resources. I rode up to the western gate with the vanguard, and when we attempted to read the proclamation, we received a volley of crossbow bolts. They are ready for us. The Eindhovein host are present in the garrison, and they will remain loyal to Sergio, and ensure the town guard do likewise.'

'This is what we feared,' Cliff said, his tone bleak. 'We cannot afford a protracted siege. Sergio will receive reinforcements from across Serendia, while cold and disease take their toll on us here. We have all experienced sieges like this before, and they rarely end well.'

'Then the people must be urged to rise up,' Crucio said, still defiant. 'You claimed that they still think favorably of me, Johann. There must be those within the town walls who would prefer my rule over Sergio's. And if there is an uprising in the town, I doubt he has enough men-at-arms to suppress it while still manning the walls against us.'

'It would not take many to cause disruption.' Frederick

spoke up. 'As long as we are able to time it well. Perhaps my son will aid us.'

Several other knights exchanged uncomfortable glances. Cliff replied to Ducas.

'Has young Jordine not abandoned his family name in favor of the Rhundis? They are thought to be close allies of Sergio. Their banner is one of those that fly from the town walls.'

'That may be so, but times change,' Frederick said. 'A small number of saboteurs, with instructions to strike at the gate at the right time, could prove more useful to us than a fully-fledged uprising. It's all we would need to get inside.'

'But how would we reach out to your son?' Cliff wondered aloud. 'Or anyone inside, for that matter. This sort of plan requires good communication, but we have no way of implementing it.'

'We must test their defenses,' Armstrong declared, pointing at a section of the town wall overlooking the Demi River. 'We know this tower is weak, for example. And they may not have the numbers to man every yard of fortification. Split our forces, and strike from multiple directions at once. I concur with the king – we must build ladders, as swiftly as possible, and mount an escalade.'

'Any action is better than inaction,' Frederick agreed. 'We still have the initiative. It's up to us to strike first.'

Alfonso and Jordine mounted Heidel's western gatehouse and looked out upon the besieging host.

The Eindhovein men-at-arms manning that section of the wall watched them uneasily, but none moved to impede them. The common folk had been forbidden from walking the walls, but their noble standing meant they could not be ordered off so easily. They had ventured up several times since the arrival of Crucio's host, gazing out at the martial array.

The dreary winter landscape to the west of the town was now a patchwork of tent lines and brightly colored pavilions, matching the equally bright banners and standards of the knights who had thrown their lot in with Crucio.

Like all young nobles, Jordine's education had included relentless memorization of the heraldry of the kingdom's aristocratic families, from the crests of the Domongatt princes right down to the emblems of poor, near-powerless knights like the Rhundis. Both he and Alfonso were able to recognize each of the standards arrayed against the capital – almost all belonged to the knights and minor gentry of the Western Marches, including the stag of Johann Cliff. The royal standard was present as well, a sure sign of Crucio's intent – one crimson lion would fight the other in the coming contest for mastery of Serendia.

Then he saw it – just to the left of where Crucio's royal standard had been planted, another length of silk fluttered in the cold air, a red field bearing a rearing golden lion. He had not seen such a crest for several years, yet it was still achingly familiar. The lion had been carved into the mantelpiece and above the doorway of the townhouse on Shield

Street, and had been woven on its tapestries decorating the walls. It was the heraldic sigil of House Ducas.

His father – his true father – was with Crucio's host. He had received no letters from Frederick for many months, certainly none suggesting that Crucio had reached the Western Marches and managed to convince Marshal Cliff and the garrison there to back his claim to kingship. That should not surprise him – why would Frederick trust him after he had abandoned his family? Yet still, it stung. Had Crucio really absolved his father and reinstated him? Were they now on opposite sides, by simple dint of the fact that Jordine was within the walls and, as a Rhundi, was still presumed to be loyal to Sergio?

'This cannot last,' Alfonso said, gazing out over the encampment. 'It could snow any day now. They surely won't have enough supplies to prosecute a siege with midwinter approaching?'

'They'll try an escalade,' Jordine said. There had already been two attempts on the walls the night before using a few ramshackle ladders, one to the northeast and another to the south, close to the southwestern tower overlooking the Demi. The sounds of hammers and saws were audible on the walls, rising from the camp – more ladders were no doubt being built. The attackers appeared intent on an escalade, a swift storming of the walls, rather than the drudgery and labor of slower siege techniques such as digging saps, breaching the walls and gate with siege engines, or undermining the defenses.

'I cannot believe Crucio was able to turn the whole

western garrison to his cause,' Alfonso said.

'Supposedly neither can Sergio,' Jordine pointed out. The king had hardly been seen since the besieging force had appeared outside the walls, all but locking himself away in the citadel. It had not endeared him to the people of Heidel, who were less than enthused at being shut up within the walls. While the town was well stocked for the winter, that wouldn't stop discontent from festering and growing.

Jordine understood the dissatisfaction, and he had no doubt Alfonso did as well. He had little love for Sergio even before Roxanne's revelations. Edward was still convalescing, and had yet to speak to either of them – Jordine didn't know whether he would admit that the reason he had lost his eyes was his refusal to murder Elysia. Even so, it was clear enough to Alfonso that the king had forsaken their family. The foundations that had held up their loyalty to the crown had crumbled.

Cliff walked the lines with Frederick, inspecting the work on the ladders.

'We'll need more,' Cliff observed, pausing at one that was nearly complete, a carpenter overseeing a trio of men-at-arms seconded as workmen, hammering in the final nails. 'But that will take time.'

'On half rations, the host can last a month,' Frederick said, leaning forward to test the sturdiness of the bottom rungs with a foot. 'After that, hunger and the weather will force us to abandon this venture.'

Cliff sighed. Having such a frank conversation with Crucio was becoming increasingly difficult, as the king grew more agitated about the lack of progress. He feared that the siege's collapse might be caused as much by Crucio snapping as by the usual campaign constraints of supplies and temperatures. Yet they had to face up to the possibility that Heidel might resist them.

'If we do break the siege, we need somewhere to winter,' Cliff said. 'We cannot withdraw all the way back to the Watchtower. That will be taken as failure, and the nobility will flock to back Sergio and prove their loyalty. Come the spring, the whole Serendian host will be marching against us.'

'The northern plain could serve for winter quarters,' Frederick said. 'But we will have to range the countryside for supplies. It will not endear us to the people, taking their food and much of their shelter in the hardest months.'

'Such are the realities of campaigning,' Cliff pointed out, thinking back to the many other brutal conflicts they had waged together, side by side with Crucio. 'At the very least, we can strike at the estates of those nobles who have declared for Sergio. Provide the men with some plunder to stiffen morale.'

'You speak as though we have already failed here,' Frederick said. Cliff gave an unhappy shrug.

'We both know the importance of a reserve. We cannot allow any failure here to prove decisive. If it does, the heads of you, Crucio and myself will be decorating that gatehouse over there.'

He nodded towards Heidel's western gate, where the blue-and-yellow stripes of Eindhovein, the royal standard and the pennants of a few other minor nobles hung from the grey walls.

Hoofbeats interrupted them, and a rider came clattering up, sawing on his reins. It was a messenger, clad in the blue-and-red checkered livery of Sir Olvario, commander of the rearguard.

'My lords, word from Sir Olvario,' he reported, remaining in the saddle. 'He says a force has been sighted approaching from the southwest, towards the bridge at Tolemo. No word yet as to their identity, but he is mobilizing the encampment for battle.'

Cliff shot a glance at Frederick, thinking the same thing. A relief force, come to attack them outside the walls? If the defenders of Heidel sallied out at the same time, they could find themselves under a simultaneous assault from east and west.

'Sound the general assembly, all men under arms,' Cliff ordered, knowing better than to hesitate. 'Then find the king and inform him I have ridden to the rearguard.'

Trumpets and horns blared through the trio of encampments belonging to the besiegers. Cliff, already armored, summoned one of his mounts and rode to find Sir Olvario.

He discovered him with his retinue on the south-western extreme of the camp, covering the dirt track leading from the bridge and hamlet of Tolemo, crossing the Demi. A wedge of spearmen in blue-and-red heraldry were blocking the roadway, the tips of their weapons and their helmets glinting in the winter sunlight. Olvario and a small number of mounted men-at-arms were behind them, watching the approach. The knight turned away from his retinue as he saw Cliff coming up.

'Any sign of who they belong to?' the marshal asked.

'None, my lord.' Olvario shook his head.

'How many are there?'

'My scouts at the bridge report between two and three hundred. But they could not see any banners.'

That was not a significant force, but it might only be the vanguard of a much larger one. Cliff's thoughts raced as he tried to work out who would be leading a host to Heidel. They had estimated it would take weeks for any nobles loyal to Sergio to muster and march to the capital's relief, but maybe they had misjudged? Perhaps they were about to come under attack from both front and behind?

'If they belong to Sergio, you must hold the roadway for as long as possible,' Cliff said. 'Frederick Ducas is bringing up the main battle to our rear.'

'We will hold them, Lord,' Olvario said stoically. Like so many of the knights from the Western Marches, he was a seasoned warrior. Cliff knew he would be as good as his word.

He was about to turn back to attempt to hasten the mustering of the main camp, and inform Crucio personally of the situation, when a shout went up from the spearmen in the roadway. Something was moving in the distance now, visible between the skeletal trees lining it. A minute later and a column of figures came into view, trudging towards Olvario's lines.

Cliff leaned forward in his saddle, damning his aging eyesight. There appeared to be no sign of cavalry, which would be unusual if this were indeed the vanguard of a larger host. The oncoming figures looked to be in no particular haste, either. They did not bear any kind of martial threat.

Olvario identified them before Cliff, his voice riven with disbelief.

'It's the peasantry.'

The knight was correct. It was no column of infantry bearing down on the encampment, but a disorganized mass of commoners, treading through the winter mud. There were carts trundling in their wake as well, heaped with sacks and barrels.

Casting aside caution, Cliff ordered Olvario's spearmen to make way and rode a short distance beyond their line, hailing the new arrivals as he went. They ceased, all bar one at the front, who walked up to Cliff with a confidence rarely displayed by a commoner before an armored, mounted marshal of the Serendian host.

Cliff did not recognize him at first, bearded as he was, and wearing rustic garb, but as soon as he spoke he knew him.

'Hail and well met, Marshal Cliff,' said Vittorio. 'It has been many years since last we met. I hear my father is a little way farther up the road?'

TWENTY-TWO

Cliff brought Vittorio to see Crucio. The approach to the royal pavilion was lined with warriors, but the former king's youngest son showed no signs of concern or intimidation as he strode between them at Cliff's side.

Crucio emerged from his tent, armored for battle. The contrast between the old, heavily equipped ruler and his plain-clad son could not have been greater. Crucio's expression was guarded as he gazed on Vittorio, and he made no greeting.

To the surprise of the onlooking retinues, Vittorio knelt in the mud.

'Well met, Father,' he said. 'Mine is likely not a face you wished to ever see again, but when I heard word of your march against the capital, I knew I could not remain in Glish and wait to hear that the remnants of my family have slaughtered one another. As proof of my goodwill, I have brought all the winter stocks that Glish can spare.

The rearmost wagons are still crossing over the Demi. The people support you, Father, and while I know you have every right to take my head now that I have broken the terms of my banishment, I implore that you seek to resolve your differences with Sergio without shedding more blood.'

Silence fell across the gathering, before Crucio uttered a single word.

'Rise.'

Vittorio did so, and Crucio gripped him by both shoulders, gazing intently into his face, as though only just recognizing his youngest son. Eventually, he released him and spoke in a voice loud enough to carry to all those watching.

'You have brought more than just food to feed this host through the winter months, Vittorio. You have brought hope to an old man who once called himself your father. I have erred in many ways over the years but never more so than when I cast you from my presence. The prediction you made on that dark day has been borne out. I was a fool not to listen. But even a fool can learn. Will you call me Father once again, Vittorio? Will you retake your place, and perhaps one day be considered my heir?'

'If you swear to do all you can to be resolved with Sergio, peacefully, then I would be honored to be called the son of Crucio Domongatt once more,' Vittorio said. For the first time since bringing him in from the hills, Cliff witnessed Crucio smile properly, before slapping a gauntlet back down on Vittorio's shoulder.

'Then it will be so! Come, let us waste no time. We shall

ride to the western gate, you and I, and call upon Sergio to treat with us immediately!'

Jordine and Alfonso had been about to descend from the walls back into the town when the sound of ringing trumpets from the encampment made them pause. They watched as a commotion gripped the distant tents, the figures of men-at-arms, archers and knights pouring from tents and drill areas and forming ranks.

'It looks as though they expect to be attacked,' Alfonso commented. On either side, the Eindhovein retinues were standing too, wary lest the sudden activity presage a major assault on the walls. But the attention of Crucio's host appeared to be in the opposite direction, back towards the southwest. Forested ground there led down to the Demi River, but the curvature of the walls and towers to the south hid most of the view from where Jordine and Alfonso stood.

Jordine was about to suggest they try and move to the nearest tower, unsure whether the men-at-arms manning it would permit them onto the upper battlements, when Alfonso pointed out movement close to the royal pavilion, at the heart of the camp. At the same time, it looked as though carts and wagons were being drawn in from the southwest.

'Are they receiving reinforcements?' Jordine wondered. It was generally assumed that lords loyal to Sergio would arrive from elsewhere in Serendia, attacking the besiegers.

Few had entertained the idea that, in fact, more nobles might declare their support for Crucio and bring their retinues to bolster the host outside the gates.

There was a further commotion, though this time it was from the gatehouse just to the right. Orders were barked to make way, and a wedge of royal guards in their full plate armor and purple cloaks took post on the walls.

'It's Sergio,' Jordine hissed. Sure enough, the king made his appearance among his bodyguards, fully armored, presumably summoned by word that an attack might be materializing.

Something was indeed approaching now from the direction of Crucio's camp, but it was far too small to be a genuine assault on the walls. A dozen horsemen cantered beyond the advance guards, making for the gate. The standard one of them was carrying streamed, crimson and yellow brilliance in the slowly gathering twilight. The royal banner of Serendia, its twin flying above the gate just to Jordine's right.

'Crucio,' Alfonso murmured. 'He's coming to treat with Sergio.'

Besides an initial declaration on the first day when the opposing host had arrived, there had been no efforts to communicate with the town. It seemed that was set to change. Jordine looked from the riders to Sergio, now standing in the center of the gatehouse, glaring imperiously down on the approaching horsemen.

The riders drew up a few hundred yards from the walls. Jordine located Crucio among them, in a royal tabard, but there was another next to him who stood out from the rest – unlike the armored knights around him, he wore a commoner's garb, though the way he rode his horse, straight-backed and confident, spoke of formal training. Though still too far out to be certain, Jordine found himself thinking back to the encounter outside Glish between Antonio and Crucio.

'I think that's Vittorio,' he said, pointing the figure out to Alfonso. 'He must have come from Glish.'

'If Crucio has accepted him back, that means he has a viable male heir who isn't Sergio,' Alfonso pointed out.

The standard bearer with the party dipped his flag, indicating a desire to parle. Crucio and Vittorio rode closer, though only a little. Jordine glanced at the archers and crossbowmen among the wall's defenders, but all of them were in turn looking at Sergio, who simply continued to glare down at his father and brother.

Jordine looked back at the riders who had initially accompanied Crucio. He was certain Cliff's stag heraldry was among them, but he couldn't tell for certain in the spreading twilight whether the golden lion was there too. Had his father truly been accepted back into Crucio's graces? He supposed if Vittorio had, then anything was possible.

Crucio spoke, his voice carrying up to the gatehouse.

'I am calling upon my son, Sergio. I do not expect you to leave the fastness of those walls, just as you would not when I visited you in Eindhovein. But I do ask that you would speak to me. I have not come here to make war upon my own bloodline and my own capital.'

Sergio let out a loud, coarse laugh, before calling back.

'You lead an armed host to my gates and make ready to storm my walls, yet at the same time you claim not to want war? Your duplicity knows no ends, Father!'

'There has been strife enough among our family,' Vittorio said. 'Let us turn back to words, rather than weapons.'

'Has he forgiven you then, little brother?' Sergio responded. 'Do you think he would ever have done so were he not lost to desperation? Do you think, when the old fool's anger next flares, you will be spared his ire?'

'Vittorio has brought us the winter stocks of Glish,' Crucio cut in before Vittorio answered. 'We have supplies enough to last through the harshest months. If you wish to subject Heidel to a siege throughout midwinter and beyond, it will be upon your conscience. The people are with us, Sergio.'

'Do not preach to me like you are some benevolent king of old,' Sergio spat, beating a gauntlet against the parapet. 'You lead a rebellion against me, your own son, after murdering my brother. You sought to steal his crown, and now you come for mine! You, and old dogs like Johann Cliff!'

He snatched the golden circlet he wore around the top of his helm and brandished it in the air, the last of the day's light catching it and making it shine.

'Well, come and get it,' he bellowed.

'You know it was not I who struck down Antonio,' Crucio retorted. 'Nor would I shed your blood, either. I implore you, one last time – open these gates, and let us talk, not as two warring rulers but as father and son.'

'Enough of your poisonous tongue,' Sergio shouted. 'You are no father of mine!'

The king snatched the crossbow from the nearest arbalist, and loosed it from between the crenels. The bolt fell narrowly short, thumping into the dirt just in front of Crucio's horse.

He and Vittorio wheeled their horses swiftly away and spurred back to their retinue, who in turn made for the camp with haste.

'Loose, you fools,' Sergio bellowed at the other crossbowmen atop the gatehouse.

A flurry of bolts pursued the horsemen, but they were already at extreme range, and in the falling darkness there was no indication that any of the missiles struck true.

'He has broken parle,' Alfonso muttered darkly. 'That will not endear him to anyone once news spreads that he refused to talk.'

'Best not to say such things here,' Jordine replied, glancing at the men-at-arms nearby. 'Come, let's return to Gallows Street. If Crucio decides on an immediate reprisal, we won't want to be caught up in it.'

A week passed before Crucio's host launched their first major assault.

It came with the dawn, a mass of grey shapes in the gloom, their armor dulled with soot, hefting ladders between them. A shout went up from the walls, and soon a torrent of bolts and arrows was raining down on the attackers.

They persevered, focusing their efforts on the stretches of curtain wall immediately north and south of the western gate, trying to cut it off before seizing it and opening it to the block of mounted knights waiting on the edge of the camp, under Crucio's personal command.

The attack failed. Those who made it atop the walls were hacked down, and the ladders were heaved off. Missiles struck down dozens of Crucio's warriors. Unable to make any headway, the attackers sheltered beneath their shields at the base of the wall, before withdrawing to the cheers and jeers of those defending the ramparts.

The new day revealed the dead and wounded littered across the ground between the town and the camp. A herald appeared at the gates, requesting parties be allowed forward to collect the wounded, but like Crucio, he was chased off with more bolts.

Word of it all spread through the town. Jordine and Alfonso had shared the events at the gatehouse in both the Golden Frog and the Lilly Valley, and the mood in both establishments was grim. Some worried what would happen if the besiegers constructed weaponry to bombard the town, though others claimed Crucio would not stoop so low as to rain death on the people he intended to rule. Others worried that if the besiegers were forced to take Heidel in a bloody assault, they would vent their rage and bloodlust on the inhabitants once the walls were taken.

By ancient tradition, the longer a town resisted a besieging host, the less mercy its inhabitants could expect if it eventually fell to a storm assault.

Jordine had been considering the same thing. It seemed inconceivable that a Serendian host would sack Heidel, yet there was no longer any doubting Crucio's determination to prosecute a siege. For the most part, the knights and warriors of the Western Marches had little connection with Serendia's heartlands, and Jordine suspected there would be some among them perfectly content to take advantage of the chaos of a storming to loot and kill.

The only way to stop that would be to end the siege as quickly as possible, but it was clear Sergio had no intention of negotiating. Most still expected reinforcements for the town to arrive in the coming weeks, at which point the tide would turn back in Sergio's favor. But Jordine wasn't sure if they would last that long.

Matters grew worse the day after the first assault. Jordine and Alfonso arrived at the Golden Frog that evening to find the windows shuttered and the doors barred. A proclamation had been nailed to the front of the tavern, stating that all such establishments across Heidel had been closed for the duration of the siege, by order of the king. Ostensibly it was to conserve supplies and keep the streets quiet, though Jordine reckoned the king knew that the ordinary inhabitants of the town were growing ever more restless.

Jordine and Alfonso returned to Gallows Street. Edward was still convalescing. Chirurgeon del Mattio changed his bandages twice daily, and was pleased to report his injuries appeared to be healing without signs of infection. He remained in bed though, and refused to say anything or do anything but pick at the meals brought to him. Jordine and Alfonso sometimes ate with him, trying to coax him out of the depressed fugue he seemed to have fallen into. They did so again after getting back from the shuttered Golden Frog.

That night, he spoke.

'It was Sergio,' he said.

'What?' Alfonso asked, looking up from his platter, clearly thinking he had misheard.

'The royal guards took my eyes, on Sergio's orders,' Edward said. He was propped up in bed, the plate in his lap untouched. 'They took a blade to me and cut them out.'

Alfonso looked at Jordine in shock, then back at his father.

'But why? Why would the king do that?'

'I refused to obey him.'

'What did he order you to do?'

'Murder his wife.'

Jordine and Alfonso sat in silence for a while, before Alfonso recovered enough to speak again.

'He wanted you to kill Queen Elysia?'

'As he ordered me to kill King Antonio. This time, I could not do it. I told him I had already stained my honor once for him, and I would not do so again.'

'Elysia is dead,' Alfonso said, still sounding disbelieving. 'She leapt from the western tower of the citadel the same night we found you.'

'She did not leap,' Edward said.

Alfonso looked at Jordine, and anger entered his gaze.

'You knew,' he said accusingly. 'You knew Sergio did this to my father! How?'

'Roxanne,' Jordine said simply, knowing he could not deny it.

'This is her doing?' Alfonso said, setting aside his platter and rising to his feet. 'By all the gods, I will go to the citadel this minute and cut down that treacherous witch!'

'She did not demand Elysia's death, or your father's blinding,' Jordine said, trying to placate his friend. 'She confronted Sergio with evidence of his involvement in Antonio's death, and told him if he would not make her his queen, she would tell all of what he had done.'

'And you didn't think to share that with me?' Alfonso demanded. 'You're a wretch and a liar, Joe, and may the gods damn the day you took up the name of Rhundi!'

He made to storm out, but to both their surprise, Edward's voice checked him.

'That is no way to speak to Jordine,' he said firmly. 'You do not understand the difficulties he has faced on behalf of this house. I was the one who made him complicit in the killing of Antonio. On more than one occasion, he has borne shameful acts so you haven't had to, Alfonso. You alone in this family still hold your honor intact, because of what I have made Jordine endure.'

'I'm sure it was a great struggle for him,' Alfonso sneered, looking at Jordine.

'It has been,' Jordine responded, surprised at Edward's

defense of him. 'I owed a debt to your family for taking me in, and I paid that debt by selling my honor. I regret it, but such things cannot be undone. I have loved you as my brother, Al, and all the pain I have caused, all the lies and half-truths I have spoken, were never intended to demean you or our friendship. In the name of what we once had, I beg your forgiveness now.'

Alfonso looked from Jordine to his father, anger and regret writ large on his features.

'Sergio has rent this family asunder,' he said, fire in his voice. 'He is a murderous brute who does not deserve the loyalty of the Rhundis. He must be removed from the throne.'

Until recently Edward would have fiercely chastised his son for speaking such treason, but now he said nothing. Alfonso went on.

'The people support Crucio. He had many faults as a ruler – not least the banishment of your family, Joe – but he was not a dishonorable murderer like Sergio. It would be best for Heidel, and all of Serendia, if this siege were ended and he reclaimed the throne.'

'That will only happen over Sergio's dead body,' Jordine pointed out.

'That is no less than Sergio deserves,' Alfonso said. 'The longer this siege endures, the greater the danger for the town, and the more Serendia as a whole will fracture. We must end it, as swiftly as possible.'

'How?' Jordine asked, wondering where Alfonso's furious train of thought was leading him.

Alfonso told them, faltering at first as he grasped the nature of just what he was suggesting, but with swiftly growing conviction. Jordine thought it madness at first but couldn't deny the allure of the plan's boldness.

Death seemed almost certain, yet if it worked, the siege of Heidel would be ended at a stroke.

TWENTY-THREE

It started on Mason Street in an old, disused warehouse that belonged to a merchant named Bobby Lauren, the owner of the Golden Frog. The siege was bad for Lauren's business, and so he agreed to do what would have seemed unthinkable just a few months earlier – he set fire to his own property.

The fire took time to catch, but by midnight the warehouse was fully ablaze. Mason Street was near the southwestern edge of the town, and the flames were easily visible from most of the southern and western sections of the walls.

In a town of timber like Heidel, fires were always treated as immensely dangerous, and it was usually the responsibility of the town watch to help fight them. Yet with the watch posted to defend the ramparts, it meant drawing some of those men away to tackle the blaze with buckets brought up hastily from the water sluices in the walls overlooking the Demi.

The area around the warehouse was consequently busy with people, rushing to and fro, carrying buckets or the belongings of those living close to the blaze who had decided to flee rather than risk staying in place. Others had come simply to gawk at the fiery spectacle, causing the streets to fill up more thoroughly than they had done since the start of the siege.

Which was all part of the plan. It enabled Jordine and Alfonso to pass without comment up to the western gatehouse. The defenders on the walls there were focused on the town's exterior, alert to any attempt by the besiegers to take advantage of the fire and the chaos it was causing within the walls.

'We have come to join the garrison,' Jordine called out to the pair of men-at-arms standing watch in one of the doorways leading up into the gatehouse tower. The pair looked suspiciously at the two new arrivals, and one held up a torch to better identify them.

Both Jordine and Alfonso were fully armored and wearing the Rhundi surcoats, the white unicorn on a red field.

'Jordine and Alfonso, sons of Sir Edward Rhundi,' Jordine announced, silently amazed at how calm his voice sounded while his heart was pounding in his breast. 'Our father is still recovering after being viciously assaulted in the street by a pack of beggars, but he would never have it be said that House Rhundi did not stand in defense of the rightful king of Serendia, Sergio Domongatt.'

Jordine was hoping that the lowly men-at-arms would

have little understanding of the intricacies of recent events or the king's role in Edward's blinding. Publicly, the Rhundis were still thought to be a family loyal to, and favored by, Sergio. And while Jordine and Alfonso were still too young to be knighted, it was not out of the question that they might wish to join the garrison.

'I will speak with the commander of the watch,' one of the men-at-arms said with a hint of reluctance, before disappearing into the gatehouse. Jordine and Alfonso were left alone with the other guard.

'There seems to be a danger the fire may get out of control,' Jordine said idly to the man, gesturing along the southern length of the wall. 'You can see the blaze from Hawthorn Street.'

'The commander won't permit any more men from the western wall to go to the blaze,' the man-at-arms said with a shrug. 'If you ask me, I'd rather be running buckets up from the sluice gate than facing the threat of another attack.'

'Well, you might find your wish is granted sooner rather than later. It looks like the flames might be catching at the Tigelli stables, along there.'

Jordine pointed higher up the road beneath the wall to the south and, curious, the man-at-arms stepped forward to try to catch a glimpse.

That was when Jordine hit him. It was a good blow, beneath the man's sallet helm, squarely into his unprotected face. The steel of Jordine's gauntlet burst his nose and dropped him with a grunt, before Alfonso slammed his foot into the man's stomach, twice, winding him and stopping him from making a sound.

Jordine crouched hastily, yanked the sallet off, and cracked his head against the cobblestones, stilling his efforts to rise.

'Is he dead?' Alfonso panted, sounding at once hopeful and fearful.

'Unconscious, I think,' Jordine said, rising. 'No turning back now, Al. Up we go.'

He drew his sword and Alfonso did likewise, the firelight reflecting on the bared steel like liquid flame. Jordine ducked through the doorway and into the southern half of the gatehouse.

They met the man-at-arms who had entered just moments earlier on his way back down. Jordine didn't give him time to work out what was happening before he hacked his sword into the man's left leg. His greave turned the worst of the blow aside, but it tripped the man, who came clattering down the stairs, almost carrying Jordine and Alfonso down with him. Jordine was able to get a foot up above him and wedge his arms against the stone on either side, while Alfonso clung onto his waist.

They kept going up, bursting into the guardroom directly to the left of the top of the gates. A single crossbowman was on duty there next to the arrow slit, while two more men-at-arms, both in the livery of the lord of Eindhovein, were trading cards and wages at a small table, their sword belts unbuckled and helmets acting as upturned coin receptacles. All three looked up in shock as Jordine and Alfonso came storming in.

To hesitate meant death. Jordine lashed his sword at the nearest of the men at the table, who threw himself desperately back in his chair, sprawling across the floor. The other one was faster, snatching up a dirk and catching Alfonso's own swing with one hand, before trying to drive the knife into the younger Rhundi's gut. The blade jarred off his plackart, but the man-at-arms moved with desperate speed, stabbing lower, trying to jam the dirk through the joints where leg met torso.

Jordine lashed across the table at him, and this time his blow connected. The sword cleaved down through the partially armored man's shoulder, and Jordine felt it hack meat and splinter bone. Blood jetted in the light of the room's torches, and the man twisted and wailed horribly, before Jordine wrenched his sword free and Alfonso ripped his wrist from the man's grip and drove him to his knees.

The one who had fallen from his chair was now on his feet, but he was unarmed and blocking the angle of the crossbowman who had been standing by the arrow slit. He took one look at Jordine and made a dash for the door leading from that floor of the gatehouse out onto the southern stretch of the wall, shouting as he went.

The crossbowman loosed his bolt. The hasty shot missed Jordine by a hand's width, embedding itself with a thump into the timber of the overturned table.

Alfonso kicked the table aside and rammed his sword at the man before he could either reach for his short sword or begin hauling back his crossbow's cord – he thrust, rather than cut this time, driving the steel point through the man's gambeson, jarring off ribs as he pierced heart and lungs.

Before Alfonso had even ripped his sword free, Jordine was throwing himself against the door leading out onto the wall, slamming it shut in the face of several more men-at-arms who, alerted by their fleeing comrade, were attempting to get inside. He bolted the door while Alfonso hurried to do the same with the one leading down to the rear of the gate, slamming it in the face of the man-at-arms they had thrown down the stairs, who was now charging back up them, shouting furiously.

'Get the lever,' Jordine shouted, as both doors started to shudder and rattle, the heavy, iron-studded oak pounded by blows.

They both moved across the chamber to the side adjacent to the gate itself. A turning mechanism was set into the wall there, along with an opening that allowed those in the guardroom to look down on the gate itself.

The gatehouses that studded Heidel's town walls were larger and did not feature as many complex defenses as the entrance to the royal citadel – there were no murder holes, portcullis or machicolations. Yet they did include an opening mechanism that meant the heavy doors could be swiftly parted without the need for half a dozen men to heave up a heavy locking bar and drag the entrance open. Given the number of times the large doors were required to open and shut during the day to admit traffic into and out of the town, it enabled far fewer members of the watch to maintain the gateways.

But it also meant that, should infiltrators manage to capture the locking mechanism, it would not take many of them to open the gates from the inside.

Jordine and Alfonso sheathed their swords and grasped the lever, beginning to crank it, engaging the system of weights and balances that caused the gate to swing open. There was a groan as the hefty timbers slowly started to part, accompanied by the wrench and rattle of chains and the creak of pulleys.

It was madness, but what Jordine had said to Alfonso was true – there was no turning back now. Either they would perish here, cornered and cut down in the gatehouse's narrow stone confines, or they would prize the defenses of Heidel wide open for the besieging host.

'It's working,' Jordine hissed as he put his weight behind keeping the lever cranking, the mechanism set into the stone to his right making a clicking noise as it kept shifting the weights. 'Send the signal!'

Alfonso abandoned the lever and scrambled to the guardroom's arrow slit. He snatched a torch from its bracket nearby, then shoved it through the slit, reaching through as far as the narrow aperture would allow him to.

'Can you get to it?' Jordine panted, struggling to keep the gate opening. The blows on the doorway leading to the walls had ceased being the pounding of mailed fists, swords, maces and polearms, replaced instead by the single, powerful strike of something large, large enough to cause splits to begin appearing in the wood with each strike. It was only a matter of time before it gave way.

'I… I can reach it,' Alfonso hissed, straining, his armor scraping where he was pressed against bare stone. At last the torch, now being waved on the outside of the gatehouse, caught and flared against the side of the Eindhovein standard hanging there.

The banners of Heidel's defenders had been draped all along the gatehouse and the nearest sections of wall, and in doing so they were unwittingly providing Jordine and Alfonso with their best hope of sending a signal to the besiegers.

The gate continued to ponderously creak open. For a short time at least, the way into Heidel was open.

'What in the name of Elion is happening?' Frederick demanded as he arrived amongst the pickets, still buckling one of his pauldrons into place. Like most of the encampment, he had been sleeping while partially armored, so that he could respond swiftly to any sudden alarm. Just such an alarm had come minutes earlier, when one of the sentries facing the western gate had entered his tent and informed him there appeared to be a commotion coming from within Heidel. A plume of black smoke could be seen rising into the night sky, blotting out the stars over the town, underlit by a flickering amber glow. It seemed as though something was on fire, just up from the southeastern tower overlooking the Demi.

And apparently, the fire was spreading. Just as Frederick had arrived on the scene, a bolt of flame had shot up the gatehouse, which stood not four hundred yards from the picket line guarding the camp. He realized that one of the banners hung from the walls had caught light.

At first, he thought it had to be some ember or falling ash from whatever was ablaze inside the tower, until one of the pickets called to him, pointing with his spear at the heart of the gatehouse.

'Look, sire! It's opening!'

Frederick saw he was correct. By the light of the swiftly burning banner, he saw that the western gate into Heidel was swinging slowly open.

It seemed hard to imagine how the fire within the town could be connected to the gate's opening – Frederick's first, instinctive thought was that it was some kind of trap, designed to lure the besiegers into a rash, hasty dash towards the defended walls. But what if there was some kind of general uprising or rebellion within the town in favor of Crucio? It was something they had discussed but had no way of directly influencing. What if the people of Heidel had decided they wished to be rid of Sergio once and for all, and had seized the gates?

Whatever was happening, it would surely not be long before the entranceway was closed once more, and the window of opportunity was gone. Frederick knew he did not have time to prevaricate, or seek either explanations or authority from above.

'Sound the rallying call,' he ordered his horn blower,

who had accompanied him to the pickets in case he discovered some sort of sally being launched from the town, and needed to signal the rest of the camp.

As the notes pealed out through the fire-shot darkness, he called for his squire and mount. The youth had only just been provided to him from Cliff's own retinue, and was still learning his trade, yet he had Cliff's big old stallion saddled and brought forward in moments, having anticipated the order. It felt strange, having gone the past two years without the amenities of squires, servants, pages and messengers, to suddenly have access to such luxuries again, just as he and Martha had started to learn how to survive on their own.

He clambered up into the saddle, drew his sword, and gestured to the small gathering of men-at-arms, comprised of those from his retinue who had followed him from the camp and the pickets who had been standing guard.

'I do not know what good fortune has led to the opening of the town gates, and I cannot guarantee that it is not a trap that will see us all slain before sunrise. What is certain is that I am going there. Into Heidel. Into our capital, to prize it free from the grip of a tyrant. I am not ordering any of you to accompany me. But I have fought many battles, and I know in my heart that this opportunity will not present itself again. So often, victory goes to a bold few, and tonight we are those bold few. For King Crucio, and for the greater good of all Serendia.'

He didn't wait for any sort of response, even for cheers, before spurring his mount for the stretch of darkness that lay between the campfires and the town walls. And beyond it those gates, still open, still promising victory if only Frederick could reach them, and hold them long enough for the rest of the camp to awaken and come to their aid.

'For Crucio,' Frederick roared as he rode, brandishing his sword. 'And the glory of House Ducas!'

TWENTY-FOUR

'They're trying to shut the gate!' Jordine shouted to Alfonso.

The western entrance into Heidel was almost fully open, but men-at-arms in the liveries of Eindhovein and the town watch were now rushing to the gates themselves, heaving against them, trying to force them shut against the weight of the unlocking mechanism. No matter how hard Jordine heaved on the lever up in the guardroom, he could not force the doors apart any further.

'Shoot them,' Alfonso urged. He was hauling the table that had once stood in the room's center over to the door leading out onto the walls, desperately trying to buttress it as one of its planks splintered apart. The door leading down and out of the gatehouse was hardly doing any better, shivering against its frame as it was beaten by members of the garrison desperate to recapture the lever that opened the doors.

The crossbowman Alfonso had run through and the man-at-arms Jordine had slain were still lying between them. Jordine abandoned the lever and scrambled over to where the crossbow itself had fallen. He began to ratchet its heavy cord back, then fumbled for a bolt, slotting one home. He had only used a crossbow a few times before, but the weapon's simplicity was its beauty.

He hurried back over to the lever and the gap in the wall that allowed its operator to look down on the gate directly. The doors had started to shift fractionally shut, more of the garrison rushing to push and shove against them. Jordine took aim at them through the gap.

The bolt slashed down and cracked off one of the cobblestones of the roadway, just missing one of the men-at-arms' feet. It was enough, however, to make them briefly stop pushing. One shouted and pointed up at Jordine, and he was forced to throw himself back as a flurry of return shots rattled and clattered from the stonework protecting him.

There was a crash from across the other side of the room. The door to the walls had almost completely broken apart. A knight in full plate armor was trying to force his way in through the splintered remnants, driving the spike of a halberd at Alfonso.

'Burn it,' Jordine shouted desperately. There was no time to reload the crossbow.

Alfonso snatched the torch he had used to ignite the banner outside the arrow slit, and thrust it in the knight's face, driving him back far enough to toss it down onto the overturned table still partially blocking the doorway. The flames caught instantly. In a few heartbeats, the door was ablaze.

Jordine and Alfonso withdrew across the room from the fire, back to the gate's lever.

'We're going to die here, aren't we?' Alfonso said as he drew his sword once again.

'Looks like it,' Jordine admitted, doing likewise as he watched the fire catching on the timber floorboards, steadily starting to spread. 'I won't lie, I'd hoped it would be a half-dozen decades from now, in my sleep, with a beautiful woman lying either side of me… but I suppose if I had to choose an alternative it'd be side by side with my best friend, swords in hand, going out in a blaze of glory.'

'There's a blaze, that's true enough,' Alfonso said, eyes on the burning doorway. 'Not so sure about the glory.'

Smoke was beginning to broil through the chamber, covering the ceiling in dark smog and making it hard to breathe. Jordine could feel the heat through his armor. Terrible visions of being cooked alive in the steel plate assailed him.

'Better to die to cold steel than the flames,' he said, moving across the room to the door they had originally entered through. It was still barred, and still shuddering under the assault of the garrison troops on the other side. Alfonso hesitated, then followed.

Jordine turned to his friend, wondering if he should say something more before the end. Apologize for enabling his father's dishonorable actions. But the look said enough.

They had both known the risk, and had chosen to embrace it together. There was nothing more to be said.

Jordine nodded and Alfonso drew back the bolt and yanked the door open.

The man-at-arms beyond it stumbled, caught mid-swing, the timber he had been striking suddenly no longer there.

With a bellow, Jordine kicked him square in the middle of the breastplate. Already off balance, he was sent crashing back into the other men-at-arms packing the narrow stairway behind him.

Jordine followed up with a shout, storming down after them. There was no room to swing his sword properly, so he used the pommel, slamming it against the helm and face of the man-at-arms as he was checked by the weight of bodies below him. He kicked again, punched downwards with his other gauntlet, using his armored body like a battering ram, driving his way down the stairs, Alfonso adding his own strength to the desperate charge.

There were no torches in the short flight, and after the brightness of the fire spreading above, it was difficult to see anything. Jordine just kept kicking, punching and pushing, feeling a blow ring against his knee plate and another against his plackart. He expected to feel the hot, piercing pain of a blade finding its way through the heavy armor, but then there was light ahead, more torchlight spilling in from the street outside. He lost his footing on the stairs, but it didn't matter – they were all tumbling down, armor crashing and clattering as they sprawled out onto the cobblestones.

Alfonso had managed to stay upright, and he rammed his sword down through the hauberk of one man-at-arms who was on top of Jordine before hauling him off and delivering a ringing blow against the helm of another who was beneath him, grappling with him. Jordine tried to push himself up, and felt Alfonso's gauntlet on his pauldron, helping drag him onto his feet.

His elation at having broken out of the gatehouse died quickly. More men-at-arms were closing in from the left and right, the street behind the gateway packed with warriors of the garrison. The nearest of them leveled spears and polearms, closing in.

Jordine lunged at one, striking aside the spear tip with a clatter and trying to get inside his guard. There were too many though – another stepped in and blocked him, parrying his sword lengthways with the haft of his billhook, the blade biting into wood. A third lunged from his left with another spear, the point ripping through his surcoat and jarring off his side.

He was forced to give ground, Alfonso alongside him, until he felt his back connect against the gatehouse wall, steel scraping the stonework. He knocked aside and parried another flurry of strikes, knowing that without room to maneuver it was over. His armor started to take more hits, the billhook crashing against his shoulder, denting metal and causing his left arm to go suddenly numb.

He snarled, fighting back all the harder, unwilling to accept the end. He threw himself in amongst his assailants, striking left and right, feeling his sword bite through leather and into flesh. Blows rained down on him from all sides, a solid wall pressing in on him, trying to bear him down, trying to crush him.

Then, suddenly, the pressure decreased. He stumbled, swinging blindly, but this time his sword cut only air.

Something came crashing through the bodies that had been surrounding him – a mounted rider, sword catching the firelight as he swung. A head flew from one man-at-arms' shoulders, blood spurting, the remains tumbling. The horseman wheeled, using his mount to further break apart and scatter the enemies around Jordine, standing in his stirrups to hack down with his sword to his left and right.

By the light of the flames, Jordine saw the heraldry emblazoned on his rescuer's surcoat. The golden lion of House Ducas.

He shouted, driving his sword against one of the men-at-arms who was trying to cut through the horse's barding and bring the beast down. Alfonso was still with him, somehow still standing, and together they helped drive back those around the rider, hacking and slashing with renewed vigor.

The horseman had come through the gate, and he wasn't the only one. Hooves clattered on cobbles as mounted men-at-arms followed after him, knocking aside or cutting down the defenders still desperately trying to slam the gate shut. They were too late. Heidel was breached.

The town guards were the first to run. Unlike the Eindhovein retinues or the royal guards in the citadel, there were few among their number with absolute loyalty to Sergio. Most had no intention of dying in the midst of a dynastic struggle.

The soldiery from Eindhovein were more steadfast, but their numbers were fewer. The riders scattered them, securing the space immediately behind the gatehouse, wheeling about to strike at any small knot of infantrymen who tried to make a stand. Jordine and Alfonso remained standing in their midst, swords bloodied and armor dented, scarcely believing they were still alive.

Jordine brought his sword up in salute to the first rider who had made it through the gate. The horseman rode alongside him, and snapped back his visor.

'Father,' Jordine said, his voice a dull croak. Frederick Ducas stared down at his son, then smiled, and returned his salute with his sword.

'Well met, my son,' he said. 'Well met.'

TWENTY-FIVE

Heidel fell.

Frederick had only a few dozen men with him, but their ferocity as they stormed the gateway convinced many of the defenders, already panicking, to throw down their weapons and make for the streets and back alleys. A retinue belonging to one of Sergio's Eindhovein knights, Sir Delfino, attempted to counterattack, but that meant abandoning a section of the wall immediately south of the gatehouse, and because part of that structure was now fully aflame, they needed to head in the opposite direction to make it down off the walls first.

By then, Frederick was being reinforced. The sounds of his horn blower calling the assembly had drawn the men from their tents, and the realization that, suddenly, the way into Heidel was open had led to an all-out attack, disorganized but ferocious. Sir Guel was the first knight to make it through in support of Frederick, accompanied by six of his men-at-arms and a trio of archers. In their haste some of them were barely armored, but they helped further secure the gates.

All that mattered was that they were kept open until more of Crucio's host could make it inside.

Cliff reached the edge of the camp, summoned from his pavilion tent, and Crucio himself arrived soon after. Vittorio came with his father, still looking for all the world like some common peasant, roused from his farmstead in the dead of night.

'What's happening?' Crucio demanded, looking disbelievingly past Cliff at the open gateway and his forces streaming through it. One of the gatehouse's two towers was now fully alight, blazing like a torch into the night sky. As the two watched, Sergio's royal standard – fluttering in the gateway's center – touched off, consumed in an instant by the spreading flames.

'Someone opened the gates,' Cliff said, not taking his eyes off the shocking spectacle. 'Frederick decided to lead an immediate attack.'

'And it isn't a trap?' Crucio wondered aloud.

'It seems not. But we have to exploit it. We need to keep going, until the whole town is ours. And the citadel. That is where Sergio will make his stand.'

'Then go,' Crucio said. 'I will be with you, as soon as I'm armored. But remember your promise!'

'Sergio is to be spared,' Cliff said, finally looking away from the gates and shouting for his mount.

'We have to press on,' Frederick told Jordine and Alfonso, pointing along the street leading from the gate deeper into the town. 'To the citadel. If we are swift, we might be able to compel Sergio to surrender immediately, or even storm it.'

'What of the rest of the town?' Jordine asked. The gate was now secure, and with more of Crucio's host flooding in beneath the burning tower, individuals and small groups were now spreading into the surrounding streets. Jordine saw several men in the livery of Sir Huscari, a minor knight of the Western Marches, kicking in a nearby doorway and charging inside, followed by screams from within. More sounds of terror were rising from the south, along with the glow of an inferno – it seemed likely that amidst the chaos and confusion, the warehouse fire that had originally been set to distract from Jordine and Alfonso's attack on the gateway was now getting out of control. A part of him feared he might have consigned Heidel to the flames.

'We need to regain control,' he carried on, gesturing at another group of men-at-arms breaking into the tannery shop that stood on the north corner of the square behind the gatehouse. 'Otherwise the whole town will be sacked tonight, or worse, reduced to ashes.'

'Cliff or the king will restore order once they arrive,' Frederick said, gesturing for two of the men who had followed him through the gate to dismount. 'If we hesitate now, the citadel will remain beyond our reach! The siege will continue, and Heidel will keep suffering! I am going, and I need every able sword-arm with me. Don't abandon me again, Jordine!'

The words were more stinging than any blow he had suffered since the fighting began. He looked one more time to the surrounding shops and homesteads, doors and windows being smashed in now by the rampant, victorious invaders, before taking the bridle from one of the dismounted men-at-arms and pulling himself up into the saddle. Alfonso hesitated, then did likewise with the horse given to him.

'Our night's work is not yet done,' Frederick shouted, addressing all the mounted men-at-arms still with him, brandishing his bloodied sword. 'But we can finish this war now, with one more blow. Follow me! To the citadel!'

TWENTY-SIX

They rode through Heidel. Streets that Jordine had trodden almost every day since he was a small child were now unrecognizable: windows shuttered and doors barred, no light from hearths and candles permitted to spill into the dark lanes and roadways. The thunder of hooves on the cobbled thoroughfare leading through the town reverberated back from the looming, shadowed buildings, like a storm that had broken in the heart of Serendia's capital.

What ruination would be revealed when dawn finally broke, Jordine didn't dare imagine. His father was right. Now was not the time to weigh his sins. All they could do was press on and on, to the citadel, crouched like a vast beast in the darkness upon its crack, the odd flicker of firelight from within the narrow windows and arrow slits of its turrets like fiery eyes glaring down upon them.

If they captured Heidel, the citadel could still endure

for months. It could withstand even the most dedicated and well-equipped besiegers, as it had done on half a dozen occasions throughout the centuries. And time was still on Sergio's side. Hold out within the citadel, and the lords still loyal to him would reach Heidel sooner or later. If that happened, Jordine's head would join his father's on spikes above the blackened ruins of the western town gate.

Such grim visions started melting away as they rode up the final approach to the citadel's gate. It stood open, the iron portcullis raised and the doors thrown wide. Bodies lay in the gap, a trio of royal guards slain by unknown assailants.

Frederick rode over the dead and straight into the citadel, just as he had done with the town gate. Jordine followed, feeling an uncontainable thrill. At that moment, balanced on the knife's edge between success and failure, life and death, at his father's side – he would not have wanted to be anywhere else.

They cantered into the courtyard, and almost trampled a clutch of figures dashing across it towards the keep. Jordine was forced to saw on his reins, his borrowed mount rearing. He made to lash with his sword, but the man below him scrambled back, holding up his hands in supplication.

'We are friends, my lords,' another shouted, likewise doing his best to avoid being trampled or hacked down by the rampant riders. 'We have secured the gate for you!'

'You acknowledge Crucio Domongatt as the rightful king of Serendia?' Frederick snapped, clearly suspecting a trap. Jordine saw that some of those before him were members of the royal guard, armored and battle-ready, the light of the nearest torches picking out their purple cloaks. The rest were servants, besides one antlered figure that Jordine recognized as the court's master of trade, the antlered demibeast Roig Mills.

'We do acknowledge Crucio as king, Lord,' one of the guards said, kneeling on the courtyard's cobbles before Frederick. The others hastened to mirror him in supplication.

'We saw that the outer walls were breached, and the imposter Sergio refused to leave the citadel, so we knew it was time to act,' the guard said.

'Where is Sergio now, and how many of the other guards and servants are with us?' Frederick demanded. 'Speak the truth, and I will ensure none of you are harmed. You have my word.'

'We cannot say for sure, Lord, but there is more fighting within the keep,' the guard said, glancing fearfully from Frederick towards the great tower. 'Sergio makes his last stand.'

'Secure the gateway, ensure none but the true king's host enters,' Frederick ordered a trio of his riders, before dismounting and throwing his mount's reins to the servants. Jordine, Alfonso and the other cavalrymen still with them did likewise, a wedge of about half a dozen approaching the keep.

What the guard had claimed appeared to be true – more bodies littered the keep's open doorway and the entrance hall within. Civil war had gripped the citadel, a fact that had to be exploited before those still loyal to Sergio were able to secure the defenses.

'The king wants his son alive,' Frederick said as they moved deeper into the keep, following sounds of battle still ringing down from the upper levels. 'Elion willing, he will cease his resistance once he realizes how futile it is.'

'And if he does not?' Alfonso asked, his tone grim.

'Stay your sword, young Master Rhundi,' Frederick responded.

They climbed the timber staircase that led up to the great hall and the throne room. A figure came reeling through the doorway before they could reach it: another royal guard, clutching a bloody wound in his side. He collapsed to his knees, and Frederick moved past him only to be forced to parry the swing of another guard who appeared to have just dealt the death blow to his comrade.

'The citadel has fallen, surrender and you may be spared,' Frederick said, stepping back in an attempt to disengage, but the guard lunged after him with a snarl, face hidden behind his helm's visor. Frederick parried again and Jordine stepped in, hacking at the rear of the guard's knee joint, where the armor was weak. The blow cut through, and the guard stumbled and was driven back and forced down by Frederick, who left him for those following behind to finish.

They swept into the antechamber before the throne room, and found the doors shut. The space was littered with more dead, the tapestries that decorated the walls torn and bloodied. Frederick strode to the doorway and beat the pommel of his sword against the timbers, but they would not budge.

'Sergio,' he called out loudly. 'It is over! The town is taken, and now the citadel as well. Your father comes to treat with you. He has no wish to see you harmed. Open these doors and give supplication, and I swear your life will be spared.'

There was no reply. Frederick tried the doors again, before turning aside.

'He has barricaded himself within,' he said. 'We need to find something to breach it.'

'That may suffice,' Jordine said, pointing at the life-sized statue that stood in a nook in the entrance hall, facing towards the doors. It was a carving of Crucio's father, which he had installed across from the throne room on the day of his coronation, all those decades ago.

'Fitting,' Frederick said with a humorless smile. 'The king's father will again make way for his son's reign.'

'Jordine,' Alfonso said as they moved to help pull down the statue and bring it to the doors. 'We don't have time for this.'

Jordine looked at his friend, surprised.

'Jarette,' Alfonso elaborated. 'We need to find her. If she isn't in the hall with Sergio, who knows what's happened to her. With the town being sacked, and fighting here in the citadel…'

Jordine felt a pang of shame – amidst all the excitement and furor of battle, he had momentarily forgotten their friend. Alfonso was right, she had to be found. If Sergio didn't have her, one of his guards could well decide to try to use her for ransom, or worse.

He was about to point out as much to Frederick when a dozen more men-at-arms in the livery of several knights from the Marches, Sir Salazaro and Sir Ulbert, entered the antechamber from the stairway, panting and flushed with exertion.

'We followed you directly from the gate, sire,' one told Frederick. 'With word that the king is coming, and Marshal Cliff. They have passed into the town.'

'Ride back and tell them we are securing the citadel,' Frederick instructed. 'I believe Sergio has barricaded himself within the throne room, and refuses to answer any summons.'

The man-at-arms bowed and departed while the others moved to begin manhandling the statue down. Jordine took his father aside.

'We must find Princess Jarette,' he told him. 'Sergio has been holding her prisoner. She is likely in danger. She may well be in the hall, but we cannot be sure until the doors are breached.'

'The king will want her safe and secure as swiftly as possible,' Frederick agreed. 'Go and seek her out. But be careful. Trust none of the guards or servants. Watch young Rhundi's back, and have him watch yours.'

'As always,' Jordine said, smiling briefly. 'I will see you again soon, Father.'

The stone head of Crucio's father broke apart the doors to Heidel's throne room.

Crucio and Cliff arrived just before the timber gave way.

'Let me lead the assault through the breach, my king,' Frederick said.

'You have already risked yourself in my cause,' Crucio replied, but Frederick shook his head.

'I esteem it as a point of honor, my liege. I have opened the town and the citadel. Let me open the way directly to your throne.'

'As you wish it,' Crucio said. 'Henceforth, you shall always command the van of the Serendian host.'

By now the antechamber was packed with the warriors of Crucio's and Cliff's own retinues. Frederick assembled those he'd led into the keep behind the improvised battering ram.

'Slay any who oppose us,' he called out between the shuddering impacts. 'But stay your hand for those who surrender. Enough Serendian blood has been shed this night.'

There was a crash as the statue broke through and splintered the locking bar. The mass of knights and men-at-arms threw themselves at the broken doors, driving them open despite the weight of furniture that had been piled up on the far side.

Frederick was the first through the gap. A flurry of crossbow bolts slashed past him, but none struck. He heard screaming behind from those less fortunate, but his sole focus was on what lay ahead – those royal guards still loyal to Sergio.

One swung a battle-axe at him, and he blocked its haft with his sword, the force of the impact jarring up his arm. The force and momentum of those behind him drove him hard up against his opponent, their armor clattering as they collided.

There was no room to swing or even stab. Frederick grappled, his helmet ringing as the guard tried to headbutt him. Another of the guards to the right went down in the press, and for a moment it cleared a space that allowed more of Frederick's men to push through, the doors further splintering and splitting apart.

Frederick shoved the guard with all his strength, breathless in the crush. His legs became tangled amidst the broken tables and chairs that had been heaped against the door, and he would have lost his own footing if the increasing weight of the press had not held him up. He managed to strike his pommel against the guard's visor, denting it, both of them pressed close as lovers.

The hall's defenders could not resist the force of the incursion. As more and more of Crucio's men-at-arms drove themselves inside and trampled the barricades, the slender line of guards who had chosen to stand with Sergio bowed and broke under the pressure. Frederick was able to breathe properly again as the guard he had been fighting finally yielded, a few straining steps at first, then more as the breakthrough became irresistible. Frederick didn't even have a chance to strike at him, losing him beneath the tide of plate and chain mail, leather and surcoats.

The melee spilled out through the hall. Frederick pulled himself free of the press, making it to the immediate right of the doorway, mounting the broken remnants of the great feast table that had once dominated the center of the hall as he looked for Sergio.

He found him almost immediately. He was armored for battle, his crown circlet atop his helm, wielding a hand-and-a-half sword overarm from the center of a wedge of purple-cloaked guards. His visor was down, but Fredrick heard his roar of rage and effort as he drove his heavy sword through the gambeson and shoulder of one of Cliff's men, almost cleaving the man in two.

Sergio and the surviving guards fought ferociously, but there was no stopping the tide. They were driven back towards the dais at the far end of the hall, which now stood empty – Frederick saw that, in his desperation, Sergio had heaped up the royal thrones as part of the barricades Crucio's men were now storming over.

He clambered back down with some difficulty and shouted for his men-at-arms to make way, trying to reach the front of the melee. If such slaughter was allowed to continue any longer, Sergio would meet his end, regardless of Crucio's order that he be spared.

He hadn't gotten far when he heard a familiar voice. Cliff had arrived, and with him came Crucio and Vittorio. Frederick changed direction to intercept them before they could reach the sharp edge of the combat.

'You should have stayed outside until the chamber is secure,' Frederick shouted at Crucio over the din of battle reverberating from the rafters. 'I cannot guarantee your safety, sire!'

'Where is my son?' Crucio demanded in response, his visor raised and his aged expression fierce. 'I will not have him meet his end in this madness, penned in and butchered like cattle!'

'He is resisting to the death, sire,' Frederick responded, trying not to snap at the king. 'He has already slain a number of good men.'

'He will heed none but his father,' Crucio said, beginning to forge forward once more. Fredrick clutched at Cliff.

'We must stop him,' he said urgently. 'Sergio will cut him down, and then all this will be for nought.'

Cliff nodded gravely, and they pushed in alongside Crucio, who was now almost at the front ranks.

Sergio and his last bloodied band of survivors had been forced back onto the dais. They had cut down their pursuers, leaving their bodies around the short flight of steps at their feet. Sergio stood at the fore, his long sword brandished, royal surcoat rent, looking every bit the warrior-king brought to bay.

The attackers hesitated, the pause threatening to rob them of their courage – none wanted to be the first to renew the assault, and become the last casualties in what were now clearly the conflict's final moments.

Frederick managed to interpose himself between Crucio and the narrow, body-strewn space between the two lines.

'Sergio, my son,' Crucio cried out, trying to make himself seen through the press. 'Cease this senseless slaughter!'

'Sire, go no further, I beseech you,' Cliff said, joining Frederick in holding the king at bay.

But then another voice again called on Sergio, and it wasn't Crucio's. All eyes turned to a figure who, unburdened by armor, had slipped between the ranks and now stepped out into the deadly space between the two sides, his feet treading in the blood of those lying slain at Sergio's feet. It was Vittorio, still clad like a rustic farmer from Glish.

'Brother, come down,' he said, his voice calm and firm in the sudden silence that descended on the hall. 'It is over. No one else needs to die this day, nor any other. No more Serendian blood needs to be shed. No more Domongatts need die for that metal circlet upon your brow.'

Sergio snapped up his visor and gazed down on his younger brother, his face flushed from combat, his expression wrathful and imperious.

'You naive little worm,' he snapped. 'Has that old dog truly managed to convince you that I will be spared? Or are you trying to lure me to an ignoble end? I will trade my blood for yours!'

Sergio lunged down from the dais. Frederick stood frozen with horror, as did every other onlooker besides Cliff. The old marshal, responses honed by a lifetime of warfare, launched himself towards Sergio as he struck at the shocked Vittorio.

Sergio's heavy sword swung, the force of his rage and the momentum of his lunge behind it. It caught Vittorio's neck and cleaved cleanly through it, cutting his head from his body.

But the killing blow had left Sergio exposed. Cliff's momentum met Sergio's, the marshal's sword punching in under Sergio's arm, piercing the armor's joint and jarring between his ribcage to drive through lungs and heart.

Sergio crashed into Vittorio's body as the latter slumped, the two brothers ending up entwined upon the throne room floor, slain together in front of the dais.

TWENTY-SEVEN

Jordine and Alfonso hastened for the upper eastern side of the citadel, passing ransacked chambers, corpses and other signs of disorder and struggle. A gravely wounded servant at the top of one flight of stairs sat with his back to the wall, face white as a bedsheet, clutching a bloody wound in his stomach. He looked up blearily as Alfonso knelt and asked if he knew what had become of Princess Jarette. The man made no reply.

They carried on, up onto the floor where Jarette's bed-chamber lay. A maidservant ran past them at the end of the corridor, screaming. Both Jordine and Alfonso began to run.

Jordine reached the chamber first. Its door stood split open. He heard Jarette's cry from within.

He burst inside. Jarette stood, cornered by a royal guard. The man had his back to Jordine, and appeared to be locked in a grapple with the princess.

He rushed to them, kicking aside a partly fallen dresser

and slamming into the guard's back, before snatching him by the shoulder and ripping him away from Jarette.

The guard half turned as he was hauled off, choking, revealing a slender dagger rammed up through his throat. Blood was gouting from the wound, the front of Jarette's nightgown messy with it, her face as pale as the dying servant they had passed earlier.

Jordine let the guard fall with a clatter. Jarette threw herself into his arms.

'Jarette,' Alfonso shouted, bursting into the chamber. Jordine eased her off him, looking her up and down.

'Are you hurt?' he asked. She shook her head, tears in her eyes, unable to speak.

'Stay with her,' Jordine told Alfonso, moving aside before heading back out into the corridor.

'Where are you going?' Alfonso called after him, but he didn't reply.

He carried on down the corridor, to Roxanne's bedchamber.

Unlike Jarette's, it was still barred. Jordine struck his sword pommel against it and called out her name. After a while, there was the grate of a bolt, and it creaked open a fraction.

He found himself facing another dagger, this one wielded by Roxanne's chief handmaid, Carolin. She glared at him, and Jordine took a pace back and lowered his sword.

'I am here to ensure your lady's safety,' he said. 'The citadel has been taken by Crucio.'

'Stand aside, Carolin,' came Roxanne's voice from

within the chamber, and a moment later she stepped into Jordine's view. Her expression was proud and stern, but there was fear in her eyes, just like when he had encountered her in Eindhovein.

'Crucio is within the citadel?' she demanded.

'He is,' Jordine replied.

'And I take it from your demeanor that you have thrown your lot in with him?'

'It's over, Roxanne,' Jordine said. 'Sergio's brutalities have ensured his downfall. Whether he is slain or simply captured, he is king no more. The throne belongs to Crucio.'

'And what of me?' Roxanne said. 'Will you ensure I suffer the same fate as Sergio? Or perhaps as Elysia…'

Jordine sighed and shook his head.

'I cannot guarantee your fate, my lady. But I'm certain you will do what you always do. Survive. Crucio was the one who rescued you from the flames when you were still a child, and adopted you into the royal household. I doubt he will have you harmed.'

'Unless word of my involvement in Elysia's death becomes known,' Roxanne said.

Jordine was sorely tempted to tell her that she would have to face the consequences of her actions, and that if she had any honor, she would admit her crimes and throw herself upon Crucio's mercy. Yet he knew she would not, and knew too that he would tell no one of it. In this case, adherence to honor would only bring more suffering to Serendia – Elysia had been the sister of King Seric of Calpheon, and word that she had been murdered by the then-king of Serendia could easily lead to a war between the two realms. Better that the truth stayed buried, than be allowed to bring about such bloodshed.

'The fewer who know about the truth of Lady Elysia's death, the better,' he said. 'If it becomes known, then it will not be because of me.'

Despite her efforts to appear reserved, Jordine sensed Roxanne's relief. She smiled briefly.

'It is for the best,' she agreed. 'But tell me, what has become of Sergio?'

'Last I saw, he was besieged in the throne room,' Jordine said. 'They were breaking down the doors as I left.'

'Is Crucio there?'

'He was on his way.'

'Then I will go down, and make my supplication to him,' Roxanne said.

'It would be wiser to remain here until the citadel has been wholly secured.'

'Are you saying the sword of Jordine Ducas is not sufficient to defend me?' she said, smiling once again. Jordine could not help but do likewise.

'None shall lay hands upon you so long as I live, Lady Roxanne,' he said. 'If you wish, follow me, and we shall see if your betrothed has surrendered his crown.'

Jordine and Alfonso accompanied Jarette, Roxanne and Carolin back down to the great hall. Jarette was clearly still shaken, but had recovered some of her fiery spirit.

'I hope Sergio suffers,' she snarled as they descended, but she grew quiet again when they entered the hall itself and found what was waiting for them.

The battle was over. The last few of Sergio's guards had surrendered, and were being made to pile the bodies of the slain along one side of the hall. The floor was littered with the broken barricades, splintered statues and ripped tapestries, and the blood of the fallen.

Despite the victory, every expression Jordine saw was grim, and as he made his way to the royal dais, he understood why.

Crucio was kneeling, bent over two lifeless bodies. Frederick and Cliff were standing over him, their expressions close to despair.

Jordine realized the bodies were Vittorio and Sergio. Crucio looked up, Sergio cradled in his arms, eyes red and face streaked with tears.

'It is over,' he said in a voice that trembled with horror. 'It is all over! My sons, my heirs… Oh Elion forgive me, they are dead! They are all dead!'

PART THREE

TWENTY-EIGHT

'You called for me, sire?' Cliff asked.

Crucio looked up slowly from the plate he had been picking at and stared at his marshal, as though unsure about whether he had, in fact, summoned him. Then realization dawned and he grunted, sliding a letter across the table towards Cliff.

Three months had passed since Crucio had reclaimed the throne, three months since the tragic, joint deaths of Sergio and Vittorio. In that time, Crucio had slipped into a deep, dark melancholy, one which Cliff had repeatedly tried, and failed, to drag him from. The coronation had been held in private, with the court not permitted to witness what ordinarily would have been a ceremony redolent with grandeur and tradition. That had set the tone for Crucio's second period of rulership.

Cliff had worked to secure Crucio's reign without any directives from his monarch. He had taken the supplications of a parade of different nobles, and when some of those loyal to Sergio had refused to answer the summons to the capital, he had marched the Serendian host to secure their allegiance by force.

Eindhovein had resisted a two-week siege, seemingly in the hope there would be a wider rebellion against Crucio's return, but it had failed to materialize. Cliff had been forced to have the instigator of the resistance, the son of Sir Ajacci – who had died during the capture of Heidel – beheaded after he would not accept the royal proclamation announcing Crucio's return to the throne.

It was a grim and brutal business. Once it was done, Cliff was able to return to Heidel and reassure Crucio that Serendia was once more his. The citizens, high and low, tired of the tumult, were just concerned with surviving the winter months.

The king hardly seemed to care. He barely ate or slept, and since Frederick had returned to the Western Marches last month to assume overall command there, there had been only two individuals who seemed able to rouse him to any kind of action – Roxanne and Jarette.

The former was sitting beside Crucio at the long dining table. She had been welcomed by the king, whose paternal instincts seemed to have fixed upon her and Jarette as the last remnants of his household. Roxanne was rarely absent from his side and treated him like some aging grandparent, an act that Cliff suspected only increased Crucio's dependence on her. He had considered warning him not to dote on her too much, but knew he had to choose the right moment. It seemed clear that making an enemy of Roxanne would be unwise.

He picked up the letter Crucio had proffered and read it. Initial relief that something seemed to have piqued the king's interest was replaced with a familiar sense of concern – the letter had come from Calpheon.

King Seric was demanding an audience with Crucio, the third in as many months. He wished for a full investigation into the circumstances behind the death of his younger sister, Lady Elysia.

'King Seric's grief is understandable,' Cliff said slowly, rereading the missive. 'But he must accept that there was nothing we could do. She took her own life. It was tragic, but we have suffered tragedies of our own. Who has not, in these hard times?'

'Dear Roxanne has recommended we ignore this latest communication.' Crucio spoke up, his voice frail. Cliff glanced at Roxanne, but her expression was unreadable.

'That might be unwise,' Cliff said, looking back at Crucio. 'Seric is not the kind of king who will accept being ignored. And we must not forget the Calpheonian devotion to Elion. Remember the first chapter of the holy scripture – Elion taught that heretics should be warned three times of their transgressions. This is the third letter we have received from Seric.'

'You claim there is nothing we can do, yet you would still respond to the Calpheonian claims?' Roxanne spoke up.

'There is a middle ground,' Cliff said. 'My advice would

be to do as we are continuing to do, and express our sorrow at Elysia's death. We cannot be held responsible for events that occurred during Sergio's reign.'

'Placation will only cause Seric's attitude to sour further,' Roxanne said. 'I am told the Xian merchants trading winter wares in Heidel's marketplace have been paid by Calpheonian agents to ask questions about the circumstances of Elysia's death. They are seeking evidence that her fate was not self-inflicted.'

'If Seric wishes to accuse my family of cold-blooded murder, he can do it to my face,' Crucio growled, displaying a little of his old fire. 'And if he does make such an accusation, it will be his last!'

'My liege, we cannot afford a war with Calpheon,' Cliff said, trying to find a way of navigating Crucio's emotions and Roxanne's meddling. 'The Serendian host has been damaged by the late conflict, and our winter supplies are almost gone. We will not see the spring without severe food shortages. I cannot in all good conscience say we could muster the host again this season without risking mutiny.'

In the past he might have expected Crucio to rage at such insubordination, but now he simply slumped back in his chair, exhausted. It was Roxanne who spoke up.

'I am not suggesting we march on Calpheon this instant, Constable Cliff. Only that we consider our preparations should Seric continue to demand an investigation. Marshal Ducas now commands the Western Marches, does he not?'

'He does,' Cliff confirmed, not liking where Roxanne was going with her train of thought.

'If Calpheon chooses to invade, then it will fall on him, and the garrisons there, to stop them, at least until we can muster our strength,' she said.

'Frederick is aware of what is happening across the borderlands,' Cliff said. 'But I will not order him to make any pre-emptive preparations. Doing so could well end up enticing Calpheon into the very conflict we hope to avoid. I ask again, sire – write to Seric, one last time. Express your continued, genuine grief at Lady Elysia's death. Remind him how much you too have lost in recent months. And ask that we move forward, in the spirit of friendship that once endured between our two kingdoms.'

Crucio was silent, gazing down at the letter resting in front of Cliff, his eyes seeming not to see it. Then, abruptly, he nodded.

'One more time,' he said. 'I will write one more time, and after that, I will consider the matter closed. Elysia's death was a tragedy, but it was one amongst many. We can only afford to dwell on it for so long.'

'Another ale,' Jordine said loudly, slamming a fistful of coins down on the bar. 'Actually, make it three!'

The barmaid failed to match his drunken enthusiasm, simply collecting the coins and heading for the keg. Jordine propped himself up against the bar, gazing a little blearily around the establishment, as though searching for anyone who might challenge his boisterousness. The few patrons present that evening knew better than to look up from their own drinks.

'This place has gone to the dogs,' Jordine grumbled as he took the ales back to where he, Alfonso and Jarette were sitting in the corner. Neither of them responded.

Neither of them had been the same since the fall of Heidel, Jordine thought morosely. But then, they weren't the only ones. Little of the town had escaped the carnage unleashed that night. While the citadel was still being secured, the host of the Western Marches had sacked the town, looting and pillaging. Few of the lords of the Marches had any affection for the capital, and their men even less so. To make matters worse, the fire initially set in Bobby Lauren's warehouse had spread, immolating nearly half of the lower town before burning itself out. Come morning, Heidel had been a scene of desolation, doors broken, windows smashed, the contents of looted households littering the streets along with drunken soldiers, a pall of ash falling as the blackened timbers in the south of the town continued to smolder.

Jordine had felt a powerful sense of grief when he witnessed the final outcome of the town's storming. Mikos had been badly injured warding rampaging men-at-arms away from the Rhundi household on Gallows Street, and many of the neighbors had been even less fortunate. The Lilly Valley had been ransacked, while the Golden Frog had burned down entirely – Bobby Lauren apparently intended to rebuild, but work had not yet started. The town

Jordine had loved so much had been wrecked, and there was a strong argument to be made that it was all his fault.

That was hard for him to accept. He had tried to convince himself that Heidel would have suffered even more acutely if the siege had dragged on into weeks and months. Looking at his friends and the places he had known, such thoughts were cold comfort.

'You'd think they could at least get some new furniture in,' he said, tracing the line of a sword stroke across the top of the table they were sat at. The Lilly Valley still bore the scars of the incursion, with half-mended furniture and broken windows covered by blankets to try to keep out the winter chill.

'You can hardly blame them,' Alfonso spoke up. 'It isn't as though business has been booming since the place was sacked.'

'Well, it should be,' Jordine said. 'They no longer need to worry about the king shutting them down for fomenting dissent!'

'It doesn't change what happened that night, Joe,' Alfonso went on. 'It was our fault. We were the ones who opened the gates.'

'And so we should be treated like heroes,' Jordine snapped. 'You didn't show any hesitation at the time, Al. If it wasn't for us, Heidel would still be under siege! People would be starving and suffering through the winter. Instead, the kingdom is at peace, and free from Sergio's misrule.'

Alfonso said nothing, in no mood for another drunken argument with his friend. Jordine looked at Jarette, expecting her to fall on one side or another as she would once have done, but she remained quiet, staring down into her ale.

That night had changed them, and Jordine knew he could only deny it for so long. Neither he nor Alfonso had ever killed a man before, and neither had imagined that when they did it would be in combat against their fellow Serendians. It seemed like a cruel joke – in the chaos of the fighting at the gatehouse, Jordine didn't even know how many he had killed or wounded.

Jarette had struggled as well – the first time the trio had reconvened in the Lilly Valley, trying and failing to recapture what they had in days gone by, she had broken down in tears, recounting the terror of her chambers being broken into, and how she hadn't even really meant to stab her attacker, that it had just happened in a blind flash of rage and fear. Jordine hadn't known how to comfort her.

Alfonso had tried to reassure her, but she had turned cold and quiet, the fire that had once fueled her quick wit and sharp tongue now burned out.

'How does your father fare?' Jordine asked Alfonso, deciding it was best to try to change the subject.

'You would know if you didn't spend all your time at the citadel,' Alfonso said tersely; then, seeming to regret his tone, he shrugged. 'He is no longer bedridden. He does not suffer as he did. But I fear he will never be himself again.'

Jordine considered that was true of all of them.

'I have been considering leaving,' he admitted. He hadn't found the right time to tell the others yet, but now seemed as good as any, his courage stiffened by the ale. They both looked at him in confusion.

'Leaving Heidel,' he clarified. 'And going west, to join my father.'

Being reunited with Frederick felt like the only good thing that had come out of the siege. Yet despite the Ducases' return to favor, Fredrick had spent barely a week with Jordine in the capital. He had been granted the title of marshal and warden of the Western Marches, but now that Cliff had overall command of the Serendian host, an experienced knight was needed to command Serendia's western border. Frederick had accepted the role, and had returned with much of the garrison of the Western Marches, taking post in the Watchtower.

Jordine had considered going with him, but Frederick had urged him to stay, perhaps thinking that was what Jordine still desired. He had instructed him to search out a townhouse fit to act as their new home in Heidel, and to help secure his position at court. It was just a few months until he was old enough to receive a knighthood and become Frederick's formal heir and inheritor, and in that time it was expected that he would take on more and more family duties.

Yet Jordine wanted little of it. Frederick's latest letter from the Marches, received just a few days ago, had spoken of growing unrest in the border region, with rumors of Calpheon agitating over the death of Lady Elysia. He also reported that Martha, who Jordine had not seen for over two years, had fallen ill. Jordine had already written requesting he be allowed to visit. All being well, he intended to make the move permanent.

'I should have gone with my family when they were first banished,' he went on. 'I have avoided my station for too long. It is time I took up the Ducas name once more, and the duties that go with it.'

'And what of the name Rhundi?' Alfonso asked pointedly.

'I have given enough to that name already,' Jordine said. 'I cannot heal your father, Al.'

'I'd go too, if I could,' Jarette spoke up. 'It feels like everything in my life is… in ruins. I just want to rebuild somewhere else.'

'We should be building together,' Alfonso said. Jordine looked at Jarette, but she just drank her ale, not replying.

That evening, Jordine returned to the place where he spent most of his nights – Roxanne's bedchamber in the citadel. She was not present when he arrived, but Carolin permitted him inside, and she returned soon after.

'You look beautiful tonight,' he said on seeing her.

'And you look drunk,' Roxanne replied, but she kissed him anyway. They slipped into each other's embrace, and when they were finished making love, Jordine told her what he had already told his friends.

'I'm going to the Marches,' he said. 'To join my father.'

She had been lying facing away from him, but rolled over to look him in the eye.

'You're sure?' she asked.

'Yes. It's time I accepted my place, as a Ducas.'

'And you cannot do that here, in the capital?'

'My mother is ill.'

'If you want, I can convince Crucio to send one of the royal physicians to her.'

'Why is it you wish me to stay?' Jordine demanded. She looked away, seemingly annoyed by the question.

'I enjoy your company,' she said.

Jordine snorted.

'I'm sure there are any number of gentlemen in the capital whose company you might enjoy.'

'Do not mock me,' Roxanne said dangerously. 'I am… fond of you.'

'Is that all?'

'Do not ask me to bare even more of myself to you, Joe. Not yet.'

'So what would you have me do? Warm your bed until you decide whether you want the same as me?'

'And what is it you want, Jordine?'

Now it was his turn to falter, frustration warring with embarrassment. He looked up at the canopy of the four-poster bed, and eventually found the right words.

'I feel a connection with you, Roxanne, and I believe you feel it too. Both of us are experienced enough to know this is more than a passing fancy. More than the "fondness" you just admitted to.'

She put a hand on his cheek, turning his head on the pillow so they were once more gazing into each other's eyes.

'Don't go,' she said. 'I do not want to be parted from you, it would be as great a pain as ever I have suffered. Yet I can make no promises. I still do not know where I stand in this new era Serendia has been plunged into. After all that has happened, I do not know if I can trust myself to simply love you, and hope for a better future.'

Jordine kissed her, and gripped her hand in his.

'Then I will stay,' he said. 'For a little while longer, at least. Destiny may ultimately force us apart, but for the next few weeks, I am yours, and you are mine. Perhaps that is all we need.'

The next day, once Jordine had departed, Roxanne dismissed Carolin and her other handmaidens from her chambers. She stood for some time gazing from the window, her outward calm giving no hint to the turmoil she was suffering within.

There was no falsehood in the words she and Jordine had exchanged the night before. Inconceivable though it might once have seemed, she could no longer ignore the stirrings of her heart, the unfamiliar emotions that the young lion of Serendia was drawing forth.

Contentment, security, even hope for the future – until Jordine, those had all been dangerous liabilities. Yet now she had tasted the possibility of a life where those things were the norm, and it had been sweet.

She had to be strong. She could not afford to falter now, this close to the end, when the goals she had worked so tirelessly towards were almost within reach. She needed to stoke the fire within, so that the flames burned hot once again.

She moved across to Mnemosyne's cage, unhooded the falcon, and whispered the words of command.

The chamber melted away, and a new reality asserted itself. Roxanne soared on wings that were not her own, circling through smoke and ash. Below her a fire blazed, devouring a farmstead, the heat so fierce she could feel it even at such a great height.

The roar of the flames carried on the wind, along with screaming, the terrible, piercing sounds of pain and despair.

Roxanne felt her eyes sting, not with the memory of ash, but with her own tears. Her personal recollections of that night came back to her, roaring like a fire that had just been fed by a gust of air. They were less clear than those of Mnemosyne, fragmented, yet even more potent.

The searing heat. Her mother's grip on her as she carried her downstairs. The screams of her father and brothers. The dark figures that had surrounded the farmstead, the firelight glinting from plate armor and chain mail and lowered visors. The man who had dragged her from the inferno, beating her smoldering dress so it did not catch light.

The face of Crucio Domongatt, younger then, cold indifference turning to remorse as he looked down on the little girl his soldiers had nearly burned alive, and heard the screams of her less fortunate family.

Roxanne hissed another arcane phrase of command, barely able to speak the words.

She was back in her chamber in Heidel's citadel, shaking, tears flowing freely. For a heartbeat she swore she could still smell ash and burning timbers and the unmistakable, sickly stench of seared human flesh and hair.

Now was not time for regrets, or remorse. Now was not a time to forget where she had come from. She had to act, or those memories would lose all meaning. It would all have been for nothing.

Wiping her eyes, she retrieved a sheaf of parchment, a quill and an ink pot, sat at the desk across from her bed, and began to write.

TWENTY-NINE

'Without evidence, the people will not support it,' High Marshal Velqez said, his voice cold and firm in the echoing space of the council chamber of the royal citadel of Calpheon.

'Damn the people,' King Seric snarled, banging a fist on the table between them and causing the little pieces atop the maps spread out across it to leap and topple, and several of his advisors and commanders to flinch.

'The Calpheon host is with you always, my liege,' Velqez said, attempting to ameliorate his previous words. 'But the war with Valencia has thinned the ranks and drained the coffers. If we wish to persecute a new conflict against Serendia, we will need the public's spirit behind us. They are weary of war, and the harvest has been poor. The revelation that the Serendians have murdered your beloved sister would likely cause enough furor to warrant an invasion, but without tangible proof of their duplicity it will be hard to win universal support. We need recruits, donations and supplies before we can make any move come springtide. And for that we need evidence.'

'What am I paying those damned Xian merchants for anyway?' Seric snapped, looking around his advisors. None met his gaze. The only one who could have adequately answered that particular question was Murillos, the king's chief spymaster, and he had not yet arrived at the session.

'The Church can provide funds, as well as the spiritual guidance that enervates the people,' Leona declared. The red-robed priestess was present as a representative of Lehard Motenon, the High Priest of Elion. The Church, always closely intertwined with the rulers of Calpheon, had been agitating for the annexation of at least the western regions of Serendia, ever since the presence of mines extracting the fabled Black Stones had become common knowledge.

The Church was as greedy for it as Seric, but the commoners would not be moved by abstract notions of arcane stones, nor the prospect of filling the royal treasury. Would the preaching of Elion priests, rousing them to righteous war, be enough?

'My learned colleagues among the priesthood in Serendia shall aid us,' Leona went on. 'They will demand that there be no resistance to your host. The people will be left without any doubts – Calpheon's cause is just. The blood of Lady Elysia calls out to glorious Elion for vengeance, and he will answer her by placing his fiery sword in your hand. Your Majesty will become a tool of divine retribution!'

Seric did not much fancy being anyone's tool, even a divine one, but he had to concede the priestess had a good turn of phrase. Just as he was wondering whether the backing of the Church would be sufficient to move ahead, the doors to the council chamber were thrown open.

Murillos had arrived. At a glance, the man wasn't much to look at – short, middle-aged, with a plain face and a simple mode of dressing. He looked out of place among the armored warriors and well-dressed nobles attending the council, like a yeoman farmer or merchant of middling wealth, called before his king. Yet besides Seric, he was the most powerful man in the chamber.

His expression was unreadable as he joined the gathering around the table and offered a short bow.

'You are late,' Seric said tersely. The spymaster proffered a letter, speaking as he did so.

'My most fulsome apologies, Your Highness. I was detained on a matter of the greatest urgency, one that pertains to this council. I have spent the morning verifying what you currently hold – the proof we have been seeking these past months.'

Seric snatched the letter, read it, then reread it. A smile spread slowly across his face. He looked up at High Marshal Velqez and his military subordinates.

'You said we needed evidence before we could count on the support of the people,' he said, raising the letter. 'Well, now we have it. Send out the call to arms. The Calpheonian host musters for war.'

'It must be war,' Alfonso said, looking with concern at Jordine. 'Even if Calpheon doesn't intend to act upon these accusations by marching against us, Crucio cannot permit such claims.'

Jordine would have agreed, but they both knew the truth behind them. He and Alfonso were standing in Heidel's market square, among a growing crowd of people gathering around a Treant timber and furniture merchant from Calpheon called Lylina. She had been giving an account – undoubtedly not for the first time that morning – of the momentous news from Calpheon.

According to Lylina, King Seric had received a letter from an anonymous member of the Serendian court, claiming that the late King Sergio had murdered Queen Elysia, and that King Crucio was actively covering up his dead son's crime. What was worse, the story being regaled wasn't the usual gossip-mongering that pervaded market stalls the length and breadth of the continent. It had come from a royal proclamation read by the herald Rubin, an open letter that Seric had apparently addressed to Crucio, calling out the unavenged murder of his sister and the duplicity of the Domongatt household.

The news stirred Jordine's anger. Seric's proclamation had refused to name the member of Serendia's court who had made such damning claims, but it could only be Roxanne. She was the only one who knew the truth of what Sergio had done, besides Edward and Alfonso.

'If the Calpheonian host marches, your father will be in the first line of defense,' Alfonso pointed out, having to speak over the noise of the crowd as they demanded more information from the timber merchant.

'I'm going to the citadel,' Jordine replied, pulling away.

'Why?' Alfonso asked, but he didn't respond. He didn't trust himself to say anything else, not until he had seen Roxanne.

The guards stopped him at the gates.

'I am here to see Lady Roxanne Domongatt,' he said, trying not to let his anger show. He had been permitted to pass by the guards without question for the past few months, on his frequent visits to Roxanne. This time, however, the one barring his way showed no sign of moving.

'You have been forbidden from entering the citadel,' he said, gazing at Jordine stoically.

'By whom?' Jordine snapped.

'By Lady Roxanne Domongatt.'

'What? Why?'

'I do not know, and if I did, it would not be my place to say.'

Jordine had to fight down the urge to draw his sword and hack his way into the keep.

This was all Roxanne's work, it had to be. She had sent word to the Calpheonians of Sergio's wicked deeds, it could have been no one else. Now, she was making sure he wouldn't have the chance to confront her.

He turned away from the guard, placing a hand against the gatehouse wall, mastering himself. He could not lose his temper, not now. Drawing his sword, or making wild accusations – both would see him either cut down or imprisoned.

He had to find another way to face Roxanne.

Over the next week, the rumors bred and multiplied. Supposedly the Calpheonian host was on the march. Some claimed they had crossed the western border and were besieging the Watchtower, others that it had already fallen and the foe were on their way to Heidel itself. It was said that Crucio had challenged Seric to resolve the dispute in personal combat, though others accused the king of doing nothing, of sitting idle in the citadel while the kingdom was invaded. A few even dared say Crucio had lost his wits, or that he was actually the one behind the murder of Queen Elysia.

Panic and turmoil threatened to engulf the realm, and Jordine felt dragged along with it, paralyzed by indecision, dragged under by doubt and disbelief. Every day he went to the citadel, and every day he was turned away. He felt powerless, used, and it infuriated him. He had hoped Jarette might be able to intercede, but apparently Cliff had advised that the royal family remain within the citadel, for their own safety, a fact that only made Roxanne even more impossible to reach.

He wondered whether any would guess that she was behind the letter to Seric. Speculation on the identity of the traitor within the court was rife, but Jordine rarely heard

Roxanne's name mentioned. It only added to his frustration, and the only person he could share it with was Alfonso.

The Rhundi heir seemed less surprised by what Roxanne had done, but then he had never tried to hide how he scorned Jordine's relationship with her. Again and again, Jordine asked himself what she stood to gain by instigating war between Calpheon and Serendia. What further lies had he failed to uncover, and was he really so great a fool that he had been misled by her yet again?

He wanted to believe she was innocent, and at times even found himself defending her to Alfonso. Could someone else have gotten word of Sergio's crime and informed the Calpheonians? Edward knew, after all, but he had not left the townhouse since the night of Elysia's death, and had scarcely seen anyone other than Mikos and the chirurgeon. Could he have confessed Sergio's order to kill Elysia to one of them?

Alfonso reacted to such thoughts with justifiable anger, only widening the rift between them. In truth, Jordine knew it was this trusting nature Roxanne had exploited in him, again and again. He had been wrong to accept all that she had told him, to believe her innocent despite the clear hand she had in Elysia's death. Now the whole kingdom was set to pay the price.

Alfonso urged him to speak out, but he knew the most likely outcome was that he would be seized for sedition. Even if he successfully argued his case, it would take too long to unpick the web of lies Roxanne had surrounded herself with. By then, King Seric could be at the gates.

A week after the first rumors had reached the capital, Cliff marched west with what portion of the Serendian host he had been able to muster at such short notice. The same day, a letter arrived for Jordine from his father. It seemed as if at least some of the rumors were true – a powerful Calpheonian host had mustered at the border and now appeared poised to strike. Frederick was marshaling what defenses he could at the Watchtower, with the expectation that Cliff's reinforcements would arrive soon.

The letter closed by stating that Martha's sickness had won out – she had passed away the night before Frederick had sent the letter. Jordine sat, reading and rereading the words over and over in disbelief. For a while, all emotion left him. There was only a cold and bitter void in which he could discern no feelings, not even a sense of self.

Then, it all came rushing back, and he wept.

It took time before he was able to compose himself and seek out Alfonso, meeting him on the landing outside Edward's bedchamber. He could tell immediately from his friend's expression that something terrible had happened.

'My mother is dead,' he told him. 'There is nothing more I can do in Heidel. I am going west, to join my father. I'm going to fight.'

'As am I,' Alfonso said, his words catching Jordine off guard.

'What about Edward?' he asked.

Alfonso glanced towards the bedchamber at his back, clearly struggling to keep his own emotions in check.

'He has said nothing this past week, since word of the

invasion spread. I fear he is broken beyond any repair. There is… it feels as though there is nothing more I can do, and I cannot bear to sit here and waste away with him. And with you gone… Will you permit me to accompany you, as both your friend and your brother-in-arms?'

Jordine embraced Alfonso fiercely, without thinking.

'Of course,' he said, clapping his hand against his back as he held him. 'Of course you can, my brother. We'll ride west together, into the fire. I should have gone weeks ago.'

'Hopefully, we can make the muster point before the Calpheonians cross the border,' Alfonso said.

'I hope so, if we hasten,' Jordine said, the prospect of finally taking some sort of action restoring a fragment of his spirit. 'Ducas and Rhundi – we'll show everyone else in this kingdom the worth of those names, and teach the Calpheonians to fear them. Together to the end, just as it should be.'

THIRTY

Jordine and Alfonso rode west.

Every inn they stayed at had different rumors about what lay ahead, though most agreed that the Calpheonians had crossed the border, and that a great battle was either about to be waged, or had just ended.

Jordine found little time to rest along the journey, riven with the need to reach his father. He should have joined him weeks ago. He had allowed Roxanne to seduce him, and now his mother had died without her only son at her side. He had to force himself not to ponder it, for every time he did a white-hot rage gripped him, one that he had nowhere to vent.

Gods willing, that would change soon. They passed into the Western Marches, where they donned the armor and weapons they had brought.

The first clear signs of conflict emerged not long before they laid eyes on the Watchtower. Plumes of dark smoke were visible on the horizon. Jordine feared it might be the tower itself, but when they crested the last rise to its east, they found that it still stood, the smoke coming from beyond it, farther west.

'The border hamlets have been torched,' Alfonso suggested. Jordine feared it was more than just that.

He spurred Greybolt ahead, skirting to the south of the Watchtower, close to where the banks of the Demi curved beneath the promontory the great defensive work was sited atop. As he cleared the slope, he was filled with dread.

The hosts of Serendia and Calpheon had indeed already met in battle, seemingly just hours before. The bridge that had once crossed the River Demi was choked with the dead and was now partially collapsed, timber struts split. Bodies and wreckage still floated downriver, and more were heaped densely around the eastern entrance to the broken structure.

The host of Serendia, arrayed under green-and-white standards and the heraldry of the commanding nobles, remained on the near embankments and the slopes below the Watchtower. The Calpheonian host stood on the opposite side of the river, vanguard, rearguard and main battle still in formation beneath standards of red, black, white and gold. It seemed as though they had attempted to storm the river crossing and press on to take the Watchtower, but had been repelled upon the bridge.

That, at least, was good news. Jordine searched for the banner of the golden lion among the standards and pennants fluttering above the Serendian ranks on the slope above him. He could find no sign of it though, until he turned back towards the river, and his heart sank.

There he found his father's men-at-arms, or what remained of them. They and several other retinues had clearly been tasked with meeting the brunt of the Calpheonian assault, and had held them at the bridge before its partial collapse. The dead were still being collected, men tending to and carrying off the wounded and separating the corpses of slain comrades from the enemy.

Jordine rode up to them. Several of the men-at-arms recognized him, or at least noted that he bore the same livery.

'Forgive us, sire,' one said, removing his battered sallet helm, his face and armor streaked with mud and blood. 'We were sent to hold the line, and your father was in the thick of the fray. He would not take a backward step.'

Jordine said nothing to the man, but dismounted and threw him the reins before running to where the bodies of the Serendian dead were being laid out in a row, close to the banks of the Demi.

At their center, set upon the lion standard, lay Frederick Ducas. His helm had been removed and placed beside him. Jordine would almost have thought he was simply in a deep sleep, were it not for the bloody rent in his side, the hacking work of a heavy polearm blade.

Jordine felt sick. He knelt beside his father's body, clutching one gauntleted hand in his. He found he could not look upon his face.

He was too late. He had been offered a second chance when he had been reunited with Frederick in Heidel. He should have followed him back to the Western Marches immediately, or at least have left far quicker than he had. Instead, he had squandered it, and now he would never speak with either his mother or his father ever again, would never atone for how he had deserted them, nor make them proud with his future endeavors. The life he had always simply assumed awaited him in the years to come was now gone, broken irreparably.

Self-loathing gripped him, and he angrily wiped away his tears, rising and speaking to the man-at-arms who had first addressed him.

'You were ordered to hold the bridge, and placed in the vanguard?' he said.

'Yes, sire,' the man replied, nodding gravely.

'Who commanded that?'

'The lord of the host, sire. Marshal Cliff.'

Jordine looked back up towards the Watchtower, and the ranks arrayed beneath it. At their center flew the stag banner, Cliff's crest.

He took his reins back and mounted Greybolt, before spurring her up the slope.

'Jordine, wait,' Alfonso called. He had been hanging back but now hurried to catch up.

Jordine ignored him. The anger and disappointment had grown too hot – it needed release. He needed to find somewhere else to lay the blame that was crushing him.

He rode to where Cliff's retinue held the center of the

line, dismounted, and strode to where he could see the marshal overlooking the river and its splintered bridge.

He failed to reach him. Half a dozen armored warriors intercepted him, and one – who Jordine recognized as Captain Armstrong – laid a gauntlet on him, armor clattering as he physically barred his way.

'No further, lad,' the scarred veteran growled. 'State your purpose for approaching the marshal.'

'I'd have him answer for the death of my father,' Jordine spat, hardly able to speak the words.

'Let him go, Armstrong,' Cliff spoke up. The captain did so after some hesitation, and Jordine was permitted to confront the marshal of Serendia directly.

'Did you leave him to hold the bridge unsupported?' Jordine demanded. Cliff, to his credit, met his gaze, his tone unwavering.

'Frederick had command of the van, which is an honor. It fell to him to hold the bridge, yes. He died turning back the invaders.'

'Why were you not at his side?' Jordine said. 'How many campaigns did he follow you on over the years, only to be left unaided?'

'I could not commit the main battle to the bridge, not when the plan was to draw over Seric's vanguard and destroy it in detail. You knew your father as well as I – do you think he would have hesitated for one moment to lead from the fore? Because of his sacrifice, we have won a victory here today, in the first battle of this war. Perhaps we have checked the Calpheonians permanently.'

Jordine bowed his head in anger, unable to deny the marshal's claim. Frederick would have known the risk of remaining unsupported while drawing a portion of the enemy host across the Demi. It was not the tactics at fault – it was Jordine's failure in not arriving in time. Perhaps, if he had been at his father's side, he would not have fallen.

Such a thought was almost more than he could endure, but to his surprise Cliff clapped a gauntlet against his pauldron.

'I didn't kill your father, Jordine,' the marshal said. 'But I can offer you the chance to avenge him. You came here to take a stand against those who would invade our realm? Then take command of your father's retinue, and I will find you a place in the host. The vanguard, if you wish it. Join us, and be avenged on the dogs of Calpheon, who slew Frederick Ducas, and would have every man, woman and child in this land subjugated under the tyranny of Guy Seric.'

Jordine considered the offer. He had intended to join his father and fight, but now that hope was gone. He could return to Heidel and lose himself in drunken misery, but he knew that if he slipped into that particular foul swamp, he would never emerge.

'My father is to be returned home, borne by men who stood by him in his last moments, from his retinue,' he said, fixing his mind on what must come next, on what might yet be salvaged. 'My mother too, if she is not yet interred. They will be buried together in the family crypt, in Heidel.'

'I will see it ordered before darkness falls,' Cliff said.

'And if I am to join you, then my friend, Alfonso Rhundi, will fight at my side,' Jordine went on, indicating where Alfonso was hanging back, watching the confrontation with concern. 'You shall have both of us, or neither.'

'I would never turn down any son of Serendia brave enough to make a stand in defense of his home,' Cliff said. 'Both it is.'

'Then we are yours, Marshal,' Jordine said. 'Until every last orc-loving, bastard son of Calpheon has been driven from Serendian soil.'

THIRTY-ONE

The host of Calpheon was arraying itself for battle, and they were now on the near side of the river.

Five days had passed since Jordine and Alfonso had joined the Serendian host, five days since the first invasion thrust towards the Watchtower had been checked at the Demi. And for most of those, the enemy had remained encamped on the far bank, unable to make a second attempt at crossing since the bridge's partial collapse, yet also unwilling to withdraw.

Until that morning, when the Serendian host had awoken to discover the enemy gone. They had left campfires burning and tents up through the night to convince the pickets keeping watch along the riverbank that they were still in place, yet it became clear once dawn began bleeding light and color back into the world that the encampment was deserted.

Which could spell disaster for Serendia. Cliff had

immediately ordered the host north, to where he predicted the Calpheonians had marched in the dead of night, a ford over the Demi known as Red Crossing, named for the crimson flowers – called 'witch's tears' by the peasantry – that grew thick on the banks on either side of the river. Sure enough, the Calpheonians were there, and worse, the vanguard of their army was already partially on the eastern side of the river.

'We need to attack now, while they're still crossing,' Jordine said urgently to Umberto, the commander of the vanguard. They were at the forefront of the Serendian host, with the other two battles that made up the main body of the force still behind them, marching along the herdsman's dirt track that led to the crossing.

'If we can get archers in range of the ford, we can stop them, or at least slow them down,' he went on.

Umberto pursed his lips, leaning forward in the saddle as he watched the Calpheonians from the small knoll they had stopped atop. At least two retinues were already across the river, mostly infantry and some light cavalry, forming on the near bank under two banners – one a trio of red crosses on a blue field, the other a green heart above crossed red swords on white. Even more concerning was the dark mass behind them – the main enemy host, thousands strong, waiting to cross over from the far side of the Demi. There were more in the process of forging through the waters, Calpheonian heavy cavalry who, if they reached the near bank, would pose a serious threat to the Serendians.

'My orders are not to engage if we find a sizeable force of the enemy already on our side,' Umberto said.

'That isn't a sizeable force,' Jordine said, trying not to let the urgency of the moment get the better of him. 'But it will be if we wait any longer. We have to stop the crossing. Our vanguard is four retinues strong, they only have two right now. If we attack, we'll outnumber them two-to-one. Wait and the odds will tip in their favor.'

'I've sent a rider back to the marshal seeking clarification,' Umberto responded.

'And it'll be another fifteen minutes before he returns,' Jordine pointed out, looking back along the track – the main battle, which Cliff was leading, was visible approaching in the distance, but it would still take time to reach the ford. The wet spring weather had turned the pathway to muck, slowing everything down.

'By the time we know for sure what Cliff's orders are, those heavy cavalry will be on our side of the river, and forming up,' he continued. 'They'll be able to sweep us away with a single charge if we aren't ready to meet them. We need to buy time!'

'Watch your tone, young Ducas,' Umberto growled. He was an old knight, experienced, but Jordine had found little respect for him in the days since joining the vanguard. Age had made him overcautious. Jordine understood prudence could be a virtue on the battlefield, but right now it seemed like madness. Every minute, more Calpheonians reached the near bank.

'The vanguard will be put into array around this rise,'

Umberto said, indicating the knoll they were on. 'That will give us the high ground should the Calpheonians push further. After that, we wait for the marshal's instructions.'

Jordine turned Greybolt away and rejoined Alfonso and his retinue without replying, seething with anger.

'Has he given the order to attack?' Alfonso asked, looking past Jordine at Umberto.

'If I told you what order he's given, I'd put you at risk of disobeying a superior,' Jordine said. 'So as far as you're concerned, I've just said yes, he's ordered us to attack.'

Alfonso looked briefly alarmed, but the retinue's two sergeants, Hildano and Eduoard, both grinned. Both were veteran warriors who had been members of the Ducas retinue for years, and had chosen to continue to serve Frederick during his exile. Their unspoken responses reassured Jordine that he was about to do the right thing.

'We attack,' he said. 'Our numbers won't be enough to close the crossing entirely, but if we can get the archers in range of the ford, that should at least slow them down. But those already on the near side will try and counterattack, so we have to hold them at bay.'

'I assume we're doing this without support?' Alfonso asked.

Jordine had considered seeking aid from the other two senior knights in the vanguard, Sir Riccaldo and Sir Tommaso, but knew there was not enough time to convince them that Umberto was making the wrong choice.

'At first, yes,' he told Alfonso. 'Hopefully, when they

understand just what is happening, we won't have to stand alone for long.'

And if that wasn't the case, and Umberto didn't ride to his aid, he'd meet the same fate as his father. That much was clear to them all, but there were no complaints.

'We go on foot, keep the formation close,' Jordine continued, issuing the instructions to Hildano and Edouardo. 'Men-at-arms in front, archers behind. Once we're in range of the ford, drive the stakes in and start to loose. We need to be fast. Any questions?'

There were none. He was relieved to see they all appeared to be with him, despite the desperation of the situation – he had never commanded men into battle before, and he suspected if he stopped to think about it, he might balk. To hesitate could only lead to defeat.

He strode out in front of the rest of his retinue, hefting his halberd and speaking as he did so.

'My father held these dogs at bay, and I'm damned if I'll let them cross over now! We won't let the invaders take another step deeper into Serendia! Not one!'

There wasn't time for more elaborate oration, and besides, the few words did what he had hoped they would. The men cheered.

'Follow me, for Serendia, and House Ducas,' Jordine shouted, and set off towards Red Crossing.

The Ducas retinue advanced beneath the standard of the golden lion.

They numbered just over three dozen warriors – a third of them men-at-arms, two thirds archers and arbalists. Most of them were veterans, and some, like their sergeants, had served House Ducas for years. None showed any hesitation as they moved with haste towards a force at least twice their number.

Jordine and Alfonso had dismounted, led the attack from the front and center of the small wedge of men-at-arms. Jordine's heart was racing as they reached the flat ground before the riverbank. As they got closer, the Calpheonian retinues now holding the near side looked larger and larger, and Jordine knew that wasn't only fear and anticipation playing tricks – he could see the first dozen heavy cavalrymen on the near side, knights in magnificent full plate armor with barded horses, the layers of steel flashing in the dreary spring sunlight, the tips of their lances glinting. They were the pride of the Calpheonian host, the finest cavalry in the western continent, and if a whole division was allowed to cross, it would smash through the Serendians while the main column was still caught on the track, trying to deploy.

Jordine quickened his pace. The grass was wet but not mucky like the path they had taken overlooking the ford, but it still felt laborious, and he felt as though he was moving so slowly.

He looked to the ford again. The sun had broken through a gap in the clouds and had bathed the main Calpheonian host, still on the far bank, in temporary brilliance – their numbers looked vast, pushing steadily into the ford beneath banners that became streaming bolts of multi-hued color in the sudden light.

The retinues directly ahead showed no sign of responding to the sudden advance. Jordine wondered if they were trying to work out what the single, small force of Serendians intended by moving so boldly away from their comrades, whether it could be a trap. At the moment, such confusion was their best weapon.

'Eduardo?' he called, casting a glance back at the commander of his archers, following directly behind the men-at-arms.

'Another fifty yards, Lord,' the sergeant urged. 'Not even the bolts will penetrate at this range!'

They kept going, now dangerously close to the Calpheon outriders screening their infantry, when finally Eduardo shouted at them all to halt. The archers set to work, thwacking the sharpened wooden stakes they carried into the ground, forming a small, bristling hedge that would hopefully deter at least the Calpheonian light cavalry from sweeping in on their flanks. Jordine found, as they did so, that they had halted just inside where the carpet of witch's tears began, the red flowers thick underfoot. He tried not to wonder what the bloody undergrowth might portend.

A horn rang out, and suddenly the Calpheonian retinues were on the move. The one with the three red crosses shifted in their direction, just as the first of the Ducas archers began to loose their arrows towards the river and those crossing it.

'Hold for now,' Jordine said, trying to gauge the effectiveness of the first salvo. The heavy cavalry were still on the move, their armor seemingly impervious to the initial flurry of arrows, which clattered and rattled harmlessly from them. Then the crossbow bolts started to hit – they were slower to load, but packed a greater punch, and Jordine witnessed the first horse throw its rider as it reared in pain after being struck, the man disappearing below the water.

'Keep it up,' he urged his archers. Then, a heartbeat later, Alfonso let out a warning cry.

The Calpheonians were replying. Jordine caught sight of a volley of arrows rising up from the retinues in front, and just had time to slap his helmet's visor down before they started to strike home. Suddenly, his world was reduced to a slit in the steel mask, his breath rasping loud in his ears.

Those men-at-arms in the retinue who possessed shields raised them, but most, like Jordine and Alfonso, had no choice but to endure the steel-tipped hail and trust in their own full plate armor. One of the projectiles struck off Jordine's right pauldron, and another skittered from his left vambrace, while more thumped into the tangle of flowers underfoot.

Thankfully, it seemed there were no enemy crossbowmen on the near side of the river yet, or they would all have been cut down in short order. But that was little comfort for the Ducas archers. They were far more lightly equipped than the men-at-arms, armored in gambesons or chain hauberks and sallet helms, and though they were behind the men-at-arms, shooting over or past them thanks to the angle of the river's ford, they soon started suffering. One fell clutching the arrow that had pierced his shoulder, dropping his bow and crying out in pain.

The crossbowmen were a little better protected – they carried pavises, large shields emblazoned with the Ducas lion, which they had planted in the ground, and were able to shelter behind as they laboriously reloaded their crossbows. Thumping sounds started to ring out as projectiles struck the timber boards, shivering where the white-fletched shafts embedded themselves.

Soon, the Calpheonian arrows had claimed another two archers, one struck through the eye, another pierced twice through the breast. Jordine knew that in just a few minutes more, they would be decimated.

'Sire,' called Sergeant Hildano, drawing his attention back towards the knoll. The rest of the vanguard were still there, showing no signs of advancing in support of the Ducas retinue, but a lone rider was braving the deluge of arrows, hunched low in the saddle. It was a messenger, and he reined in just behind where the men-at-arms were standing like men caught in a hailstorm.

'Lord Umberto commands that you retire,' he called down to Jordine, flinching as an arrow whipped past him.

'Tell my Lord Umberto that we will do no such thing,' Jordine replied, anger once more overcoming fear and doubt. 'Tell him I will stop that river crossing, or die trying. He can stay back and watch fellow Serendians die, or he can come and stand with us.'

The messenger wheeled away without protest, kicking his horse back towards the knoll, desperate to be out from under the steel rain.

'We have to go forward,' Jordine said to the men around him.

'You mean attack,' Alfonso clarified, his voice muffled by his visor.

'Yes. We attack them, they won't have the space they need to push farther out from the ford. We bottle them up.'

'And we'll all be dead in a matter of minutes,' Alfonso pointed out.

'Minutes that might save Serendia,' Jordine said. He knew what he was doing was beyond rash, but they were committed now, and he was in the grasp of battle-fury, the heady rush that left no room for any concern or hesitation.

'We're with you, Lord,' Hildano said, seeming to relish the prospect of such a lethal challenge. Jordine nodded.

'Keep your aim on the river,' he told Edouard, knowing the temptation was for the archers to turn their bows against their Calpheonian counterparts in the nearby retinues. 'We have to keep putting pressure on the crossing!'

Edouard acknowledged, and Jordine signaled to his men-at-arms to advance once again. Across the bloody flowers, and into the heart of the enemy.

King Seric was watching the river crossing from the roof of a poor farmstead on the slopes overlooking the Demi. Calpheonian scouts had already looted the place and driven out its occupants the night before, leaving no one to disturb the king and his entourage as they observed what, until moments before, had seemed like the maneuver that would win the war.

The Serendians had been wise to check the invasion at the Demi, and their successful resistance beneath the Watchtower had infuriated Seric. The river was high, cold and swift, in the grip of spring floods, and for days he had argued with his advisors and generals about what to do. There appeared to be no way across, at least until the spymaster, Murillos, had again brought Seric the news he wanted to hear.

There was an unguarded ford upriver. The Calpheonians had stolen a march on their foes, and now Seric was convinced they need only get the heavy cavalry division, comprised of his finest knights, across the river. The main Serendian host was visible in the distance on the far bank, still struggling to catch up and array itself on either side of its vanguard. They would not stop the pride of Calpheon.

Then Seric saw the enemy advance. What looked like just a single retinue, a small cluster of men, were abandoning the rest of the vanguard and moving against the lead Calpheonian forces already across the ford. It had seemed at first like nothing but sheer madness, but once the Serendians were in range of the ford their archers began to loose bolts and arrows on it. The salvos were not great, but they were enough to cause casualties, and injured horses disrupted the crossing, already made difficult by the high, quick-flowing waters.

'For the love of Elion,' Seric snarled, scarce believing what he was seeing. To make matters worse, he realized a portion of the Serendian retinue were now actually advancing. Their resistance against such numbers would surely not last, but as long as they stood and fought, they constrained the space the Calpheonian host had to deploy.

'Ride to Sir Hernandez and tell him not to just stand there like an idiot,' Seric snapped at one of his message riders, intending him to deliver the instructions to the commander of the Calpheonian vanguard already across the river. 'Tell him to push forward and wipe that damned little retinue out!'

Rather than send a messenger back to Umberto, Cliff rode forward from where he had been overseeing the main column, accompanied by Captain Armstrong and the mounted division of his retinue, two dozen of the most heavily armored knights and men-at-arms in the Serendian host.

He thundered up to Umberto, who was still astride his mount on the knoll, the other three retinues comprising the rest of the vanguard arrayed beneath him, idle.

'Sir Umberto, what—' Cliff began to exclaim as he reined in, then stopped, staring down towards the river, at the scene playing out at the ford below.

'By all the gods,' he murmured, as he watched one lone retinue, identified by the golden lion heraldry of House Ducas, driving alone into the midst of the Calpheonian host.

THIRTY-TWO

The fear came back to Jordine as he saw both Calpheonian retinues start advancing to meet him.

There was a track leading directly up from the ford, and over the years, the cattle driven along it had created a rut. It was shallow, but its banks, thick and red with witch's tears, offered a minor obstacle that could protect the retinue's flanks better than open ground.

He led his men onto the track, the last yards of space between him and the enemy rapidly closing. He could feel the pounding of his own heart, the dryness in his mouth. His body felt leaden, slow. He was going to die here. He wanted to stop, to turn back, but he made himself go on. Then Hildano shouted.

'For Serendia!'

Jordine echoed the cry, and the rest of his small band did likewise. It acted like a release. Suddenly there was no more time for fear. He remembered his father, lying dead on the banks of the river, and the fury of that memory drove him the last few yards.

The two sides clashed. Jordine picked his man, a Calpheonian in full plate at the forefront of their advance, his surcoat emblazoned with the triple crosses, bright red on their dark blue field. He was carrying a two-handed war hammer, and he swung as Jordine closed with him.

He brought his halberd up, and the long wooden hafts of the two weapons collided with a *crack*, stopping the hammer's four-pronged head from slamming home against Jordine's helm.

There wasn't any time for either of them to recover. The Ducas retinue had built better momentum than their opponents, and those behind Jordine carried him into the foe.

Armor crashed and clattered. Jordine was rammed up against his opponent, long weapons pinned between their two bodies, momentarily useless.

The Calpheonian headbutted him, helmet to helmet. The steel absorbed the worst of the blow, and Jordine heaved on his enemy with a roar, driven by pure rage. Someone behind gave way and sent the Calpheonian slipping in the track's muck, giving Jordine enough space to beat his halberd's haft on the man's breastplate and then his pauldrons, trying to further unbalance him and get him down in the mud, where he could deliver the killing blow.

The Calpheonian fought back, jabbing his own weapon's haft against Jordine's plackart, while one of his comrades behind rammed a billhook forward, the weapon's flared head clashing off Jordine's breastplate and almost snagging his gorget.

Jordine shortened his grip on the halberd and chopped down with it, trying to hack the axe-head through the Calpheonian's upper armor. He didn't have enough space to swing, but after a few short, ferocious blows the joint between right pauldron and gorget buckled, and blood jetted from the wound, painting the burnished steel red.

The Calpheonian gave way under him. Jordine doubted he was dead yet, but there was neither space nor time to finish him – he was still being driven forward, and had to trust that someone in the rear ranks would stoop to slip a dagger through a visor or under an armpit.

The man's fall had at least given him more space to swing properly. He splintered the haft of the next Calpheonian's billhook, then jabbed the halberd's spike at his face. The wicked length of steel punched through his mail coif, and Jordine felt it shatter teeth and crack bone.

For a little over a minute, the Ducas retinue drove like the tip of a lance into the heart of the invaders. The track's embankments meant the Calpheonians couldn't immediately lap around the smaller formation, and the Serendians could funnel between the raised earth, forcing their way into the enemy.

With his visor down it was almost impossible for Jordine to see anything to his left or right. He was vaguely aware of Alfonso on one side and Hildano on the other, both hacking and slashing with their own polearms, driven into the foe by those behind. Along with one other man-at-arms, they comprised the whole frontage of the Ducas formation, filling the cattle track.

Jordine brought down the man whose face he had gouged and felled a third with repeated strokes of the axe-head of his halberd, ignoring the counter-blows from a falchion that deflected from his armor – suddenly, the killing was easier. As was customary, the most heavily equipped men in the Calpheonian formation comprised the front ranks, while the men-at-arms in the rear of the formation were less well armed and armored. There was little they could do to stop the Serendians from pushing through.

For a wild moment, Jordine felt invincible. It seemed as though they could cut all the way to the river itself, routing the enemy entirely, winning the battle without the support of even the rest of the Serendian vanguard.

Then, reality reasserted itself, as the rest of the larger Calpheonian retinue they were engaged with came scrambling up and over the embankments on either side, trampling the red flowers and surging down on the flanks of Jordine's men.

'Circle!' Hildano bellowed, taking a step back from the melee. 'Form circle! Rally!'

They pressed together, a last-ditch attempt at holding back the rising tide. Alfonso was weathering a flurry of blows from a glaive-wielding Calpheonian, but Jordine forced the man back with a desperate swing of his halberd, giving his friend time to disengage.

He almost tripped over someone on their hands and knees, vomiting blood – he bore the Ducas surcoat, but Jordine didn't get a chance to see his face. He had to parry off another assailant, his back clashing against another of his men, who was now facing in the opposite direction, smashing a mace against the helm of a Calpheonian knight who was grappling with him.

There was nowhere to retreat to. Blows came from all sides. Jordine felt panicked, desperate as the swing of another falchion hacked deep into his halberd's haft, the heavy blade splintering it. He snapped it off and wielded the halberd's head like a battle-axe, frenziedly hacking it into his opponent. The man went down in a welter of blood – he didn't know if he had killed him, didn't know how many of his own men were still with him.

A sword rang like a bell-stroke from his helm, almost knocking it askew. He was vaguely aware of someone – Hildano, he thought – going down on his left, felled by the repeated blows of a Calpheonian mace.

He slammed a shoulder into the gambeson of the man in front of him, but found himself grappling, one of his attacker's arms locked around his midriff while the other clutched at a slender dagger and tried to ram it up under Jordine's arm and between his ribs. He desperately grabbed at the man's vambrace, straining to hold the knife at bay, while beating his broken halberd against the man's helm. When that failed to do anything, he planted the spike at the weapon's head against the man's visor slit and rammed it forward before he could turn his head aside.

The point punched through the Calpheonian's eye and into his skull. Jordine twisted the weapon, screaming with battle frenzy, feeling fierce exultation twinned with raw relief as the life-or-death grappling abruptly ceased.

But there was no reprieve. Another blow crashed against his helm, and he staggered and fell, momentarily blinded by his own twisted visor.

Rage was replaced by panic. He dropped his halberd and fumbled with his helmet, trapped in breathless darkness, expecting to feel the agony of a blade slipping between his armor plates, or the brutalizing blows of a polearm against his back.

He managed to rip the helmet off, panting, finding himself face-down in the mud. He struggled to rise amidst the thicket of legs around him, realizing one of his men-at-arms lay beside him. It was Sergeant Hildano. He too had lost his helmet, and a blow had pulverized half of his head. Blood was pouring down, turning the mud into a dark paste, fragments of skull showing white through the mess. He was on his hands and knees, looking as though he was trying to say something to Jordine, his movements sluggish, one eye lazy and unseeing. Instead of words, he vomited blood.

Jordine tried to get up. He had fought in tournament melees before, and had been trained in combat by Cliff, and one particular lesson had been hammered home by both experiences – the warrior who fell rarely lived for long.

He managed to get onto his haunches and drove himself up with a bellow, slamming back a Calpheonian who had been trying to force his way into the space he had vacated in the packed formation. Alfonso was still standing and fighting, and he managed to clear more room with haymaker swings of the mace he was now wielding.

It was hopeless. The Ducas retinue were being crushed in the Calpheonian vise. Surrender now offered the last, slender chance of survival. Jordine was damned if he would yield to the invaders, to the dogs who had slain his father.

He was about to vent his defiance at the surrounding foe when a crash rang through the air, and bodies slammed against him from his left. He struggled to stay upright, carried against Alfonso, who held firm.

Suddenly, the attention of the Calpheonians was no longer on them. A series of shapes came thundering in from the left – horsemen, mounted men-at-arms and knights. Lances splintered and cracked like shattering tree boughs, and the thunder of hooves, the clatter of armor, and the cries of men and horses filled Jordine's senses.

He stared in disbelief as the wedge of riders carved like a blade through the flank of the Calpheonian envelopment. He saw a standard above them, one he knew – the stag. Serendian cavalry, Marshal Cliff's own retinue no less.

Alfonso gripped him by the arm. Though his visor was still lowered, he could sense the unbridled joy in his voice.

'They came! By all the gods, Joe, the bastards actually came!'

Jordine looked back, and saw his best friend was right. It wasn't just Cliff's mounted retinue that had ridden to their rescue. The whole vanguard had come pouring down from the knoll after them, and the infantry were now moments from crashing into the Calpheonians on either side.

The enemy didn't stay to receive them. They were running, back towards the ford, where their heavy cavalry was now completely stalled, under a punishing hail of arrows and crossbow bolts being delivered by the reinforcements flooding to the aid of the Ducas retinue.

Jordine felt the emotions drain from him, leaving behind only a dull, disbelieving relief.

The battle of the witch's tears was over.

'Kneel,' Johann Cliff said.

Jordine and Alfonso exchanged a brief glance before obeying. Each went down on one knee in the mud.

They had returned, with the bloodied, battered remnants of the retinue, to the knoll overlooking the ford. The space below them was now packed with Serendian infantry, the host's main battle blocking the passage across the Demi. The Calpheonians stood on the opposite bank, just out of bowshot, their route deeper into the kingdom once more barred.

The two could scarcely believe they were still alive. Jordine was certain he had suffered minor injuries that he hadn't yet registered, but he seemed largely unharmed.

Few other members of the retinue could say the same. Half lay slain, laid out now on the slope behind, where Jordine had demanded they be carried as soon as the Calpheonian assault had been repulsed. Sergeant Hildano was dead, and almost everyone else was wounded to some degree or another. Yet they had survived, and not only that, they were victorious.

Cliff had led the vanguard into the fray just in time. The marshal hadn't tried to disguise his fury with Umberto for his indecisiveness, and had ordered Jordine up onto the knoll, where he and Alfonso now knelt.

'By the authority vested in me as high marshal of Serendia, and in the name of King Crucio Domongatt, I hereby knight thee, Sir Jordine Ducas,' Cliff declared before both his assembled retinue and what remained of Jordine's, tapping him on both shoulders with his unsheathed sword.

'Let this blow be the last you accept without reply,' he added, finishing the ceremonial rite by lightly striking Jordine on the face – he had removed his gauntlet, so it merely stung.

'I accept this honor, my lord,' Jordine said, looking up at Cliff, burning with a bittersweet surge of both pride and regret. 'But I wish it to be known that I do so on behalf of my father, slain defending these lands from the Calpheonian invader, and for his retinue that now serves me. Over a dozen good men lie dead beneath us. I led them to that death.'

'Such is the price of command,' Cliff said sternly. 'All who follow you understand they may be called upon to make the final sacrifice. Therein is both the honor and the burden that every knight worthy of the title must bear.'

Jordine inclined his head in acceptance. He had

dreamed of being knighted, of fully joining the ranks of Serendia's martial nobility, but now he wished only that his mother and father were present. Combined with the deaths of so many of the same men his father had led for so long, the honor felt hollow.

Cliff repeated the ceremony with Alfonso, and warned them both that the king would have final say over their knighting, once word of it reached Heidel. He expected, however, that news of their valor would make the ratification a formality.

'You are both still young, but you have proven yourselves on the field this day,' Cliff finished. 'Arise, and see to your men once more. I, and Serendia, will have need of you both again before this war is over.'

Cliff raised the sword he had knighted them with, and announced them to the surrounding host: 'Sir Ducas, and Sir Rhundi!'

The retinues cheered, letting up a racket of weapons and gauntlets on breastplates and shields, seeming for a while to shake the very hill itself with acclaim for the two new knights of Serendia.

THIRTY-THREE

The side-chapel of the Church of Elion in Heidel was quiet, quiet enough for Roxanne to hear the soft swish of robes and the light tread of sandaled feet behind her, marking the approach of the chief priest.

She was kneeling on a plush prayer-rest before the altar, alone until that moment, enjoying a period of private contemplation. As a member of the royal family, she had exclusive use of this particular side-chapel, though until recent weeks she had only been an occasional visitor.

More news of the Serendian victories to the west continued to come in day by day – it seemed the Calpheonian invasion had stalled utterly upon the banks of the Demi, and would soon be turned back. Such triumphs had seen an apparent upsurge in Roxanne's piety. When the likes of Jarette had argued that the Elion priesthood were siding with Calpheon, and were preaching sermons that bordered on treason in churches up and down Serendia, Roxanne had claimed that they had to make an effort to show the people this was not a holy war against the Domongatts, despite what Guy Seric and the Calpheonian high priest might claim. The royal family of Serendia still worshipped the Lord of Fire, and had not been forsaken by him.

Privately, Roxanne doubted that, but an excuse was all she needed.

'Might I ask what it is you are praying for, my lady?' said the chief priest. She stood, genuflected towards the altar, and turned to face him.

'For a swift end to this bloody war,' she said, smiling and producing a small pouch that clinked as she placed it in the wooden bowl the red-robed priest was carrying. 'A donation, for the upkeep of the church.'

'My lady is most generous, as ever,' the priest said with a sallow smile and a short bow. 'I will see that my superiors receive word of your good deeds.'

'It is enough that great Elion knows,' Roxanne said, that smile remaining fixed as she brushed past the priest and departed, leaving him with the pouch containing her coins and a scrap of parchment that stated, in cipher, that Princess Jarette intended to make a surprise visit to the front lines in two days' time.

'Why have we stopped?' Jarette called through to the driver of the royal coach.

'An obstruction on the roadway, Your Highness,' came

the muffled reply. 'It seems a coach carrying one of the brothers of Elion has thrown a wheel.'

'Can't we go around?' Jarette demanded, in no mood to offer aid to a servant of Elion. As far as she was concerned, that damnable faith had done nothing but undermine Serendia since the start of the war. The Church's ties to Calpheon were common knowledge, yet despite Jarette's entreaties, Crucio had refused to order their churches be closed for the duration of the conflict.

Then again, Crucio had very few orders of any kind to give these days. He had grown even more withdrawn since the start of the invasion, refusing to speak to his councilors or issue royal decrees. There was a void at the heart of the rulership of Serendia, and Jarette had found herself having to take up the mantle of leader more and more.

On Roxanne's advice, she had decided to journey to the front lines in an effort to meet with Marshal Cliff and inspire the Serendian host. That was not a duty that would normally have been expected of a young princess, but there was no one else left to fulfill such a role, and Jarette had never been one to shirk the prospect of danger. The war had been going unexpectedly well, with two victories checking the Calpheonians before they could cross the Demi, as well as rumors that a pack of harpies had unexpectedly assaulted their supply lines at Delphe Castle and Keplan. A royal presence rallying the Serendian host might just help win a last, decisive engagement. Besides, it was a relief just to get out of Heidel, where rumors and speculation about the progress of the war and Crucio's mental and physical state constantly circled.

'Can it not be dragged aside?' she demanded of the coach's driver, but there was no reply. She was about to step out and check on the delay for herself when she heard a shout.

More followed, as well as the shriek of horses and the clash of steel. Jarette's heart began to race. She looked at her new handmaid, Carolin, provided for her by Roxanne, but the woman seemed as confused as she was.

Jarette flung open the carriage door, and found herself at the side of a forested track. The coach's driver was at her feet, dead, a crossbow quarrel in his neck.

The royal guards escorting her were under attack. Cloaked and masked figures were swarming from the thickets on either side, slashing at the horses and mobbing the riders when they fell. Others were armed with crossbows – one of the guards right in front of Jarette cut down an attacker with his sword, and began to shout at Jarette to run, when a bolt slammed through his breastplate, pitching him from the saddle.

Jarette snarled and made to lunge back inside the carriage to grasp the sword she had brought. Wielding a weapon was not befitting of a princess, but Jarette had never had much time for propriety, and ever since the incident during the sacking of Heidel she had insisted on carrying some sort of weapon at all times.

To her surprise, Carolin blocked her. The handmaid snatched her wrist before stepping out to join her.

'You must not, my lady,' she said, fear in her eyes. 'There are too many! What will your father do if you are murdered in the woodland by brigands?'

Jarette instinctively wanted to deny her maid's words, but she could not deny the evidence of her own eyes – the last of her guards were being cut down, hooded attackers closing in from all sides.

Reluctantly, Jarette let the sword go.

Jordine smashed his mace against the Calpheonian's helm, striking with such force the spiked weapon staved the sallet in, driving a wedge of steel down through the man's skull. Blood ran thick and dark down one side of his face, and he collapsed – Jordine had to put a foot on the man's breastplate and wrench the mace with both hands to free it.

He looked for another opponent, but there were none. The Calpheonians were running back towards Red Crossing, abandoning weapons and what armor they could easily shed in an effort not to be weighed down in the fast-flowing current.

Teeth bared in a snarl, Jordine made to pursue them but was checked by Alfonso. He rounded on him, expecting his friend to rebuke him. It had been nearly three weeks since their victory at this same ford, and in that time Jordine's need to avenge his father by cutting down the invaders had not abated. This latest attempt at forcing a crossing – in the face of the entire Serendian host – was only feeding Jordine's fury.

But Alfonso had not stopped him because he feared his friend's bloodlust would carry him too far. The Rhundi heir gestured up at Cliff's stag standard, planted on the knoll that had become the lynchpin of the Serendian positions.

'We are being summoned,' he said.

Jordine caught the pealing of a horn, blowing the command for the knights of the host to attend the marshal. In the throes of combat, he had completely missed the order.

'Why is he calling us to him when we should be pursuing?' Jordine growled. 'If Cliff were down here in the melee, he'd understand that.'

'We've checked them again,' Alfonso said. 'Pursue them across the ford, and we'd turn another victory into defeat.'

Jordine could not argue that point – while the latest attempt at a crossing had again been repelled, the main body of the Calpheonian host yet remained on the far bank in array. Trying to counterattack across the Demi would undoubtedly give the same result in reverse, men-at-arms struggling against the current and a deluge of missiles before being hemmed in and cut down on the far embankment.

They had the Calpheonians where they wanted them. Another week at most and their supplies would be gone, and they would be forced to withdraw from Serendian soil. Yet the trumpet peals ringing out from the knoll seemed to indicate that something more than the latest failed assault across the ford was occurring.

'It sounds urgent,' Alfonso went on. 'We should hasten.'

The finest warriors of Serendia gathered under the banner of the stag.

Jordine and Alfonso were the last to make it to the assembly – Cliff had just started to speak. His expression was grim.

'Moments ago, I received word from the south. While we were engaged here, a small Calpheonian force was able to cross the Demi and mount an escalade against the Watchtower. The defenses there have fallen into their hands. It seems the renewed attack here was a diversion.'

There were murmurs of dismay from those around Jordine.

'How could they have managed to cross, after the bridge below the Watchtower collapsed?' one knight spoke up.

'It is unclear, but we suspect boats were used. They may have been rowed from Delphe. There is also a report that King Seric himself is among the division that has crossed over and seized the tower.'

'If they repair the bridge, and can hold it from both banks, there will be nothing to stop them shifting their whole host across,' Armstrong pointed out. 'Then we will have to meet them in open battle, before they can march on Heidel. The odds will be in their favor.'

'We will respond immediately,' Cliff said. 'But this threat could also represent an opportunity. The bridge below the Watchtower is still broken, and if we are able to seize the boats the enemy crossed over with, we can cut them off on our side of the river, away from the main Calpheonian battles. Come tomorrow, we may have captured Guy Seric.'

The Serendian host divided. Half remained facing the main Calpheonian force across Red Crossing, under the command of Captain Armstrong, while Cliff took the other half, including all the heavy cavalry the host possessed, and headed south with all possible speed.

Jordine and Alfonso were with them. The entirety of the vanguard had been chosen, along with Cliff's own retinue and several from the host's main battle. There was a sense of expectation, and though no one had yet dared voice it, all hopes were focused on the marshal's claim – that if they could capture King Seric himself, the war would surely be at an end.

The anger that had been animating Jordine for weeks flared anew as they drew within sight of the Watchtower, and saw the white eagle on a red field, the crest of Calpheon, fluttering from its uppermost turret. It seemed the report that had reached Cliff had been correct – rowing boats lay on the near banks of the Demi, not far from where the timber bridge stood. Efforts were already underway to repair it, with figures hurrying to lay down planks across the broken span.

'We ride now, before they can complete the work,' Cliff said after he had again called his commanders to him. 'Cut off the western and eastern tracks to the Watchtower first, and isolate it from the bridge. Then, we demand their surrender.'

'Why not ride straight for the tower?' Jordine spoke up. Cliff shook his head.

'We risk Seric's escape if we throw ourselves into an immediate assault. Better to cut the other routes first. Then, with a little patience, we shall have our prize. Vengeance will be yours soon enough, young Ducas.'

At first, the plan went well.

As soon as the Calpheonians working on repairing the bridge spotted the approaching Serendians, they fled back towards the Watchtower. There was no further movement within it, and no attempt was made to stop Cliff's two prongs from cutting off the eastern and western approaches to the small rise the stone structure was sited atop.

'Perhaps they intend to surrender without a fight,' Alfonso murmured as Jordine and the other knights joined Cliff in the tower's shadow.

'More likely they'll bar the doors and hope they can resist a siege until the rest of their host makes it over the river,' Jordine responded, eyeing the arrow slits above.

Cliff's bannerman had swapped the stag standard for a white flag of truce, and Cliff called out to his knights as they began to urge their mounts slowly up the final approach to the tower's main door. 'Say nothing, and offer no provocation unless I order it. We have come here to end a war, not renew it until all are slaughtered.'

Jordine could sense Alfonso looking at him, as though doubting whether he would be able to keep his temper in check. He didn't deign to respond to the unspoken criticism.

The knightly entourage rode to within a hundred yards of the western doorway, within easy bowshot of the parapets. There was movement up there, and behind the arrow slits in the walls, yet for a while the Calpheonians made no sign that they intended to acknowledge the parle. Jordine half expected bolts and arrows to start raining down on them, but there was no sign of that either.

Then, with the scraping of locks and the creak of old, heavy timber, the main door in the tower's flank opened.

Men-at-arms in liveries that Jordine assumed were Calpheonian stepped warily out, followed by others in more familiar blazons – the remnants of the garrison left to hold the tower, now prisoners.

The captives, around two dozen, were made to kneel outside the walls. Only then did a cohort of heavily armored Calpheonian knights step out, forming a protective wedge around the figure at their center – King Seric.

'Have you come to surrender to me, Marshal Cliff?' the ruler of Calpheon called out, a hint of mockery in his voice.

'Not unless my king demands it of me,' Cliff responded. 'And that king is Crucio Domongatt, rightful ruler of Serendia.'

'Are you certain of that?' Seric said. 'It seems Serendia's monarch changes with the seasons. Are you sure he even still reigns, back in Heidel?'

'Whether he does or not, that is no concern to the king of Calpheon. You are in the wrong realm, Guy Seric. But if you will parle with me, we might yet come to an agreement that will allow you to return home without further bloodshed.'

'You speak as though it was Calpheon who started this,' Seric barked, pushing to the forefront of his retinue and gesturing down the slope at Cliff and the Serendian knights. 'But it was your former king who first shed noble Calpheonian blood. My sister, a good and noble woman, murdered at the hands of a Domongatt, her own husband!'

'Your accusations are well-known, but that does not make them any truer,' Cliff replied, his tone staying resolutely level. 'Your sister's death was a tragedy, but my king had no hand in it. There is no need for this slaughter to continue. If you will agree to return to Calpheon, today, and not enter the lands of Serendia again so long as you or your heir reigns, you may leave this place freely. I offer this in spite of the many good and noble Serendian lives your invading host has claimed these past months.'

'You speak as though you hold the advantage here, Marshal,' Seric pointed out.

'Because I do,' Cliff said. 'You may have made it across the river and repaired the bridge, but now you are cut off and surrounded. The main body of your host is too distant to come to your aid. If you choose to continue down the path of violence, I shall order my warriors to storm this tower. Many will die, but at the end of it, you too will lie among the slain. That, or you will be captured, and taken to the dungeons in Heidel citadel. There, you can remonstrate with King Domongatt in person, if he will deign to see you.'

'You are an arrogant old dog, Marshal Cliff,' Seric snarled. 'And a fool for thinking me trapped here.'

He snapped an order to his retinue, and several more Calpheonian men-at-arms emerged from the Watchtower. They were dragging a figure between them, and Jordine felt pure disbelief as he realized who it was – Jarette. The princess's fiery red hair was unmistakable. She was wearing a muddy dress, and had her hands bound and her mouth gagged, yet she struggled defiantly in the grip of her captors.

Stunned silence greeted her appearance, and Seric laughed.

'Not quite so bold in your demands now, are you? What will you offer me in exchange for the life of the last living child of old Crucio Domongatt, hmm? Don't worry, I already have a few suggestions. Firstly, you will withdraw your host to the north. You will also leave the bridge below us intact. Do that immediately, and I may consider further negotiations.'

'This is an outrage—' Cliff began to say, but Seric shouted over him.

'The only outrage was the murder of my sister! Now withdraw your retinues, Marshal, or I'll cut your little princess's throat myself!'

He drew a dagger, brandishing it against Jarette's neck. Alfonso started forward, pale-faced with fury, but Jordine snatched his mount's bridle and checked him.

'Stay your hand, or you'll get us all killed,' he hissed. 'Including the princess!'

'I will withdraw, for the time being,' Cliff told Seric. 'But you will not harm her, nor even threaten her again. Not one of you will ever leave Serendian soil if you do!'

'We have an understanding,' Seric said, smiling. 'Run along now, and tell your king that his only living child will continue to enjoy my hospitality until he admits to his family's crimes.'

THIRTY-FOUR

'We have to do something,' Alfonso said.

He was shaking with rage. Since the withdrawal from the Watchtower, he had done nothing but pace up and down the makeshift camp the Serendian host had established on the ridgeline north of the fortification. Jordine had never seen him so distraught, not even after the brutal attack on his father.

'We will,' he told him. 'But we won't manage anything alone. We need to talk to Cliff.'

'There's been enough talk,' Alfonso hissed, pointing towards the marshal's pavilion. The commanders of the Serendian host had entered it over an hour before, and had not yet emerged. The sun was dipping below the horizon, casting a bloody red hue over the landscape below and shining on the damnable Calpheonian standard that waved mockingly atop the Watchtower's pinnacle.

'We still don't know how they were able to capture

Jarette,' Jordine pointed out. 'Was she seized in Heidel? Is the capital itself under threat? Whatever the case, it is likely treachery was involved. Cliff cannot proceed until we know more, and what of Crucio's will? Does he even know Jarette has been taken?'

'How can you sound so calm?' Alfonso demanded, rounding on him. 'Our best friend has a knife at her throat, and we're just standing here doing nothing!'

Jordine snatched him by both shoulders and looked him in the eye.

'You were the one urging restraint at the ford,' he told him. 'You know how much I want to drive these imp-rutters from Serendian soil. To avenge my father. And now, to free Jarette. But we won't manage any of that if we rush in. We'll likely all end up dead. Remember Heidel, and the capture of the west gate. We need at least the beginnings of a plan.'

'So let's make one,' Alfonso said, before breaking free from Jordine's grasp and striding to the pavilion. He forced aside the guard, who seemed unsure whether he should stop a Serendian knight from entering, and left Jordine with no choice but to follow him inside.

Candlelight illuminated tense faces within, Cliff and a gaggle of the most senior nobles in the host clustered around a campaign table. A look of irritation crossed the marshal's tired face.

'Not now, young Rhundi—' he began to say, but Alfonso would not be stopped. Words tumbled from him like an avalanche, his face flushed red.

'We cannot just while away the night with a princess of the blood being held captive under our very noses! For the love of all the gods, Marshal, give Sir Ducas and I even half of your retinue and we will see her rescued before the sun rises!'

Cliff's expression became one of outright anger. He gripped Alfonso and marched him from the tent, then dismissed the guard outside, so that he and the two younger knights were alone.

'I would thank you not to interrupt your superiors in such a fashion,' he said in a low, cold voice. 'As knights on campaign, you are expected to obey my commands, even those you disagree with. Any further insubordination and I will rescind my recommendation to the king regarding your new status, and order your return to Heidel.'

It said much about how angry Alfonso was that he still opened his mouth to argue, but Cliff continued before he could speak.

'For what it's worth, I am as concerned about this turn of events as either of you. I have had no word from the capital, nor the king. Do you understand the predicament that leaves me in? I do not have the authority to negotiate with Seric, especially when the princess's life is at stake. I have no recourse other than to wait for direction.'

'With respect, Marshal, that doesn't sound like your usual course of action,' Jordine spoke up, trying to pick his moment better than Alfonso. 'I attacked with only my retinue when we found the Calpheonians at Red Crossing because I knew we couldn't wait for orders. Would you hold back and await instruction in the midst of battle if you saw an opportunity for quick action presenting itself?'

Jordine expected Cliff to demand to know just what opportunity Jordine claimed to have seen, and was preparing to admit that he didn't have a plan as such, but instead he found the marshal hesitating, glancing to the side, as though checking to see if anyone might be able to overhear them.

Alfonso sensed the sudden furtiveness too, and the pair waited for the marshal to speak. When he did there was reluctance in his tone, but also a hint of guarded optimism.

'We have no means of recapturing the Watchtower by conventional methods. We don't have the equipment necessary to lay siege to it. But we do have one advantage. Presumably, this is the first time any of those Calpheonians have been inside the Watchtower, but I could walk its corridors and stairways blindfolded and not misstep. I know its strengths and weaknesses. I know, for example, of a covered way, that leads from the cliffs on the riverside farther south to a secret entrance in the tower's base, just above the dungeons. It's designed so that the garrison has a means of escape should it find itself cut off and overwhelmed. But it could equally be used by a small band to infiltrate the fortifications.'

Jordine and Alfonso exchanged a glance.

'Then we must take it,' Alfonso said. 'It is our best chance of rescuing Jarette. Our only chance, before it is too late! Who knows what the king will command when he hears she's been seized? He may well surrender the entire kingdom! We have to intercede, both for Jarette's sake and Serendia's.'

'We don't know where she is being held,' Cliff pointed out. 'If she's in the dungeons, there's a chance, but if Seric is keeping her in one of the upper chambers, we would never make it to her. There must be over a hundred men-at-arms in that place right now.'

Yet Jordine could tell that, despite his protestations, he too was tempted. Alfonso was right: the king's mind was fragile, and every moment Jarette spent in Seric's power, Calpheon's grip on Serendia grew.

'We should go,' he spoke up, putting a hand on Alfonso's shoulder while looking at Cliff. 'Just Al and I. If we are slain, you have only lost your two youngest knights.'

'Do not speak so low of yourselves,' Cliff remonstrated. 'What if you too are captured, and turned into another bargaining chip?'

'We won't be captured,' Jordine said firmly, looking at Alfonso and nodding.

'Either we return with Jarette,' he said, 'or not at all.'

Cliff looked pensive, his gaze again roaming, as though in search of eavesdroppers.

'I cannot in good conscience let you both go unaided,' he said. 'But trust doesn't go far right now, not while we still remain unsure as to how the princess was captured. I have doubts about even my own retinue… because of that, I will accompany you personally.'

It was Jordine's turn to remonstrate, but Cliff cut him off.

'You must learn when to hold your tongue, Ducas. In all my years of campaigning, I have never shirked a battle plan because of its boldness.'

The old marshal smiled, and Jordine knew his mind was made up. Despite himself, he felt a sudden sense of anticipation. Again, they would carry the fight to the invaders, against all odds. He wanted nothing more.

'The three of us, then,' Alfonso said with a determined expression. 'For Jarette, to the end.'

They waited until the depths of night before making their move. The heavens themselves seemed intent on aiding them – the clouds were dense, hiding the stars and casting the surrounding landscape into near-total darkness.

Cliff joined them at the agreed spot, to the north of the ridgeline encampment. According to Cliff's instructions, there would be a five-minute gap in the rotation of the sentinels there.

'We must be swift, and silent,' the marshal instructed before they moved off, his shadowed form silhouetted by the dying embers of the campfires at his back. Like Jordine and Alfonso, he had reduced his armor to just his breastplate and a simple, visorless steel helm, to ensure speedier, more silent movement, and had donned a cloak.

'And you must follow my orders to the letter,' he went on. 'It isn't only our lives at stake here. I will not have the princess's death on my conscience. Is that clear?'

Jordine nodded, and after a pause, Alfonso did likewise.

They set out, slipping from the camp and following the base of the ridge until they heard the waters of the Demi, and caught the faintest glimmer of its current rushing by. From there they followed its banks south, until Alfonso hissed at them to pause.

They crouched amidst the riverbank's reeds, and Jordine caught what Alfonso had first picked up – the clattering drumbeat of hooves on wooden boards.

'The bridge is just ahead,' Cliff whispered hoarsely. 'That must be the Calpheonian heavy cavalry, crossing over onto this side.'

'They're stealing another night march, and reinforcing the tower,' Jordine said, feeling a sense of frustration. If they hadn't been required to abandon the bridge because of Seric's demands, they would have been able to demolish it again and keep the Calpheonian king cut off on the near side of the river.

'Hopefully the infantry of their main battle are still catching up, on the far bank,' Cliff said.

They waited until the sounds of horsemen had receded. There was a brazier burning at the near entrance to the bridge, the dark shapes around it undoubtedly Calpheonian guards left to keep the crossing secure, so they crept a little way around them, towards the tower, trying to thread between it and the sentries. The structure loomed above them, a dire shape made vaguely visible by the pinpricks of firelight that flickered behind its arrow slits and slender windows.

They had to pause after catching the sound and scent

of cavalry again, likely the same division they had almost run into crossing the Demi, now forming up under the Watchtower. That was the signal to turn back to the riverbank, and, soon after, they found the stretch of boulders and cliffs that hid the tower's secret, remote exit.

It was there that disaster almost overtook them. Eager to locate the passageway, the trio practically ran into a pair of Calpheonian cavalrymen. They were dismounted, and had six horses down by the riverside, watering them.

Cliff, now in the lead, tried to warn Jordine and Alfonso at the last instant, but it was too late. One of the Calpheonians had caught sight of movement in the darkness, and called out a challenge.

Jordine cast back his cloak and threw himself at the man. He could see nothing but indistinct, shadowed shapes, but that was enough. He swung his mace, feeling it meet steel, repeating the blow again and again as he bore the man down into the mud, until something gave way with a crunch.

Alfonso and Cliff had tackled the second man, but he fought back more ferociously than Jordine's opponent. He heard the scrape of steel, and a muffled grunt of pain from Alfonso, before there was a splash. Cliff had borne the man down into the water at the river's edge, and managed to hold him under until he ceased struggling.

The horses the pair had been attending to were shying and whinnying with distress, and several had broken free from where they had been tied – the trio crouched in the darkness, straining to hear if they had been detected.

At length, the horses calmed themselves, and quiet returned. There was no sign of any approach from the direction of the tower, or the bridge upriver, but Jordine could tell just from Alfonso's ragged breathing next to him that something was wrong.

'You're hurt,' he whispered.

'I'm fine,' Alfonso retorted, his voice tight with pain.

'It doesn't sound like it. Where did he hit you?'

'Left leg,' Alfonso admitted. 'Not a proper strike, didn't break the skin.'

'But it could have broken bone,' Cliff pointed out. 'Can you walk?'

'I landed badly,' Alfonso admitted. 'But I'll be fine!'

'You won't be if you can hardly walk,' Cliff responded, voice low and firm. 'We need to be quick! In and out before they understand what's happening. Doubly so now we've dispatched these two. Their absence will be noted.'

'Help me stand,' Alfonso demanded. Jordine felt for him in the dark and gripped him under the arm – though he managed to straighten up and remained silent, Jordine could sense from the trembling in his body that he was in pain.

'You can't go on,' he told him. 'You won't even make it to the tower, let alone out again once we're being pursued.'

'I'm not going back,' Alfonso replied fiercely.

'Then stay here, and guard the exit,' Cliff suggested. 'The comrades of these cavalrymen may come looking for them before we return, and we can ill afford to make it out of the tower with the princess only to find our escape cut off by the knights of Calpheon.'

'We will be swift,' Jordine added, patting Alfonso's back where he was holding him. 'We cannot afford to be anything else!'

'Very well,' Alfonso said eventually. 'But by all the gods, Joe, you'd better come out with her!'

'I swear it, my brother,' Jordine said firmly.

THIRTY-FIVE

Cliff located the hidden passage amidst the rocks, feeling along the cliff face that rose for a brief stretch along the river's edge until he came across the necessary crevice. He directed Jordine to it, and they plunged into the blind blackness within.

On Cliff's instructions, Jordine put a hand on the marshal's shoulder and felt his way along behind him. His fingers brushed cold, wet stone and hard-packed earth, and he understood why Cliff had urged that they come lightly armored, and in small numbers – the place was narrow and uneven, and would have taken time and effort to traverse covertly and with more men.

Thankfully, the passage did not last long. Cliff's hissed warning alerted him to a set of steps, which they mounted until Jordine caught a glow above – firelight, faintly outlining an iron grate.

They used it to traverse the last few steps, and Cliff

signaled for him to remain still and silent. Then he carefully gripped the grate and lifted it away. It looked heavy and it seemed unlikely a man would be able to maneuver it without some difficulty, but Jordine realized that was probably artifice to help conceal the entranceway within the tower. Cliff removed it without any strain.

They both squeezed through the spherical gap that remained, Jordine again thankful he had worn only his breastplate. Beyond was a low stone storage cellar, presumably part of the complex of chambers dug underneath the tower. It was stacked with barrels and sacks, most of which helped conceal the grate. They edged out from around them and Cliff paused to whisper instructions.

'The door beyond leads to two more. The left-hand takes us down to the dungeons. That is hopefully where Jarette is being held. Stay as silent as possible, and let me go first.'

They eased out into a landing room with two sets of spiral stairs, one leading up and one down. Jordine let Cliff take the lead, and they descended. At the bottom, the enemy spoke to them.

'About damned time,' said a Calpheonian, seated at a table at the entrance to what appeared to be a corridor of cells, carved into the bedrock the Watchtower had been built atop. He and another man-at-arms were sitting playing a card game, both so engrossed that neither actually glanced up. Jordine just stared for a second, and realized they must have thought the two figures they had heard descending the spiral stairs were their shift relief.

Cliff swiftly disabused them of that notion. He slammed the war hammer he was wielding through the back of the head of one, while Jordine lunged at the other. Briefly, he was back in the gatehouse at Heidel, but where that had been all desperate haste and panic, now he felt only cold, controlled fury. He killed the man with one blow of his mace before he could even rise, blood ruining the cards upon the table.

A shout came from farther down the corridor. There was another guard there, carrying a torch as he patrolled the passage between the cells. He drew his sword and cried out again, trying to raise the alarm, his voice painfully loud as it rang through the stone space and echoed up the stairwell.

Jordine and Cliff charged him, side by side. He went down in a flurry of blows, his warning silenced, but it seemed impossible that more of the tower's occupiers hadn't heard him.

The prisoners certainly had. There was scuffling from within the cells, and exclamations of joy and disbelief as faces appeared at the bars – the Watchtower's Serendian garrison, those who had survived the sudden Calpheonian assault and been captured.

'Marshal, is that really you?' one called out.

'Who else?' Cliff said with a slight smile. 'Come to give you boys a second chance to drive out these Calpheonian bastards.'

They ransacked the bodies until they found a set of keys, and started opening the doors. The first prisoners came tumbling out, grinning and eager, and Cliff ordered them to take the slain enemy's weapons.

'Is Princess Jarette with you?' he asked as he freed them.

'The last cell,' one said, pointing up the corridor. 'They've kept her in isolation.'

'It's the biggest key on the ring,' Cliff said, tossing the jangling assortment to Jordine. 'Get her out. I'm going to marshal this lot and secure the stairway and the tunnel entrance. Bring her up as soon as you can.'

Jordine nodded and raced off to the far end of the dungeons. He could hear voices now, not just the prisoners as they were freed, but barked orders ringing from higher up in the structure. There was no doubt anymore that the Calpheonians knew they had intruders.

He reached the last cell in the row. This one had a heavier oaken door with only a small, barred slit near the top. Jordine could see nothing but darkness within. Trying not to rush, he found the biggest key and opened the cell before stepping inside.

The torchlight that spilled inside illuminated a small, dank chamber and its only occupant. Jarette looked up at him with wide, disbelieving eyes. She was sitting in the dirt, shivering, but rose hastily as Jordine came in.

'Jordine,' she said in shock.

'We have to go,' he told her, taking her hand, then realizing that she was chained to the wall – a manacle was clamped around one ankle, both her feet bare.

'Damn it,' he hissed, and crouched, starting to hunt for the right key.

'How did you get in here?' Jarette asked, looking from him to the open cell door.

'A hidden passage,' he said. 'Marshal Cliff knows about it. He's with me.'

'Is Al here too?'

'He was, but he was injured and had to stay back at the riverside.'

'Will he be alright?'

'He will be once he sees you're safe. All being well, we'll be with him soon. But I'm going to have to break this lock.'

'My ankle is twisted. I'll only slow you down. You should go without me, get the other prisoners out.'

'We came here to get you, and I made a promise that I'm not leaving without you. I've broken enough of those in recent times. I'm not going to renege on this one. Now, hold still.'

He pulled taut the chain connecting the manacle to the wall, and started to strike it with his mace. He sensed Jarette tense up in pain, but it couldn't be helped – after six or seven strikes, the chain links started to deform, before finally shattering.

Jarette stepped away with a heavy limp and a pained expression. Besides a twisted ankle, Jordine could see how the manacle had bitten into her pale skin, drawing blood that now ran down her foot.

'I… I don't think I can walk,' she admitted, sounding more angry than pained.

'You won't have to,' Jordine said. 'Put your arm around my shoulder.'

She did so, and he lifted her in both arms, causing her to give a little yelp of surprise.

'Hold onto me,' he advised, and stepped out of the cell. The passage outside was now almost empty, the last of the freed Serendian archers and men-at-arms hurrying upstairs. As he followed them, Jordine could hear the unmistakable sounds of combat from above. He began to climb.

There were bodies on the level they had initially descended from, both Calpheonian and Serendian. It seemed a rush of foes had been driven back or, more accurately, forced into the storage room Jordine and Cliff had first emerged from. The problem was that they had now either barred or barricaded the doorway. Cliff and another Serendian had been beating on it, but the marshal stepped back as Jordine arrived.

'Your Grace,' Cliff said, offering Jarette a short bow.

'Her leg is injured,' Jordine said, explaining why she was in his arms.

'You should leave me and go,' Jarette repeated fiercely, but they both ignored her.

'They've cut us off from the tunnel,' Cliff said, his voice riven with frustration. 'I'm not sure they've even realized it, but by the time we've broken this door open the whole garrison will be alerted. We'll be cornered in the dungeons and slaughtered.'

'Then we have to go out through the front door,' Jordine said. It sounded like far too bold a plan, but Jordine assumed the ground entrance to the Watchtower was just above them. 'Unless you know of another sally port, it's our only way out.'

Cliff nodded, and another of the former Serendian prisoners, now clutching a falchion retrieved from a Calpheonian corpse, spoke up.

'We can buy you time, Lords. It's the least we can do, after losing the tower on our watch. Damned if any of us will be taken prisoner a second time!'

There were growls of agreement from the other escapees.

'Very well,' Cliff said. 'We'll try to open the front doors, and once outside make for the bridge. If we can get across and break the planks after us, the Calpheonian cavalry won't be able to follow. But we must be swift. We have a few minutes at most before more reinforcements arrive from upstairs. Jordine, keep the princess by my side.'

They climbed up to the Watchtower's ground level. Cliff led the way, no longer making any attempt at infiltration. With a roar, he smashed down a Calpheonian at the top of the stair and drove his way out into the hall beyond. Jordine did his best to keep up, feeling defenseless with Jarette in his arms, half his attention fixed on making sure he didn't trip on the narrow, spiraling stone steps.

A force of Calpheonians attempted to block the assault, but had clearly been caught off guard by the attack from below, expecting their enemies to be outside the walls. Most of them were only half-armored, and the Serendians mobbed them furiously. A number of the prisoners, without any armor and with few captured weapons of their own, were hacked or beaten, but the others were able to drag down their killers in turn and, led by Cliff, had soon seized the front door into the tower.

There was no respite. Even as they began to unlock and haul it open, a fresh rush of Calpheonians came charging down from the two separate stairways that led up into the tower's midsection. These ones were better prepared. The nearest Serendians died with little resistance.

'Stand for a moment,' Jordine urged Jarette, setting her back on her feet as gently as possible before snatching the mace from his belt. He did so just in time to meet the sword stroke from one of the new attackers, batting it aside with his weapon's haft, fortunate the enemy's blade didn't scrape down it and cleave through his unprotected hand.

He attempted to grapple with the man, to stop him getting in another swing that Jordine doubted he'd be able to parry without losing half his fingers, but to his surprise he found someone else already gripping the Calpheonian's sword-arm. It was Jarette – using both hands, she held the attacker at bay before delivering a wicked kick between his legs, enough to cause him to double over. Jordine seized the chance to strike a trio of short, hard blows against the man's back, sufficient to drop him. Despite himself, he grinned at the return of Jarette's infamous ferocity.

'That's more like it,' he said, looking back at the tower's front door, which had now been dragged open by Cliff and a few others. 'But you can't fight them all alone. Take hold of me again.'

Jarette looked as though fighting her captors

single-handedly was exactly what she was planning on doing, but Jordine grabbed her arm and pulled her towards the door.

'Men are dying so that you can be free,' he urged her. 'Don't let them die in vain.'

Despite her reluctance, she again allowed Jordine to lift her. The remaining Serendians parted to let them past.

'To the bridge,' Cliff said, pointing with his bloodied war hammer out into the darkness. 'We need to try to make it across before the cavalry out there see what is happening, and ride us down.'

'I'll stay, buy you more time,' one of the Serendian men-at-arms said, to a chorus of agreement.

'We'll split our numbers,' Cliff said. 'There are guards at the bridge, and we'll need to force the crossing. Ideally, we can bring it down behind us, to cut off their pursuit.'

'Whatever you need, Marshal, we're with you,' another of the loyal Serendians declared.

Cliff swiftly divided the impromptu escape force, and those chosen to head out pushed into the darkness beyond the doorway, while the others made their gallant stand. Previously such valor would have impressed Jordine, but now he expected nothing less – he had seen war up-close, had known such loyalty from his own retinue, who had followed him to what had seemed like certain death. He had also witnessed how Cliff inspired instant obedience and veneration from his men. He was a leader, of that there was no doubt.

He bore Jarette out into the night. Dawn was beginning

to show itself, outlining the tower at their backs and lifting the worst of the darkness that clung to the surrounding landscape, as though jealous to relinquish its grip. Jordine could dimly make out the shapes of the Serendian men-at-arms who had gone ahead, down the winding track leading from the tower doors to the bridge. He began to traverse it, as swiftly as he dared, not wanting to risk stumbling in the dark.

'I can carry her, if you need,' Cliff offered as he followed. Jarette was light, but bearing her up from the dungeons and now out and down towards the bridge was causing a slowly mounting strain that made Jordine's arms tremble and his back ache.

'I'm fine,' he said regardless, refusing to give up his burden. He could feel the warmth of Jarette's body, and her trembling as she clung to him, he suspected more from the cold than fear. She had a warrior's heart, he decided – it was in her nature to want to stand and fight.

He caught the sound of the men-at-arms who had remained to hold the doorway doing just that behind them.

'For Serendia, for Princess Domongatt,' came the cry as they tried to hold back the pursuit, the sound of weapons clashing ringing out into the night.

As they neared the bottom of the slope, a bell, high up in the Watchtower, began to toll. Jordine wondered briefly where King Seric was, whether he was watching the desperate flight of the prisoners from one of the tower's upper windows. It seemed the Calpheonians in the tower, possibly at his command, were attempting to use the bell to signal to their troops on the slopes and at the bridge that their prisoners were escaping.

Jordine saw that the greatest dangers now lay to the left and the right – the strengthening light was revealing the Calpheonian cavalry they had heard crossing the bridge in the darkness. It was, indeed, their heavy horse, divisions of armored knights bearing lances and snapping pennants. Most seemed to be on the slope farther right, facing the ridgeline where the main Serendian host was encamped, but as Jordine caught sight of them he heard orders barked and trumpets shrilling, and the bulky formations began to slowly wheel about and spur in their direction.

'Keep going,' Cliff urged.

The ground was starting to level out, and the bridge was near. Jordine realized he was retreading the ground where his father had fought and died not a month ago, trying to defend a bridge now lost to the enemy. The anger that came with such a realization renewed Jordine's strength.

There were guards at the bridge, but thankfully it seemed none of the knights who had already crossed over had been detailed to reinforce them, and there was not yet any sign of the Calpheonian infantry from their main battle that were presumably on their way to cross over to the eastern side of the Demi. With the enemy closing in from behind and on both flanks, the bridge offered the only feasible means of escape.

So Jordine ran for it, as best he could. Ahead the guards had moved to block them, and the last of the Serendian men-at-arms charged them. A desperate melee broke out in the mouth of the bridge, and Jordine saw one of the Calpheonians bellowing at another to lay the torch he had pulled from the brazier there against the timbers.

'They're going to burn the bridge,' he shouted to Cliff as they tried to push their way through the combat.

'We have to get her over,' Cliff responded, before beating in the helm of one lunging Calpheonian warrior with a resounding *clang*.

Jordine was forced to all but drop Jarrette as a struggling Serendian and his opponent collided with him. He swung in to help, but the Calpheonian had already managed to plunge a slender ballock dagger through the Serendian's throat. Jordine avenged him with a vicious strike of his mace.

Thunder was rising all around, the noise of the Calpheonian heavy cavalry. They were coming from both the left and the right, bearing down on the small band of surviving escapees, set to ride them down before they could make it to the bridge. Ahead, Jordine saw flames starting to catch on the timbers, licking and spreading as though to aid the strengthening dawn light.

Another minute and the bridge would be ablaze, and the knights of Calpheon would be upon then.

He looked for Jarette in the press, and felt a brief sense of panic when he couldn't see her. Then he understood why.

Cliff had her. He had hoisted her up onto his back, and was now breaking through onto the bridge. He bore her through the flames before they rose to fully engulf the boards that had been laid across the ruined span, fire licking at his heels but not catching.

Jordine made to follow, but found himself barred by another Calpheonian. He was able to drive the man back, taking a sword stroke against his breastplate and another that cut open his sleeve and grazed his skin. He snarled, knowing he was almost out of time, driving against his opponent and pitching him from the edge of the bridge first. He almost accidentally followed him over, but managed to keep his balance.

He made to cross after Cliff and Jarette, but saw that it was too late – the fire had taken hold of the bridge's center now, rising to a conflagration, its heat making him flinch back. Through the flames and smoke, he saw Cliff still going, reaching the other bank. He caught Jarette twisting to look back at him, calling out and gesturing, but Jordine couldn't hear her, and Cliff didn't stop.

A sense of anger and abandonment gripped Jordine. Cliff was leaving him to fight and die, just as it seemed he had left his father to fight and die upon this very same ground.

Such thoughts were only brief. Cliff had done the right thing – he hadn't hesitated. If he had, they would all have been caught or cut down. They had come to the Watchtower to free Jarette, with the understanding that it was unlikely they would survive the attempt. Whatever happened now, at least it had not been in vain.

The last of the escaped Serendian men-at-arms were fighting to the death. Jordine looked to the Calpheonian knights closing like a tide of steel upon the bridge. There would be no resisting them. Above, the Watchtower was a column of darkness silhouetted by the rising sun, its long shadow cast across Jordine and the burning bridge.

The last Serendians died, defiant to the end, leaving just Jordine, with the Calpheonians to his front and a rising inferno to his back.

He did the only thing he could think to. He dropped his bloodied mace and reached back to unbuckle his breastplate, casting the fitted metal into the dirt. Then, with the enemy knights almost atop him and the thunder of their hooves filling his senses, he mounted the edge of the bridge and leapt from it into the rushing waters below.

THIRTY-SIX

Alfonso caught sight of him downriver, and managed to drag Jordine up onto the bank despite his wounded leg.

'Is she safe?' was the first thing he asked.

'She's across the river with Cliff,' Jordine panted, drenched through and beginning to shiver.

'On the Calpheonian side?'

'Well, a good number of the Calpheonians are now on this side. They'll work their way back to the host, I'm sure. As we should too.'

'Was she unharmed?'

'A twisted and cut ankle,' Jordine said, making himself humor his friend's frantic questioning. 'Otherwise she's fine.'

'What if—'

'She's out,' Jordine cut in, his patience at an end. 'At the cost of likely two dozen men. They gave their lives without hesitation. There was nothing more we could have done. She's in Marshal Cliff's hands now.'

The two of them ventured south then east and north, attempting to skirt the Watchtower as the sun rose. It was slow, painful going with Alfonso's leg, but Jordine supported him, and eventually they were spotted by outriders from the main Serendian host on the ridge north of the tower. They rejoined the camp by late afternoon, where they discovered there was not yet any sign of Cliff and Jarette. Riders were sent seeking them across the ford to the north – ironically, the Calpheonians there had all gone south. Jordine wondered if they had managed to douse the fire on the bridge.

Alfonso reluctantly submitted to the chirurgeon, who splinted and set his leg. Jordine changed into dry clothes and ate, before falling into an exhausted sleep in his tent.

He woke to a figure standing above him.

He reached instinctively for the dagger he kept beside his blanket, then let go of it when he realized who it was.

Jarette was standing in the tent. She was dressed in borrowed clothes – a doublet and hose – and looked briefly embarrassed at having disturbed him.

Jordine rose, clad in just his long undershirt, trying to find the right words to express his relief at seeing her.

'When did you get here?' he asked.

'Just an hour ago. They said you were asleep, I didn't mean to wake you…'

'Did Cliff make it too?'

'Yes. He carried me almost all the way. We had to lie low in an abandoned farm at one point, when the main divisions of Calpheonian infantry were passing by. Judging by the smoke, the bridge is still burning.'

Jordine had expected to feel relief, perhaps even a sense of triumph. They had rescued Jarette from within the very midst of the enemy. Yet all he felt was exhaustion, and the smoldering hum of his need to be avenged against Calpheon for his father's death. It never went away or dimmed. He was starting to fear that particular craving could never be satiated.

'Have you seen Alfonso?' he asked, trying to focus his weary thoughts. 'He was desperate to see you.'

'I wanted to find you first,' Jarette said. 'To thank you. Not only for carrying me out, but for convincing me not to give up when I wanted to. It would have been an easy thing, to stay behind.'

'Not so easy for those who died covering our escape,' Jordine pointed out, trying not to sound morose.

'You know I would have stayed and fought if I could,' Jarette pointed out. 'I ordered Cliff to go back and not leave you behind! But he said his duty was to see me safe, which I suppose it was.'

'You should have been a warrior-princess,' Jordine said, looking her up and down. 'You look good in this garb. Add a few plates of armor and you'd fit in perfectly well with one of the retinues.'

'I would rather that than waste away with Father back

in Heidel,' Jarette said, her tone rediscovering its old edge. 'He does nothing but eat, sleep and stare from the citadel windows. He is a broken man. I refuse to let myself slip away in the same fashion.'

'We must get news to him as swiftly as possible, to let him know you are safe,' Jordine said. 'Otherwise, he may grant concessions to Calpheon.'

'We should be fighting them, not conceding,' Jarette growled. 'Can I not remain with you? I can fight! You've seen that now, multiple times. I want to do my part.'

Jordine suppressed his laughter, knowing she was being sincere.

'I don't think, having just broken you free from the clutches of the enemy, that either your father or Marshal Cliff will much approve of you being thrown back into harm's way on the front line.'

'Damn their opinions. I'm a princess,' Jarette exclaimed, pouting. 'Does all my supposed power count for nothing when there is actual work to be done, or danger to be shared?'

'If it were up to me, I would have you on one side and Alfonso on the other the next time we meet the foe,' Jordine said. 'But I can make you no promises, and in truth, I fear the tide may now have turned. The enemy's heavy cavalry are on our side of the river. Even if many of their infantry have yet to cross, they will repair that bridge eventually, and we do not have the strength to drive them back. We will be forced to face them in an open, pitched battle, the very thing we have been trying to avoid by holding the river. Their cavalry will be almost impossible to stop, unless we choose the ground for our stand exceedingly well.'

'You speak as though we are already beaten,' Jarette said, sounding disapproving.

'It's just a matter of facing reality,' he replied. 'I'm glad it won't be my job to decide our next course of action. For now, all that matters is that you are safe.'

He expected her to brush him off, to respond to such affection with her usual cutting wit, but instead of affected mockery, she kissed him. It was so swift and sudden that it was over before Jordine really understood what was happening, and it seemed no less of a surprise for the princess. They just stared at one another in the aftermath, before Jarette spoke abruptly.

'I… I'm going to find Al,' she said, turning away, face almost as red as her hair. Jordine tried to think up the right response, but she gave him no time, disappearing out of the tent without another word.

THIRTY-SEVEN

In the end, there was no great battle to decide the fate of Serendia. The war with Calpheon died away like old, charred embers, rather than in the blazing white heat of combat.

Jordine's fears were realized. According to the rumors that ran rampant in Heidel, news of Jarette's unexpected capture caused Crucio's mind to completely unravel. Despite the princess's protests, Cliff had her escorted back to Heidel almost immediately, but even her safe reappearance did not renew the king's spirits.

The Serendian host was ordered to withdraw back towards the capital. Cliff was forced to play a cat-and-mouse game with the oncoming Calpheonians – the enemy's numerical superiority, especially in heavy cavalry, forced him to keep to high ground and defensible positions, but now that the Demi had been crossed and there were seemingly no more harpy incursions on the

Calpheonian supply lines, the enemy's numbers were continually increasing.

After several weeks of back-and-forth between the king and his few remaining advisors, Crucio's will won out. There was to be no more resistance. Rather than see the flower of the Serendian military slaughtered in a last pitched battle to defend Heidel, or risk the capital being sacked for a second time in less than a year, Crucio would meet Seric's terms.

'It's a disgrace,' Jordine said harshly when he saw Cliff, not long after the marshal had delivered the damning news to the host's commanders. He looked as angry as Jordine felt, but that did not ease the young lion's own mood.

'What choice do I have but to capitulate?' Cliff demanded, clearly in no mood to debate with Jordine. 'Do I defy our king's direct instructions and lead us all to be slaughtered? Gods know, I'm tempted to do just that. I wouldn't survive such a battle, and maybe it's for the best.'

'Our honor would be intact,' Jordine pointed out.

'But how do you weigh honor against the blood of others?' Cliff responded. 'You and I may be ready to sell our lives for the glory of Serendia, but can we demand the same from our men?'

'They would follow you as they did at the Watchtower. You had no compunction leaving those men to die.'

The point was barbed, given Jordine had been counted among those left behind, but Cliff did not rise to the bait.

'There was a purpose to that,' he said. 'We managed to bring the princess to safety.'

'But all for nothing,' Jordine responded bitterly. 'My father's death was in vain.'

'Not everything in life carries meaning, Jordine. The older you grow, the more you will learn that. You speak of your father – do you think he would throw his life away in a doomed assault on the foe, after being commanded not to by his king?'

Jordine sighed, having expected the marshal's riposte. 'He would not,' he admitted.

'Nor would he wish you to. The war is over, Jordine. You are the one charged with bearing the noble name of Ducas now. Live, and bring honor to it. This is the duty Frederick left to you.'

According to the terms of Serendia's surrender, the host was to give up its arms and armor to the Calpheonians. Instead, Cliff permitted the nobles and their retinues to depart back to their own homes and estates, keeping only a token force to pay homage to Seric. The Calpheonian king was furious, but there was nothing he could do about this small, last act of defiance.

Jordine paid and dismissed the last survivors of his retinue and rode back into Heidel with Alfonso, just ahead of the Calpheonians. Their moods were equally morose – Alfonso had barely had a chance to see Jarette before she was ordered back to Heidel, and Jordine sensed he was still bitter about having had next to no involvement in her rescue. He hadn't told him how he had literally carried her from the Watchtower, much less the brief, sudden kiss.

He still did not fully understand his own feelings towards Jarette. For so long they had been good friends, and nothing more. But the princess was fully grown into her womanhood, and the sharp-tongued, quick-witted companion he had known now felt like something more. It was one more uncertainty to add to the legion of doubts mounting up all around him.

He bade a terse farewell to Alfonso at his father's house, and rode to the Lilly Valley. The streets were busy, and he was the tavern's only patron. There was panic in the air – it had been publicly stated that the Calpheonian host would not sack Heidel, and that only Seric and his royal guard would enter and take possession of the citadel, but the people were afraid, and understandably so. It seemed impossible that the kingdom had fallen, and Jordine was glad there was none but the barkeeper to quiz him about how it had come to this.

He needed time alone, time to think. He refused to endure this defeat the way Cliff had, yet he also understood that open defiance right now would only result in a meaningless death. Cliff had been right about that. He had to bide his time, and plan carefully.

Eventually, there would be a reckoning with Calpheon, that much he swore.

There was another target he intended to hunt down first, one closer to home. Jarette had told him that it was Roxanne who had urged her to ride to the front lines, before she had been abducted by the Calpheonians. A great deal of the kingdom's woes, perhaps most of them, seemed to stem from that accursed woman. Jordine felt like a fool for having ever trusted her, let alone loved her. It fed his anger, building it into a roaring pyre.

He knew if he went to the citadel right now, he would simply be turned away again. Soon, King Seric would be in control, and he had no doubt he would reward Roxanne. Perhaps he would even install her as a puppet ruler, or Crucio's formal heir? It would not matter – Jordine would encounter her sooner or later, and pay her back for the pain she had inflicted, not only on him, but on all Serendia.

THIRTY-EIGHT

Roxanne stood in the upper-west corridor of the citadel of Heidel and watched as the Serendian lion standard was dragged up from the gatehouse and the white eagle of Calpheon was unfurled in its place.

A cheer resounded around the courtyard below, loosed by the Calpheonian royal guards packing the space.

Roxanne had expected a fiery joy to take hold once she witnessed the crest of the hated Domongatts dragged away. But there was no triumphant exultation, no sense of wrongs avenged or weight lifted. No release. Only a nothingness that made her dread what she had become.

They would be coming for her, she knew. She, Crucio and Jarette had been commanded to gather in the throne room, where they would formally swear fealty to King Guy Seric of Calpheon. Crucio would then be dragged away to face a rigged court in Calpheon, where he would be made to answer for the murder of Lady Elysia, a murder he had no inkling of, and in which Roxanne had played a far greater part.

Instead of being punished for such treachery, Roxanne would be rewarded. Seric had offered much in exchange for, initially, evidence that the Domongatts had murdered Elysia and, later, delivering Jarette into his hands. She could expect wealth and station in Calpheon or, if she wished to remain in Serendia, rulership as its queen, albeit tied by oaths of obedience to Seric.

She would accept no such positions, though Seric did not yet know it.

How she had dreamed of this day, on rare nights when her sleep was not riven with fire and screams. Crucio Domongatt believed she had forgotten how his soldiers had burned her home and her family, had forgotten everything before her adoption into the royalty of Serendia. But Roxanne had not forgotten. Her nightmares had reminded her, and her memories, dredged up by Mnemosyne. The recollection of her family – her real family, not the vain, ruthless, privileged brutes that bore the name Domongatt – had remained with her, held close even as she had learned, while still a child, to deny any recollection of those who had first born and raised her, who had loved her with all their hearts. They had been ordinary farm folk of Valencia, the Fiazza family, and they had died in agony during one of the joint Serendian-Calpheonian campaigns that had ravaged their homeland.

The fire that had reduced her family to charred bones still smoldered within her. It had kept her warm, had ensured she never lost sight of what she sought in the darkness – vengeance.

Vengeance on Serendia, but most of all vengeance on the Domongatts. The fire had seared away her pride, so she could stomach living among them, learning their ways while she acted the obedient daughter and royal adoptee.

In the end it had been simple enough to start the conflict that had torn them apart. She had only sown the seeds. Their hubris, ruthlessness and pride had done all the rest. Crucio's sons had slaughtered one another, and he had been left a broken old man, king of a conquered realm, doomed to witness the end of his lineage.

Only Jarette remained unpunished. Once, Roxanne had imagined fates as cruel and deadly as any that had befallen her brothers for that spirited girl. Yet the desire to inflict further suffering had wilted over time. She had watched Jarette grow, and had come to love her as a little sister. Betraying her into Seric's hands had been almost more than she could endure, and she had secured assurances that Jarette would not be seized or in any way punished. If Seric kept his word, she would be granted the rank of duchess, her inheritance as a princess of Serendia stripped, but much of her privilege and standing in the newly annexed realm still intact.

As she watched the Calpheonian eagle take the place of the Serendian lion, Roxanne knew it was done. Now the fire was gone, burned out, and it had left her cold and empty.

She thought about Jordine. There had been an

opportunity there, and to deny it would have been a lie. She could have stopped. He had offered her the first real happiness, the first unadulterated joy, she had ever really known. But how could she have stopped and embraced a life with the lion of Serendia, when the fire still burned, and the nightmares still came for her whenever she closed her eyes? Maybe over time it would have receded, and she could have found peace with the heir of House Ducas.

The regrets threatened to choke and overwhelm her. There were tears in her eyes, but it was too late now. Too painful to go back. She could only go forward.

So, she unhooded and uncaged Mnemosyne, and stepped up onto the ledge of the upper corridor window. Then out, into the nothingness, allowing it to embrace her whole being.

For a moment she was soaring again, the falcon's cry ringing in her ears as the bird took flight with her. Free and unburdened.

She knew joy again in that moment, and then, nothing.

'She's dead,' Jarette said as soon as Jordine opened the door to the room he was renting, upstairs in the Lilly Valley. 'Roxanne is dead.'

Jordine stared at her, then spoke.

'How?'

'She jumped from a window in the citadel, not an hour ago.'

'Seric's work?' Jordine asked, wondering if he had

decided to avenge the murder of his sister in the most literal way possible.

'It seems not. She left a letter describing… all the things she's done down the years. To us. To my family. It seems she was behind it all, or almost all.'

'I can believe it,' Jordine said darkly, moving aside to let Jarette into the musty little room. 'I'm surprised Seric allowed you out of the citadel.'

'I have a Calpheonian guard, but I convinced them to wait outside. It isn't like I have anywhere to run to. And they have no real need of me. Serendia belongs to Seric. He didn't even blink when he was told Roxanne had killed herself.'

The thought that Roxanne would forever remain beyond his plans for justice filled Jordine with a cold and bitter rage. He turned away from Jarette, not wishing her to witness his anger, his fists clenched and shaking.

'She deceived us all, for years,' Jarette said, seeming to sense his thoughts. 'Don't blame yourself for not seeing through her. By all the gods, it's almost admirable, what she managed to do. I know I couldn't stomach living among people I hated so much. People who killed my parents. She played the longest game of all.'

Jarette seemed not to consider the irony that she was almost describing what was expected of her now, with Calpheon's triumph.

'But I didn't just come here to tell you about Roxanne,' she said, dragging Jordine's thoughts away from his former lover. 'I came to apologize for what I did after you rescued me. The kiss…'

'Just a moment of relief after the ordeal you had endured, I'm sure—' Jordine began to say, feeling an unfamiliar sense of embarrassment.

'I think it was more than just a momentary release,' Jarette said, her expression deadly serious. 'I think… I've had feelings for you for a long time, Joe. And after everything that's happened, it has made me realize I should have pursued those feelings sooner than I have. Nothing is certain, and it's better to cast the dice and speak your mind than live with regrets.'

'You know that Al is in love with you?' Jordine asked bluntly. Jarette's expression faltered.

'I suspected as much, yes,' she said. 'He's a good man, and he'll make a fine knight of Serendia. But I've never thought of him the way I think of you.'

It all felt so sudden, but a part of Jordine wasn't surprised. Everything either of them had known had come crashing down over the past few years, and they were the last of the old certainties remaining for one another. He wondered if that was the root of their feelings – the hope for stability and the yearning for a simpler, happier time, one that was now forever lost. Was that the reason for their sudden attraction, rather than genuine love?

'I also fear Seric will order me to marry one of his piggish generals or nobles,' Jarette admitted. 'He'll try to bind Serendia even more firmly to Calpheon, but I'll never accept that. I would rather die.'

'So you would take me instead, just to keep the wolves at bay?' Jordine asked, more sharply than he intended.

'No,' she responded, just as sharply. 'What I told you is the truth. I feel something for you, Joe. I can't be certain yet whether it is true love, but it is too strong for me to either ignore or deny. Do not scorn me for my honesty.'

'I would never,' Jordine said. 'I just fear I am not… a suitable husband for a princess of Serendia.'

'House Ducas was one of the wealthiest noble families, and can be again. If it is my father's approval you're concerned about, I wouldn't worry. I fear we may never see him again, and if he survives the Calpheonian court and is permitted to return to Heidel, he will not be the same man who left us.'

'I wasn't referring to Crucio, or the etiquette of royal marriage,' Jordine said. He crossed to the window, where he eased the shutter a little wider so he could gaze down on the street outside, and the small cohort of Calpheonian guards who were waiting to escort Jarette back to the citadel.

'You said you will never marry one of them,' he said, his voice quiet, but the anger still evident. 'Nor can I ever serve them, not honestly. We are a conquered people, Jarette, but it will not always be so. I will not rest until Serendia is free again, but achieving that will take time, and care. That is a lesson Roxanne taught me, one I will not forget. I intend to live among my enemies, and wait until the time is right.'

He looked back at Jarette, and was gratified to see equal determination in her gaze.

'Then we are of one mind,' she said. 'I will stand by you,

for as long as vengeance takes. I understand the dangers you will face, and the risks. But our goals will remain the same.'

'Serendia lies sundered,' Jordine said, moving across the room and taking her hands in his, looking down into her eyes. 'But one day, we will remake it, together. And when we do, Calpheon will suffer, for every drop of blood spilled and for every insult offered. Whether it takes months or years, the balance will be redressed, and my family will be avenged.'

ACKNOWLEDGEMENTS

My thanks go out to the publishing team at Titan, especially my ever-patient and talented editor and author-wrangler, Daquan. Similarly, my thanks to the Pearl Abyss team for always being on hand to guide me through the realms of *Black Desert*.

ABOUT THE AUTHOR

Robbie MacNiven is a Scottish author and historian. His published fiction includes over twenty novels in genres ranging from sci-fi and fantasy to historical fiction. He has also written novellas, short stories, audio dramas, comic scripts and graphic novels, has worked on narrative and character dialogue for multiple digital games, and has written color text and branching narratives for multiple RPG and game rulebooks, including the award-winning Undaunted series by Osprey Games. In 2022 his X-Men novel, *First Team*, won a Scribe Award for tie-in fiction.

For more fantastic fiction, author events,
exclusive excerpts, competitions, limited editions and more

VISIT OUR WEBSITE
titanbooks.com

LIKE US ON FACEBOOK
facebook.com/titanbooks

FOLLOW US ON TWITTER AND INSTAGRAM
@TitanBooks

EMAIL US
readerfeedback@titanemail.com